Obviously, Aliens
Jennie Goloboy

ISBN 978-1-7343603-4-9
Library of Congress Control Number: 2021947222

Queen of Swords Press LLC
Minneapolis, MN
www.queenofswordpress.com
Published in the United States

Cover Design and Interior Design by Terry Roy of Teryvisions

JENNIE GOLOBOY

OBVIOUSLY, ALIENS

CONTENTS

TABLE OF CONTENTS, CONTINUED....

ACKNOWLEDGEMENTS

THANKS SO MUCH TO my friends who've helped with drafts of this manuscript, including Clarissa Ryan and Tim Shea. Special thanks to my wonderful writers' group, the Writers of a Certain Age, Tim Boerger, Aimee Kuzenski, Anika Stafford, Susan Taitel, and Rachelle Wright. Thanks to the kind and talented writers of Viable Paradise 20 for inspiring me with their love of the craft.

Thanks to the fantastic Catherine Lundoff of Queen of Swords for picking my novel out of the submissions pile and making it a real book, and thanks to her enthusiastic team, including Terry Roy, amazing cover artist.

Thanks to Steve, Al, and Matthew Sigmond, for being the best family ever.

INTRODUCTION

It might not be obvious, but this novel was inspired by my childhood love of *Scarecrow and Mrs. King.*

I have always been a huge fan of spy stories. I love the promise of revealed secrets; I love watching brutal and impenetrable security systems get defeated; I love the way spy fiction plays with identity and disguise. And what I love most of all is the amateur spy story—the average Mrs. King who gets handed a mysterious package and is told to deliver it to the contact, because the fate of the world is at stake. I love watching Mrs. King come into her competence, discover the truth, and save the world.

There's a Kurt Vonnegut quote I often think about, from his introduction to his spy novel, *Mother Night*: "We are what we pretend to be, so we must be careful about what we pretend to be." It seems to me that we can flip this quote around—if we pretend to be better than we are, we can become the people we should have been all along.

Thank you very much for reading my novel. I hope you enjoy it.

PROLOGUE

ALLRHL SWAM CLOSER TO the window of the spaceship, noticing that the water was warmer as he approached the opening. Obviously he wasn't the only one who had paused here to look at the new planet. He widened his second set of eyes and strained to see it. And there it was: a small smudge, like a single fertilized egg at the bottom of the Crevasse.

He sensed Lrrkt hovering behind him, the churn of his fins making ripples in the current.

That's it? asked Lrrkt.

I think so, he replied.

Doesn't look like much.

It didn't, did it? What a strange thing it was, to be totally unhooked in the universe, with only his ship and the eight others to hold on to.

Home was gone, and he felt no connection to Earth at all.

PART 1

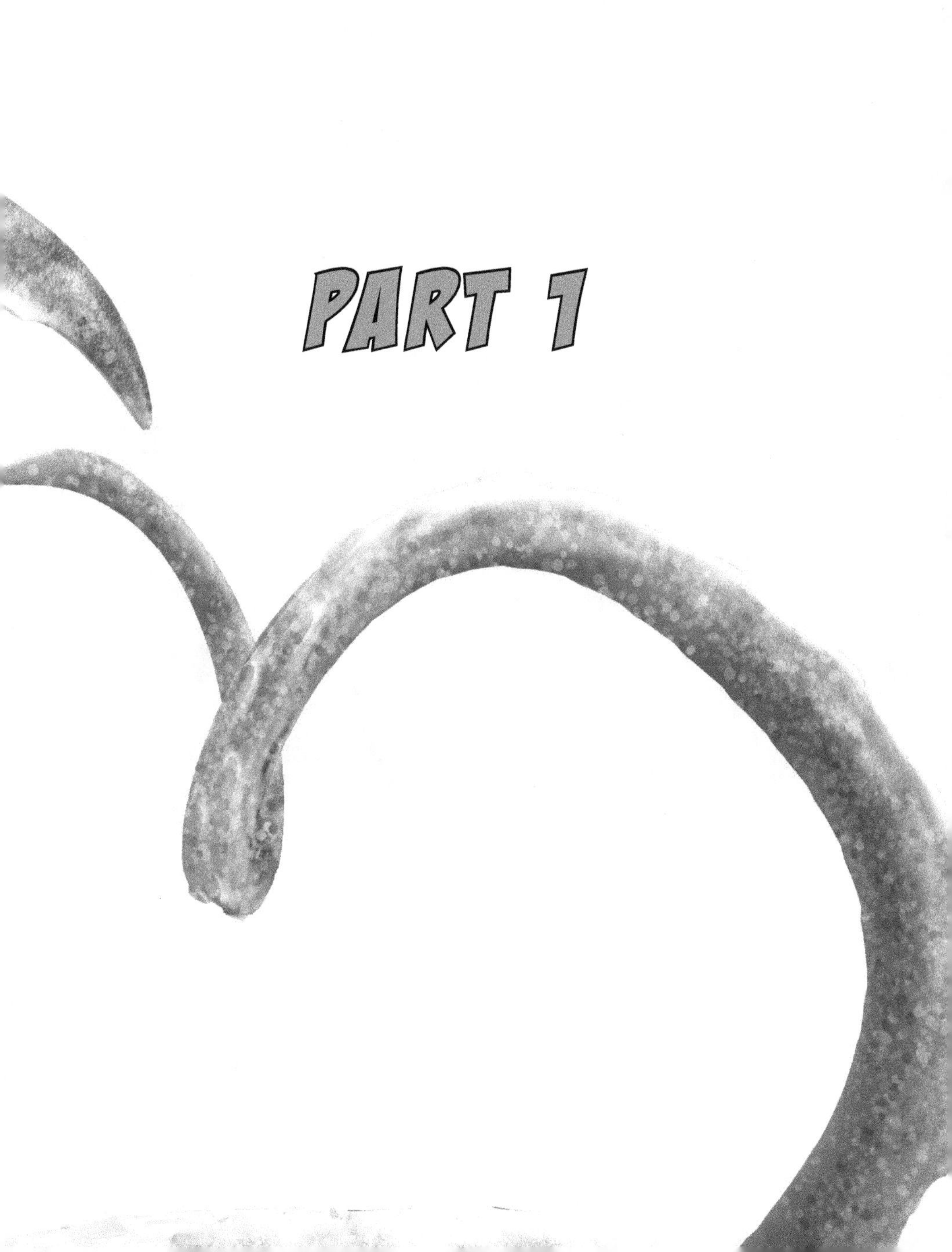

CHAPTER 1

Dana Elson sat in her rental car, rain pounding against the windshield, and thought about Rainbow Daydreams, and the pitch that was going to change her life. She imagined striding into their office in her chic dress, tights, and boots, her statement earrings swinging, her sample tucked in her briefcase. She'd shake hands confidently with the whole acquisitions team. Then she'd tell them how her new series would fit into their roster of calendar-based gift items.

After that, she'd open the carrying case, revealing her sample. A beam of sunlight would emerge from a nearby window to illuminate its hand-painted glory. Everyone would be awestruck. Then, they'd give her a million dollars, cash.

Sure, why not?

Dana sighed and watched the rain. Less than twenty-four hours until her real presentation, and she was making herself crazy. But how was she supposed to relax when she knew how important this deal would be?

What she really wanted to do was call her mom, who always knew how to tell her when she was worrying too much. If only that were possible.

She picked up the soda in the cup holder and took a big swig. Dana would later reflect that this was the exact point at which her life had forked from its intended direction, because *her* soda bottle was still in her briefcase. The soda she'd drunk from had been left by the car's previous occupant and something terrible had happened to it. A slippery lump of something disgusting slid down her throat and caught, slowly oozing downward.

Dana choked, gagged, swung the driver's side door open, and caught herself just before throwing up on a stranger's shoes.

The shoes belonged to a man who was giving her a sharp, cold, terrifying look that made her burrow backwards into her seat. Automatically she noticed the details she would put into a sketch: he was bald, blue-eyed, thin, and very pale. His jeans, grey hoodie, and black leather jacket were sodden with rain, but he didn't seem to notice.

He glared at her and she bit the inside of her lip, willing herself to keep silent and still. "That's mine," he said. He reached over her and took the empty soda bottle from the cup holder. Then he shut the door and walked off into the rain.

Suddenly Dana was eager to leave, no matter how nauseous she was.

DANA MANAGED TO CHECK into her hotel even though she was shivering with fever, and she could still feel the gooey lump slowly oozing down her esophagus, heating her as it went. Sprawled out on the bed, the ceiling spinning above her, she thought about when she was sick as a child and her mother used to wrap her in a blanket and put a cool, wet washcloth on her forehead. Now she wanted her mom more than ever. *No, don't think of that.*

She was sick and alone in a hotel room, and she was going to have to call Rainbow Daydreams in the morning to cancel her appointment. God only knew when they'd be willing to see her again, and she was out the plane fare and the hotel room. Plus maybe hospital fees, because if she didn't start feeling better really soon she was calling 911 to take her to go get her stomach pumped. *Hello operator, I'm the biggest idiot you've talked to today...*

And great, now someone was knocking on the door. She didn't have to answer that. *Nope nope nope...* But the door was opening. Housekeeping must be confused. She pushed herself off the bed and stood up, ready to explain she had plenty of towels, thanks. But it wasn't housekeeping. It was the weird white man from the rental car parking lot, and he was just as scary dry now that he'd dried off. And he'd closed the door behind him.

"What are you doing?" she said, trying to keep the fear out of her voice. "Get out of here."

Dana had always been good at reading people and this man's unblinking stare told her he was about ten seconds from slamming her head into the wall. And that letting him know how terrified she was would only make things worse.

"You have something of mine," he said. "Give to me, and I'll leave."

Surely he couldn't be talking about the rancid soda. Why would he care about that? "I can't give it to you. I drank it."

"What?" He looked her over suspiciously. "Why?"

Because it was a soda? She braced herself against the wall, which was nice and cool. This fever was weird. It was like the swollen hot feeling you got when you stubbed a toe, only all over. "I think I need a doctor."

Had she only thought that or said it out loud?

The man moved closer, but she had bigger problems. Her body felt wrong, too short, too weak, the wrong taste inside her mouth, the wrong smell on her skin, like someone else should have been standing in this hotel room instead of her. A ripple of heat went through her and for a terrifying moment, she felt her body melt. *Yuck.*

And then it felt like the room had shrunk. It took her a moment to realize that this was because she'd grown a few inches. She could feel the strength in her muscles, especially in her arms, because she was now a man. Very, very definitely a man. She tried to move her head to look in the mirror, but she couldn't. She couldn't open her mouth, either. She was stuck in her body like a passenger, without being able to control it.

Dana was always in control. She didn't like this, not at all.

The man from the parking lot had his arms wrapped around himself like he was cold. "Jay?" he asked. He sounded scared.

She felt her face crinkle into a smile. "Adam," Jay said, with her mouth.

"Oh, God," Adam said. "It actually worked." He grabbed them by the shoulders and kissed them, a hard, desperate kiss that Jay returned with enthusiasm.

This was not, in any way, how Dana had planned to spend her evening.

What the hell just happened? Who are *these people?*

This was stupid. She was not going to let the people who'd stolen her body get away with it. She knew what she was supposed to feel like, and all she had to do, was to pull everything back in—

She must have closed her eyes while she changed. When she opened them, Adam had moved back a step and was pointing a gun at her.

"Shoot me and your boyfriend dies," she said. She was proud of how calm she sounded.

"Maybe not," Adam said, with a little smile that made her shiver.

"You want to risk it?"

He paused to think. Without taking his eyes off her, Adam slowly set the gun on the bedside table. That only made her feel a little better—a guy that confident with a gun could probably kill her with his hands.

"What did you do to him?" Adam asked.

"Nothing. He's right here." She put her hand where she could feel Jay lurking inside her, a strange ball of warmth right at the solar plexus. If she paid attention, she could even pick up some of what he was feeling—a mixture of confusion and love, and for some reason, grief.

She tried to pat her curly hair back into shape and scowled. She'd like to be more put together—she especially wished she wasn't wearing her acid green yoga pants and an old Space Invaders T-shirt—but this was as good as it was going to get. "What happened to me?"

Adam crossed his arms. "You drank a reboot of someone else."

"Your boyfriend, Jay."

He glowered at her, refusing to confirm anything. *You called him by name, dipshit.*

"Great," she said. "How do I get him out of me?"

A brief pause while Adam considered. "I don't know."

"All right, then. Who does know? Jay?"

Adam gave her another silent, threatening stare. It was really starting to piss her off.

"Look," she said. "Work with me here. You really don't want to have your boyfriend sharing a body with some random woman, do you? Or was that, in fact, the plan?"

"This wasn't supposed to happen. I was supposed to use a cadaver."

"Where were you going to get the cadaver?"

He smirked a little. "You don't want to know."

It was high time Dana took control of this conversation. "I don't have time for this. You can grimace at me as much as you want, but I've got to practice my pitch for tomorrow."

"Pitch for what?"

"Ever hear of Rainbow Daydreams? Biggest manufacturer of contemporary memorabilia west of the Mississippi?"

Adam looked confused. Dana opened her briefcase, and pulled out her sample. Inside the box was a plasticine Shiba Inu with an open umbrella carried crosswise in his big grinning mouth. It was probably her best work ever.

"What the hell is that?" asked Adam.

"It's Mr. March Doge. For my series, Doges of the Month."

Adam emitted a weird laugh. "You've got to be fucking kidding."

"Here's the deal: I have a meeting at ten o'clock tomorrow morning. They have indicated interest in making the entire series. If I don't go to this meeting, it will cost me thousands of dollars. I'm going to the meeting and I'm going to give the best pitch of my entire life. Afterwards, I'll leave with you, and we can figure out how to evict your boyfriend." She closed the box and gently put it back in her briefcase.

"That's not how it's going to work."

"Just because you have the gun?"

"No. Because you're not going to make it that long."

"Is that a threat?"

He smirked. "Not from me." He picked up his gun from the table, examined it, and put it back in his holster. "Jay and I just quit our jobs. Our boss isn't going to like that, so I've got to get something that will make him back off."

That was almost completely unhelpful. And what kind of job could a guy have that would turn him into a human jello shot?

And why was this her problem, anyway?

"Here's the thing, Adam." He flinched when she said his name. Good. "No one knows where Jay is, right? So he's safe. And I'm just some woman who drank the wrong soda, so I'm safe. As far as I can tell, you're the only one in danger. So all you have to do is to fuck off for a few hours, and we all get what we want."

That was when the shotgun blast came through the door. Dana dropped to the floor. *That wasn't housekeeping*, she thought.

Adam had flattened himself against the wall. He looked uninjured. "Let Jay out," he said.

"What?"

"He's better than you at this. He'll keep you safe. Let him out."

Are you there? she thought, feeling a little silly.

Got it.

She felt herself melt back into Jay's shape. It was easier the second time, but it still took a few anxious seconds, while Adam returned fire over their prone body.

"What's the plan?" said Jay.

"I brought a bubble," said Adam. He turned quickly and shot at the window, which shattered, fragments dropping to the street below.

Jay got to his feet and bolted towards toward the open window, grabbing her briefcase along the way. *Stop! Stop!* she thought, but he ignored her and jumped, hurtling downwards towards the sidewalk.

Of all the stupid, crazy ways to die.

As Jay fell, he looked up at Adam, leaning out the shattered window. Adam threw something out after them, and then jumped onto it as if it were a surfboard. He steered it downwards, passing them, and catching Jay onto the steadily growing surface. The sides grew up rapidly, sealing at the top. It looked like it was made from smoked glass, and there were no visible controls.

A woman with long red hair holding a rifle leaned out of the shattered window and scanned in all directions.

She can't see us? asked Dana.

We're safe in here.

How do we land?

It's preprogrammed.

To where?

"Where are we going?" asked Jay.

"Manitou Springs," said Adam. He was still clutching his gun in both hands. "We're okay. I've got a plan; I'll keep you safe."

She felt Jay moisten his dry lips. "Adam, how did I die?"

CHAPTER 2

"SHE'S LISTENING, ISN'T SHE?" said Adam. He looked a little creeped out.

"Her name is Dana Elson," said Jay. "And of course she's listening."

Adam looked out of the bubble, and put his gun back in his holster. "She shouldn't know about any of this."

Where did you get this kind of technology? Do you work for the government?

Jay sighed. "Don't tell me you're still loyal to Greg?"

"I'm doing her a favor." A faint smile bloomed on Adam's thin face. "You always like it when I'm nice to people."

"Adam. Tell me how I died."

Adam scraped the side of his shoe against the floor of the bubble. "Greg shot you. He told me that he was sick and tired of my attitude, and the only reason I wasn't dead too is that I was worth more than you were. He thought he'd gotten me in line. Wasn't that stupid of him? So I got all my money together, and I bought your reboot from Tanya, and she dropped it off in a rental car in Spokane, and now they can all fuck themselves."

You DON'T work for the government. Dana's thoughts were a mess. Who else would have this kind of weird technology?

"We used to work for the Mahler Corporation," said Jay.

The plumbing people? They made my bathroom stuff!

At the same time, Adam said, "Jesus, Jay!"

"That's Adam Shapiro. I'm Jay O'Toole. And it's the same company, which is why everything in your bathroom probably leaks because the real reason that Mahler is still around is because of Roswell."

Roswell? Dana felt a chill as she realized that these two were also from New Mexico. Only a few hours' drive from her home in Albuquerque. *Did Jay just hear me think that?*

Luckily, he was busy arguing with Adam.

"I can't believe you're telling her—" said Adam.

"I want Dana to help us, and she won't do that if we lie to her. You've heard of Roswell, right, Dana? Back in 1947, an alien crashed in New Mexico."

It was a weather balloon.

"Nope, no weather balloon. A single-person alien craft, manned by an alien named—say it for me, Adam, you say it better than I do."

"Skzzx."

"Right. So the government panics, knows they want to keep this off the books. And there's a guy named Greg Mahler, who owns a plumbing manufacturing company—"

Wait, said Dana. *Why would they give an alien to someone who made sinks?*

"Mahler was an old friend of some government bigwig," said Jay.

Oh, thought Dana. That still didn't make sense, even though Jay and Adam seemed to think that it did.

"Exactly. So here's the deal: the Mahler Corporation gets everything it can out of Skzzx, it passes it on to the government, and no one in Congress knows anything about the alien. But it worked out a lot better for Mahler than anyone thought because Skzzx knew a lot more than anyone thought, especially if it kept him alive and maybe getting to see his home again someday. I mean, like, science stuff that's almost magic."

Like you.

"Yeah, like me."

"Back from the dead," Adam said softly.

But you're not, thought Dana. *The original Jay is dead. You're just some kind of copy.*

She felt the flush of Jay's anger. *Don't tell Adam that.*

"You want to know the really weird part?" Jay said aloud. "Greg Mahler's still alive and he looks like he's about thirty."

"That's only one of the many, many weird parts," said Adam. "Looks like we're here."

The bubble came to rest outside the entrance to the Pike's Peak RV Park. *Pike's Peak, that's Colorado,* thought Dana. *How did we get here so fast*? Once the bubble rested on the ground, it popped like it was made out of soap.

"I think I'd better change," said Jay. "Less chance of getting recognized."

Dana felt herself shrink down to her normal shape.

"Yeah, that doesn't get any easier to watch," said Adam. "We're just walking a few blocks that way."

"Let me grab my shoes," said Dana. On a whim, when she'd been stuck at an airport, she'd bought a pair of the slippers you were supposed to keep in your purse for when your high heels hurt. They were a nice carroty orange, Pantone 15-1262 TCX, one of her favorites. Now it looked like she'd be wearing them for a while.

Apparently, they were in a town called Manitou Springs, which looked like an old mining town, now given over to tourists. You could buy yourself a beer, a plate of nachos, and a T-shirt. And the entire thing seemed to be slanted uphill.

"Can't you walk faster?" asked Adam.

"It's been kind of a day," said Dana. And there was still the Rainbow Daydreams presentation scheduled for tomorrow—how was she going to make that happen? How could she even explain what had happened to her without sounding nuts?

Adam roughly took the briefcase out of her hand. "There. Hurry up."

"Hooray," she grumbled.

As they trudged up Manitou Avenue, Dana took a closer look at Adam. He was younger than she'd thought at first—late twenties at most, a few years older than she was—and from the black stubble on his pale scalp, it was clear that he wasn't naturally bald. He smelled like a combination of Ivory soap and gun oil. Even though he was wearing multiple layers of clothing, she could tell by looking at his face and hands that he was very thin. In fact, it looked like his jacket and pants were a little big on him, as if he'd recently lost weight. If she had to describe him in one word, that word would be *jumpy*—when a car door slammed down the street, Adam turned around with his hand on his gun, ready to return fire.

There. When the time came, she could draw an excellent picture of Adam Shapiro for the FBI. All she needed was a sketchpad and a charcoal pencil, and they'd have their man.

She followed Adam into an old-fashioned arcade. It was a place she would have liked under ordinary circumstances, packed as full as possible with old games, practically a test of how many skee-ball machines you could fit within a given space without causing an explosion.

Adam reached into his jacket pocket and pulled out a wad of tickets. She followed him to the redemption counter, willing to play along with Adam's mysterious plan, within reason, so she could get her life back. A bored clerk sat behind the counter, playing with his phone. "Can I help you?" he asked.

Adam pointed at an enormous, dusty elephant. "I want that. For my girlfriend."

The clerk wrinkled his nose. "Really? Don't you want a newer one? That one's been there forever."

"Please?" said Dana, and a look of horror passed quickly over Adam's face. *You know I can really mess things up for you right now? But I won't.* "I love elephants."

Adam leaned over the counter. "My lady loves the big trunks," he said, grinning. "The really big, thick ones."

From the look on his face, they'd grossed out the clerk. "Okay, man," he said. He set his phone down and picked up a long stick with a hook taped to the end of it. With practiced skill, he unhooked the elephant and set it down on the counter, letting loose a cloud of dust that made Dana sneeze.

"Here you go, babydoll," said Adam, bowing like she was the queen. "All yours."

CHAPTER 3

AT THREE A.M. THE next morning, Dana was at the Greyhound bus station with her briefcase, waiting for the next bus to Spokane. It was a twenty-six hour trip, so she'd get there a day late. She had no idea whether Rainbow Daydreams would be willing to move her appointment forward; no one would be in the office until she was already on the bus. But at least she was headed in the right direction, right?

The two men had opened up the elephant as soon as they'd gotten to the hotel room. Inside was a giant purple crystal that looked a lot like an amethyst. Jay had explained that this crystal was Skzzx's power supply from the spaceship, stowed long ago by another agent in what was supposed to be a safe place. And wow, had Adam been thrilled to have Jay share another little secret. His hand had rested on his gun for a bit until Jay had told him to quit frightening her.

Then the two men had spent the evening celebrating their find, starting with room-service steaks and whisky. About three glasses in, Dana had been out for the count. She'd woken up, thought *fuck these guys*, and made her way to the taxi stand. Her bus wasn't leaving for another four hours, and it was hard to stay awake, but Dana was pretty sure that as soon as she nodded off someone would steal her briefcase, including

Mr. March Doge. It didn't help that she could feel Jay drowsing warm and snug inside her, right below her heart. It wasn't an unpleasant sensation—it was kind of like having a cat sleep on your lap.

She'd have to figure out how to get Jay out of her sometime, but the Doges came first. *Just give me a day or two, Jay. You can understand that, right?*

A shadow fell over her and she looked up. It was a familiar angry man in a grey knit cap and black leather jacket, and she could see the outline of his gun against his jacket pocket, pointed at her.

"What the hell do you think you're doing?" Adam asked her.

She was too tired to even pretend she was frightened. "Adam," she said, "we both know you're not going to shoot me in the middle of a Greyhound Bus station."

He sighed and slouched down in the chair next to her. "You can't go back to Spokane. Tanya's watching your hotel room and car. She's trying to get Jay's reboot back before anyone notices she stole it. You don't want her catching you."

"How did you find me?"

He probably put a tracer on you, thought Jay.

Oh good, we're all awake. "You put a tracer on me?" she added.

Adam scowled. "If you'd stayed put, I wouldn't have to. Come on, let's get back to the hotel." He put his hands on his knees as if he were about to stand up.

"We're just going back to the hotel? And sit there? Why? What's your big plan here?"

He scraped the side of his shoe against the floor, looking down at it. His leg swung back and forth a few times, and when he was done there was a pale, clean streak on the linoleum. "There isn't one."

"What?"

"I thought they'd have killed us by this point. I didn't think this would work."

She felt Jay's urge to comfort Adam, to put his hand on Adam's shoulder, and tucked her own hand under her thigh. "So now we're going to hang around in Colorado with your boyfriend stuck inside me until your bosses catch us and kill us all? That's the worst fucking plan I ever heard of. That's worse than 'Let's all go to Bolivia.'"

Adam was silent for a moment. "Why would we go to Bolivia?"

"I can't believe it," said Dana. "I'm the brains of the outfit."

Yep, said Jay. *That's probably true.*

THEY SPREAD EVERYTHING ON the bed. Dana's pile included several packs of chewing gum, her phone, her wallet, her house keys, a bunch of pens at various levels of chewedness, and the box containing Mr. March Doge. Adam's pile was a phone, a car key, a wallet, a bunch of small metal trackers, a gun, and a surprisingly large pile of ammunition. Together, they had $4100 in cash, a large purple crystal from an alien spacecraft, and an eviscerated, dusty elephant.

"Now what?" asked Adam.

Adam might be the one with the gun, but she was the one making the decisions. She wondered if Adam had realized it yet. "First of all, we get more clothes, because I'm sick of your giant boyfriend stretching out my yoga pants."

Adam smirked.

"Then," she added, "we have to deal with this purple glowing thing. We have to figure out how to get Mahler to take it in exchange for getting Jay out of me, and letting us all go free."

"You really think you can do that?" asked Adam.

"I haven't figured it out yet, but I will," said Dana. She pointed at him. "You're lucky you kidnapped a smart person."

AS SOON AS IT was morning in Spokane, Adam called Rainbow Daydreams. His phone made it look like he was calling from the Deaconess Hospital ER where Dr. Adam Isaacs said that they'd taken Dana Elson with food poisoning. The company delayed her presentation for a week.

One week to get Jay out of her without getting them all killed. No problem.

Luckily, there was a store selling clothes and gadgets for hikers a short walk from the hotel. While Adam played with the Swiss army knives, Dana picked out some new clothes for herself, and, with Jay's help, some things for Jay. She locked herself in the changing room and thought, *this is so incredibly strange.* Especially for her, a natural planner and organizer, a person who made up her calendar two months in advance. One of her ex-boyfriends had called her the most boring artist he knew. (Which was why he was an ex, honestly.) When was the last time she'd even been on a spontaneous road trip? Let alone a spontaneous road trip spent fleeing from a mysterious and powerful corporation, with a strange man trapped inside her.

This kind of thing *never* happened to Dana.

She tried on her clothes—Jay being very silent for once—and then stripped back down to her underwear again.

Your turn, she thought.

I just want to tell you a couple of things, first, he said. *Now, when it's just the two of us.*

All right.

Everyone always says I'm the best roommate they ever had. I'm not in the way, I clean up after myself. Okay?

Okay. Why was he telling her this? How long did he think they were going to be like this?

Not to say I'm staying here forever, just that I'm a good roommate for as long as I am. Okay?

I already said okay.

Also, when you said I wasn't really Jay—you're right. I'm a copy of Jay. The real one died.

There was a wave of sorrow that went with that, and she could feel it as if it had been her own.

And what that means, he continued, *is that I'm starting fresh. All the stupid things I did last time are not going to happen again. And that's true for Adam, too. Okay?*

Was it meant to be reassuring? They were stuck together. It didn't matter if she liked or trusted either of them. Well, she did like Jay; it was hard not to. He was like a high-school football player, not the quarter-back, but one of those big solid defensive types, large and sweet natured, gone a little old and regretful. She wondered how he'd ended up working at a place like Mahler. Maybe he really had been different before.

She peeled off money from her giant roll of bills to pay the cashier. The man at the cash register counted it out loudly, like he was sure she had shorted him. Already irritated, she felt a presence looming directly behind her, breathing on her neck. A presence that smelled like Ivory soap and gun oil.

It was Adam. "You and I have the exact same hair," he said.

"I wouldn't know."

He smiled and peeled back his knit cap, revealing an eighth of an inch of black stubble. "It looks a little thin in front when it gets long, so I just shaved it off. But now I look like a doorknob, which is why I'm wearing this hat."

"Huh," she said. She'd never seen him in such a good mood. It dawned on Dana that Adam was actually very attractive when he wasn't trying to scare the crap out of her. Not handsome, but attractive. You could picture him as a character on a cop show in the Seventies.

"I brought the car over," Adam said, with a full-on grin.

She nearly said, "What car?" until she realized what he meant.

It was a brand-new black BMW. She could feel Jay's subvocal excitement. "You're going to steal someone's Beemer?" she whispered.

"My key opens the door," said Adam, demonstrating. "That means it's mine." He leaned in and whispered in her ear. "Go change in the coffeehouse bathroom and let Jay drive. He's the best driver I've ever seen."

Really? And then she realized, *given the choice, which of us would I rather have drive the stolen car? Me or the other guy?* She stomped towards the coffeehouse to let Jay out.

CHAPTER 4

I AM RIDING IN A *stolen car,* thought Dana. *I am riding in a stolen car driven by the guy sharing my body.* The freaky part is that neither Jay nor Adam seemed rattled by the idea. In fact, Jay was trying to calm her down. He was also really enjoying driving the BMW. Adam had been right about one thing—Jay was an excellent driver.

"I thought we'd head west for a bit on 24," yelled Jay over the godawful country music he was blasting. "We probably want to get pretty far from Manitou Springs before we let them know we have the crystal, right? Because that's the first place they're going to look."

That made sense. It was very quiet where they were—it was a two-lane highway leading into the mountains, and she'd only seen a few cars.

Still, Dana didn't much like letting Jay take control like this. And she didn't like his taste in music, either. She also really, really didn't like riding in a *stolen car.*

Behind them was a long-haired woman on a motorcycle. She was getting closer, looking like she was trying to pass. And then she pulled out a gun out of her jacket.

GUN! Dana screamed, trying to get Jay's attention, just as the rear window shattered.

Adam turned, pulling the gun from his holster, and shot through the opening. Two efficient shots. In the rearview mirror, Dana could see the woman fall backward from the motorcycle.

She was dead. Dana had just seen Adam kill someone. She was lying on the highway behind them, next to her fallen motorcycle.

No. She couldn't let this happen. She grabbed control of her body from Jay, the car weaving wildly over the road as he fought her, until she was able to pull to the shoulder and stop.

"Don't do that while Jay's driving! You'll kill us all!" said Adam. No reaction about the woman he'd just shot. None.

"I will not be party to murder," she said. She pounded at the touchscreen until the radio turned off.

"That was manslaughter, maybe, at most," said Adam. "But I'd call it self-defense."

"I'm done," she said. "We're turning around, we're going back to Manitou Springs, and we're doing what we should have done originally, which is call the FBI."

"You think the FBI doesn't know about Mahler? If you don't want to die, right here, right now, either get driving or let Jay take the wheel."

"I'm so sick of you threatening me."

Now he looked angry. "I'm not threatening you!"

She could hear something behind them. Loud thumping noises, coming quickly. She turned around and looked. It was a woman in motorcycle boots running towards them. At something like forty-five miles an hour.

"Jesus," said Adam.

She threw the car into reverse and drove backwards until she heard a wet crunch. Then she tossed it back into drive and sped away. She didn't look behind her. She knew she couldn't take it.

"What was that? What was that, Adam?"

"That was Tanya."

"You shot her in the chest! She was down! And can she usually run that fast?"

Adam laughed, a weird strangled noise.

"What?"

"I will not be party to murder," he said, in a high, squeaky voice.

"Shut up," she said.

"I will not be party to murrrrder."

"Shut up." She could feel Jay trying to cheer her up. It didn't help.

CHAPTER 5

DANA KEPT THINKING OF the sound Tanya's body had made hitting the car. Driving helped; driving was nice and mindless and it took her away from thinking about how right about now she should be hearing whether Rainbow Daydreams would be buying the series or not if all this hadn't happened.

"I don't think you killed her," said Adam. "Tanya's pretty indestructible."

I ran over her with a car.

"They've been messing with us all at Mahler. Everyone who works there." He was looking out the window, away from her, so all she could see was the edge of his knit cap. "Weird alien technology stuff."

Us, she thought. *Did that include Adam too?* "What did they do to you?"

"I was supposed to be able to teleport, but it doesn't work right," He swallowed. "The other guy they tried it on got stuck halfway in a wall. It took him like half an hour to die. But Jay's cloning thing worked, so I bet Tanya's did, too."

You suck at cheering people up, she thought, but she kept her mouth shut, because she'd just realized something—this was the first time Adam had told her a secret when he didn't have to. Which was, she guessed, his way of trying to be nice to her.

At least we don't have to worry about contacting them now, she thought. *Obviously they know we stole the crystal.* "How do you think they found us?"

He turned back towards her.

"Because there are probably some other things squirreled away here and there that you could have stolen for leverage, right?"

I thought we'd be going for the thing in Coeur d'Alene, thought Jay.

"They put a tracker on me," said Adam, as if it had just occurred to him.

"Oh, they put a tracker on you? What a rotten thing to do." She still hadn't found the one that Adam had stuck somewhere on her body and she let that anger creep into her voice.

He reached over and pinched at something just above her hairline, right at the base of her neck. He held it up in front of her and crushed it.

He opened the window and tossed it out.

If he's got one on him, I didn't see it, Jay said. *And I pretty much saw everything.*

She didn't want to think about that part too much. *Okay,* she thought. *Maybe it's on something he brought with him.*

"Jay thinks it's on your stuff," she said.

Adam reached into his jacket and took out his phone. Then he threw it out the window. Next, a palmful of trackers. He took his gun out of the holster and looked at it. "I'll have to trust the gun," he said. "And the ammo. But I should get more ammo soon. And the car key, I guess. But everything else has to go." He unfastened his seatbelt. Off came the hat, which went out the window. Then his shoes, and then he slid forward and she heard something unzip.

Don't look, thought Dana. *Don't look don't look don't look*

She could feel the edge of Jay's amusement. *Don't crash the car trying not to look at my hot boyfriend. Even though he's NAAAAAKED.*

"Where am I driving, anyway?" she asked, pretending she couldn't hear Jay.

My uncle has a rifle range in Minnesota. We could go there.

"Jay suggests his uncle's rifle range in Minnesota," she added.

"No, Mahler's got to be watching it," said Adam, muffled slightly by the grey T-shirt he was pulling on. "And it's got to be someplace hard to get a signal, in case the tracker is in something I swallowed." He held up his leather jacket. "Goodbye, jacket." He threw it out the window and sighed. "I liked that jacket."

Dana was considering something really stupid. Because she did know a place where it was really quiet, with almost no one around and bad cell coverage. And she was thinking about bringing Jay and Adam there. Not because she had decided to trust them. She knew they were both keeping secrets from her, especially Adam. They were just three people who were temporarily driving in the same direction.

She might be making a huge mistake. But ever since she was a little girl, this place was where she had always run when she was scared or sad or troubled, and she needed that safety now.

"I've got a place," she said.

SHE'D TAKEN PEOPLE TO her late father's house before—it wasn't too far north of Albuquerque where she lived—and the reaction was always the same. First people would scan the walls full of gold records, reading off the labels of Press Elson's hits from the Fifties and Sixties, all moonlight-and-magnolias with a rock-and-roll beat. But they always ended up in the middle of the entry hall, staring at the black leather pants and jacket in the big illuminated glass case. The famous suit that Press Elson had worn in his triumphant comeback concert in Hawaii. Adam was no exception.

"Holy shit," said Adam. "Dibs."

"No," said Dana.

"I don't even have to pick the lock. If I climb that bookshelf over there—" He whipped around and looked at her. "Dana ELSON."

"I'm his kid. My parents had me a couple of years before he died."

Sometimes people asked Dana what it was like being Press Elson's daughter. The thing that was hard to explain was that it was normal to her. Her father was like the sun; she was like a little moon, touched by the glow of his fame. That's the way it had always been. She didn't even remember meeting the man, since she'd been a toddler when he died.

It did tend to take other people as a shock, though. She was enjoying the goofy, confused look on Adam's face. "You're Press Elson's daughter. So why aren't you rich?"

That was the next question they usually asked. "Because there are about seventy-one of us, last I heard. Dad would travel the country performing, and he'd pick up a girl in every town. We all inherited a share of this house. But every time they find a new Elson kid, my share gets cut, so we're not talking about a lot of money here. Besides, this place is in the middle of nowhere. It used to be a sulfur springs resort where gangsters hung out in the twenties. Dad bought it for nothing in the fifties, and it's kind of fallen apart since then, but the gas and lights work, most of the time. It really needs a new roof, but we've got to get a majority to agree on it, and that's nearly impossible. Now we all just show up whenever we feel like it."

Can you sing? said Jay. *Sing "Buttercup Time." No, "Sweet Evelina"!*

"I am not going to sing," said Dana.

Adam was still staring at the jacket. "This is nuts," he said. "You're Press Elson's kid."

"If it helps, I met him like five times and I don't remember any of it because I was a toddler when he died. Mom said he was a very sweet man."

"I'll bet," said Adam. She could hear the sarcasm in his voice.

Privately, she agreed with Adam. Dad had been the central fact of Mom's life, her big story. And Mom had just been one night in Dad's, some anonymous half-hour in an endless life on the road. What had it been like to be him, to go and go and not care what you were leaving behind you?

Very sweet. Right.

There was always some food in the kitchen, though you had to be careful about the expiration dates—Dana had once accidentally eaten some cereal that predated the first Bush administration—and they were able to pull together an early dinner out of canned soup, crackers, and apples. They reclined in the sunken, carpet-lined living room on the big hairy sofas. Dad had had it redesigned in the 70s in what the decorator called "South Sea Islands" which only made sense if the South Sea Islanders had a big thing for fake tiger fur.

There were a lot of big furry chairs and a glass coffee table with an etched-in checkerboard, and an enormous (for the 70s) television, also covered with tiger fur, which no longer worked. One of Dana's siblings had mod-podged a picture of Dad to the screen. Half-dead spider plants hung from macramé suspended from the ceiling. It was ugly—hideous—and sometimes Dana found dried, crusty, scablike *things* stuck in the shag carpeting, but somehow everyone wanted to hang out in there in spite of all of that. If anyone else were at the house, this is where they would have been.

Dana watched Adam peel his apple with a Swiss army knife she was pretty sure he'd swiped from the clothing store in Manitou Springs. She couldn't feel too guilty about it.

"What do you think Mahler's doing to find us now?" she said.

"I think Tanya would have realized that she can't handle this alone," he said. "They'll probably have a team in Manitou Springs, and they might have kept some folks in Spokane. And then they'll try to figure out where we're headed next."

"So you think they're just going to try to find us, kill us, and take the crystal back."

"No reason not to, from their perspective."

Dana ground her foot into the carpet in frustration. "We have to make them think that if we die, the crystal goes someplace they wouldn't want it to go. Who can we give it to? Maybe a big energy company?"

"They know about it already. They're all paying off Mahler to keep it hidden."

"Maybe a newspaper?"

"Mahler owns a bunch of newspapers. I don't know which ones."

"The government?"

"Are you kidding?"

Dana sighed. *Any thoughts, Jay?*

Not yet, no.

"Good news is I think we'll have a quiet night," Adam said. "It's pretty hard to track two people in a car—three people, I mean—and we switched the car, which helped."

She did feel bad about taking the Ford from the used car lot they'd passed. Eventually they'd ditch it somewhere, hopefully without any bullet holes in it. They'd kind of ruined the Beemer.

"So what I'm wondering now is if maybe Jay can come out," he continued.

She'd been dreading this conversation. "Yeah, I wanted to talk about that. I mean, last night, I have no idea what went on, and that's okay. But today, I'm here, I'm awake, and this is really, really weird."

Adam looked up from his apple and squinted at her. "Are you saying you want to be more—involved?"

Yes, she was attracted to Adam—he had an amazing body—but it was stupid to be attracted to Adam. For many, many reasons. She picked the most tactful of the reasons. "Adam, you're gay. You're like a Kinsey Twelve."

He grinned. "It's not that I don't like you. You're cute, and you're a smart-ass." He took her hand in his. His fingers were cold and hard, and a little sticky with apple juice. "Two months ago, I saw Jay die in front of me and now he's right here. I can pretend you're not here if I have to, because there's a bunch of things he really likes I haven't even had time to do yet, and I don't want to wait until we figure everything out because we might not get another chance. Okay? No one has to know. No one ever has to know."

That was the worst attempt at seduction she had ever heard in her entire life, including high school, and normally her answer would have been a hearty *hell, no.* But it was a little hard to think clearly, with Adam's face so close to hers, those desperate blue eyes looking into her own. Jay's warm thoughts washed over her, telling her it wasn't just about the sex for Adam, it was about Adam trying hard to be a good person, and this is what he needed to do it, the chance to feel warm and safe and loved.

Please, Dana, she felt Jay think. *Please, please, please.*

It was getting very difficult to remember why she should say no, and her lips opened, the words about to come out of her mouth, when all three of them heard the car on the gravel road outside.

"Who is that?" asked Adam.

"I don't know," said Dana. *Did they find us already? How did they find us already?*

He picked up the gun that had been sitting beside him. "See who it is," he said, his voice harsh. "I'll be behind you."

She got up and walked towards the door, not wanting to open it. How had Tanya found them already? Her heart thumped in her chest. The door was going to open, and she was going to die.

She heard the door unlock and then swing open, revealing a woman holding two big grocery bags. It was one of her favorite half-sisters, Sierra. Dana sighed with relief.

"Hi, Sierra," said Dana, trusting that somewhere behind her, Adam was making his gun disappear.

"Dana! Good to see you!" said Sierra. "Who is this?"

"Sierra Elson, Adam Shapiro," said Dana. "Guess what, Sierra? I found another half-brother."

CHAPTER 6

BEAMING AT THEM BOTH, Sierra put her groceries down on the kitchen counter. She was about ten years older than Dana, and no one would have taken them for half-sisters, though Sierra claimed that they had the same teeth, whatever that meant. Teeth were teeth. Sierra had long blond California hair, and she favored loose hemp clothing and lots of handmade beads. "Who's ahead then? Boys or girls?"

"Girls, I think," said Dana. "By two or three."

"Well, come here," said Sierra. "Welcome to the family." She hugged Adam, which had to have been a lot like hugging a lamppost. She held him by the shoulders, scrutinizing him. "You've got Dad's eyes, I think." Given any two people in the world, Sierra could find a family resemblance.

"Why have you got all those groceries?" asked Dana.

"There's more in the car," said Sierra. "I hope you guys don't mind, but I'm having some friends over tonight. I got a new job, Dana! I'm working at a company that's working on developing solar wind energy."

"Solar and wind energy?"

"No, solar wind energy. We're going to be putting sails in the desert to pick up solar wind. It's *awesome.* It's like the best of both worlds. Come on guys, help me get all the hummus out of my car." She turned towards Dana and beamed. "This is great! I love finding a new brother. It's like a birthday present!"

On paper, Sierra should have annoyed the hell out of Dana because nearly everything she believed was demonstrably nuts. But in actuality, she was one of her favorite people in the world. She was totally non-judgmental. You could tell her that you believed the moon was actually a giant egg and she just would have nodded and smiled. And she was also incredibly positive. She would have agreed that it was just so *cool* that the moon could hatch into just about anything you could imagine. Maybe it would turn into a giant space-dragon! Wouldn't it be awesome?

None of Dana's half-siblings looked all that much alike—not surprisingly, because Dad hadn't had a physical type so much as an interest in women who would sleep with him on the basis of listening to him play in concert—but they all seemed to have inherited a weird artsy streak that came out in unpredictable ways. Sierra's showed up in the way she wanted to remake the world out of rainbows and unicorns and sparkle-magic.

And I make collectible dogs, thought Dana. *Doges.* She was proud she could support herself as a commercial artist, but some days, she wished she were a little less commercial, and a little bit more of an artist. Dad never listened to the record labels about what was fashionable—Dad was always just Dad.

THE HOUSE DID HAVE a formal living room, which some decorator in the fifties had filled with hard, white furniture and lined with smoked glass. But usually it just sat cold, alone, and empty during parties. It turned out that no one liked to watch himself get drunk. Instead, everyone collected in the Island Pit, even though it was impossible to get really clean, though Dana, Sierra, and an oddly quiet Adam had given it a good shot. Also Sierra had watered the nearly dead plants, because that was Sierra.

As the party burbled along in the Pit, Dana and Sierra sat in the kitchen together, drinking a sororal beer.

"How did you find him?" asked Sierra.

Dana really didn't like lying to her sister. "Mom left some stuff behind for me to deal with."

"How's that going?" Sierra took a sip of her beer.

Dana sighed. Oh yes, now she had to think about her actual life problems. Sierra remembered things like that. "There's still a lot of stuff in the house. And the house itself is pretty much a ruin. You know how she got. She wouldn't fix it and she wouldn't let me fix it."

Dana had to have been something like twelve years old when she looked at Mom and realized that Mom was a kind, sweet woman, but in many ways, her life had frozen in place the day a star reached down from the stage and took her by the hand. Dana had planned to spend a good chunk of her life taking care of Mom. Now Mom was gone, and Dana was at loose ends, because nothing else she did seemed as important as taking care of Mom.

And wasn't that a selfish way to think about it?

Sierra looked her right in the eyes and squeezed her upper arm. It was weirdly comforting, even though Dana felt something at the edge of her mind, something she'd forgotten.

"I miss her a lot," Dana admitted. "I don't feel like myself."

"Of course not," said Sierra. "It's only been six months. Why should you be back to normal?"

There is no normal, thought Dana. Someday the house would be cleaned out and sold, and Mom would still be dead. There was always going to be a Mom-shaped hole inside her.

How did you say something like that? Sierra would feel obligated to try to cheer her up, and then Dana would have to pretend that it had worked, to avoid disappointing her sister. Better not to say anything, better to just drink her beer and tough it out like a good little soldier. It wouldn't always be like this, would it?

What had she forgotten?

Sierra set her beer down. "Why don't you show me the art you've been working on? The Shiba Inus?"

Dana liked how Sierra always called it her "art." She got up, trailed by Sierra. To get back to her bedroom, she had to pass by the Pit. In the hairy sofas reclined five hippy-ish people, and Adam. Five rumpled souls who had dressed in the cleanest things from the floor, sprayed themselves with patchouli, and gently wandered into the world, and her monochromatic, precision-machined "brother." *That's what I was forgetting.*

He's drunk, said Jay. *Please don't leave him.*

Why? Do you think he's dangerous? Does he shoot things when he's drunk?

She felt the edge of Jay's anger.

I'm not being unreasonable.

Adam tilted his head upside down on the back of the couch to look at her and grinned. "Hey, little sister."

A fifty-ish man with a thin grey-blond ponytail was talking. "And by the time we got the sail up it was almost midnight. Cold and dark. Marta saw them first. It was five lights, zooming back and forth across the sky."

"It was really weird," a young woman in a worn-out Pixies T-shirt said. "They'd hover there, and then they'd zoom off in another direction. It wasn't meteors."

"I think it was aliens," said the older man.

"I've heard a lot of people say they saw aliens out in the desert," said Sierra. "I think there might be some truth to it."

"I saw an alien once," said Adam.

Oh, fuck, thought Jay. *Dana, you've got to stop him.*

How?

Jay was silent.

"It was greyish and covered with tentacles," said Adam, looking at the ceiling, "and you could almost see through it. About forty feet away from me. And they'd painted a line around it, and they said never cross that line, because back in the forties he ate a guy. Just sucked him in, screaming."

"Where did you see that, Adam?" asked Sierra.

Adam swallowed, concentrating. "Huh, I'm drunk. Does anyone else get drunk like that? Like I'm fine I'm fine I'm fine and now I'm drunk? Like a light switch drunk? Anyone else a light switch drunk?" He looked at Dana. "Jay, it's your job to tell me to stop."

"Okay, big brother," said Dana. "Time for bed."

Adam Shapiro woke up in the pitch dark and realized two things: he was alone, and he really needed to find the bathroom.

He snapped on the light by the bed and winced. Was he sober yet? He thought he probably was. But his mind didn't feel any clearer, and he had no idea what to do next. None.

He'd spent ten years working as one of Greg Mahler's problem-solvers. Greg would say, "Adam, I need you to get some papers out of a lawyer's office." Adam would get the blueprints for the lawyer's building, check out the place out in person, and draw up a plan to steal the papers. It was fun; he was good at it. Or Greg would say, "Adam, get that state representative to leave us alone." And Adam would figure out the best way to make that happen, which might involve scaring someone a little, or something stronger than that. He was good at that, too.

So life had gone on until one day Jay had asked him, "Do you like your job?"

Adam wasn't used to thinking about how he felt. Usually he just got on with things. But it had dawned on him as he looked in Jay's warm, brown eyes, that he wasn't happy, not at all.

He'd wanted to leave the Mahler Corporation, but he'd only gotten as far as suggesting to Greg that maybe he could pick his assignments in the future. And the next thing he knew, he'd been called to Greg's office, and Jay was waiting in there, a confused look on his face. Adam had looked at Jay, not Greg, and he'd heard the first gunshot before he'd even seen Greg was armed.

He knew what he needed to do now—he needed to figure out a way to get Jay away from Greg for good. But all Adam's skills were ones he'd learned at Mahler; he couldn't outrun or outthink Greg. He could stretch things out, but ultimately, they were fucked. Greg wouldn't let him go as long as he was still having fun playing with him.

Adam trailed his hand along the wall of Press Elson's hallway, feeling for the bathroom door. For some reason, he felt safer here. Maybe it was because they were so far out in the desert. It was so dark and quiet—no lights or other people for miles. Or maybe it was that it felt like someone's home. A nest, a den, safe little animals peeking out at the world. This is what it would be like having an actual family, rather than his asshole mother and the rest of his dirtbag relatives. He could go back to Worcester but he'd never feel this safe in his mother's apartment.

He was so tired and he felt like he'd driven off the edge of the world.

Jay, what should I do?

He snapped on the bathroom light—ow—and avoided looking at himself in the mirror. He knew how it was going to end for him. Back at Mahler, working for Greg, until Greg finally got bored with him and shot him. But until then—

What if he really were Dana's lost half-brother? What if they just kept on pretending it was true for a while?

"No complaining," Dana said. "Drink your orange juice."

Adam squinted at her and drank. His scalp was covered with uneven stubble, and he was well on the way to having a moustache and beard. He'd fallen asleep in the clothes he'd been wearing and he was still in them, and still covered with the comforter she'd draped over him before shutting the door. Jay found his smell soothing, but Dana thought he could really use a shower.

"How much did you drink last night?" said Dana.

"Doesn't matter. I just can't drink beer."

"Well, then you shouldn't drink beer."

He smiled. "Don't piss off a guy with a hangover and a gun."

"Did you really see an alien?"

"Did I say that? Jesus." He sighed. "Yeah. When I first started working at Mahler. We all did. It was like, 'This is what you're protecting the world from.' But you kind of had to feel sorry for him. He comes all the way to Earth, and they stick him in a glass box for seventy years. If I were him, I'd grab the first guy who got close enough, take his gun, and shoot everyone between me and the door."

"And then he'd still be trapped on Earth."

Adam shrugged, winced, and took a sip of his orange juice.

There were a lot of things that Dana wanted to ask him. Mostly, she wanted to know what he'd done for Mahler and why he'd decided to stop. But she didn't think she'd get a real answer, either from him or from Jay. And in the end, maybe she really only needed to know that he loved Jay enough to bring him back from the dead. She crossed her arms over her chest. "I had an idea."

He looked at her over the edge of his orange juice glass.

"The really valuable stuff we have is the stuff inside your head. All the other Skzzx goodies squirreled away here and there that you know about."

"Jay knows a few things too."

"Okay, and Jay. The threat is not that hey, we have this magic rock. The threat is what else might we take? So I say we drop off the rock somewhere, and while they're busy finding it, we go steal something else."

He squinted at her.

"We need to show we have leverage over them. Because they know how to get Jay out of me and I don't want to talk to them until they're worried about what we can do to them."

"So your plan is to drive around the country, stealing things."

"What do you think?"

He shrugged. "Sounds like fun."

CHAPTER 7

THEY PULLED UP TO the first parking lot by the Grand Canyon and got out, the crystal securely held in Dana's jacket pocket. She looked around. No one was around, so she set it down on a picnic table. *Goodbye, weird alien crystal,* she thought.

Without saying a word, she and Adam continued along the trail to the edge of the canyon. The two of them stood there and looked at it. There didn't seem to be any words, but it was one of the few things in her life that really lived up to the hype. It was huge, and it was beautiful, and it looked like it had been there forever. It even smelled good, like pine trees.

I've never been here before, thought Jay.

"I've never been here, either," she said.

"Neither have I," said Adam, leaning over the edge and looking down.

He looked different to her after a few days on the road, like proximity to Jay had softened him. He looked tired and still a little hungover, but somehow lovable. Which was strange, because by all objective measures, Adam was an angry, weird gun nut.

No one should be judged by objective measures. Was that her or Jay thinking? Or both of them?

"You know, I don't mind Jay being in here," she said, touching the place under her breastbone where she could most feel his presence. "He's just kind of warm and sweet and nice."

"Not like us," said Adam. He kicked a small rock over the edge, watching it fall.

No, she thought. *Not like us at all.* "Adam?"

"Yes, Dana?"

"Is that Dad's jacket you're wearing?"

He looked away from her, considering. "It's cold. And I think Dad would have wanted me to have it."

And what was she going to say? "You know he's not really your father?" *What the hell,* she thought. *Dad was a generous soul. You might even be right.*

MIDWAY THROUGH THE FOUR-HOUR drive to Las Vegas, Dana was losing focus. There wasn't much outside the windows but the endless highway. It reminded her of Mom's well-worn copy of *Press Elson Speaks*. Mom had let Dana read it, pretty much as soon as she could read, so Dana could know something about Dad. Her favorite parts were the early chapters, back when Dad had been a young, broke musician, driving around the Southwest with Eddie Harris, the bassist, and Bob Crispin, the drummer, in a rusted-out bread delivery truck, trying to get momentum behind their first single, "Okay Baby."

"Half the time the radio didn't work," Dad had told the interviewer. "The other half, it was some preacher talking about the end of the world. I got to appreciate the way Bob and Eddie squabbled all the time. Kept me from falling asleep at the wheel." He talked about meals in greasy spoons where the three of them shared one hamburger, and nights where they all pigged up under a blanket in the back of the bread truck for warmth. It all sounded so wonderful when Dad wrote about it—like he could sense the whole world opening up to him, and he was ready to meet it.

But she'd always been dubious, especially as she grew up. Maybe it was all rosy sunrise in retrospect but at the time, she bet it was hard, and cold, and hungry, and a little scary.

Now here she was on a grand adventure. But to be fair to herself, it wasn't her fault. She was a totally straight-laced individual, always had been. She was the kid who did her homework on a Friday night. This made her sort of a rarity in the Elson family. Press Elson had faith that everything would come out all right. Dana Elson did not, so Dana Elson planned in advance.

This trip was just a vacation for her. Soon enough she'd figure out how to get Jay back in his own body and Jay and Adam would go back to their lives, and she'd go back to hers. Dad would say she ought to enjoy herself while it lasted. Maybe she'd even get to see an alien on the way. That would be interesting.

She looked over at Adam in the passenger seat, his head tilted against the window like he wanted to fall asleep but couldn't quite manage it. It was overly warm in the car, and for once he wasn't wearing a jacket. She would have expected someone like him to have some tattoos, but he didn't. "Talk to me," she said. "Keep my mind from wandering."

"About what?"

"I don't know. Tell me something about Mahler."

He thought for a moment. "Did I tell you about the spa?" he asked. "There's a spa."

Plumbing supplies, a captive alien, and a *spa*? "Adam, that makes no sense."

"Well, they do sell plumbing supplies, right? The spa is where they show everything off. Luxury sinks, that kind of thing. And there's the secret reason, too. Greg told me he built the Mahler Spa so there would be an excuse for important people to stay in Roswell when they came to talk to the alien." He shrugged. "I don't know. It's nice, though. I took

Jay there for an overnight on our first anniversary. They've got a hot tub in every room. And they've got showers you could wash a car in."

That was a really *great trip,* thought Jay. *REALLY great. So we were in the hot tub—*

Jay had apparently decided (a) Dana was a prude and (b) teasing her was fun. "Okay!" said Dana. "Don't tell me anything else, Jay!"

Adam snickered.

"But what about the alien?"

"What do you mean?"

"You said people came to talk to Skzzx. You said Greg got the alien to teach them how to do things, right? Like the reboots and the bubbles and things like that?"

Adam shrugged.

"How did they talk to him? I mean, it's an alien. They don't show up speaking English, right?"

"I don't know, Dana. I only saw it once, and it didn't talk. It just hissed. I don't think it even had a tongue." Adam got a faraway look on his face. "Huh."

"It's probably not important," said Dana. "I'd just like to know."

"There you go," said Adam. "Always thinking."

THERE ARE CASINOS IN Las Vegas that look like James Bond might be there, playing roulette while wearing a tuxedo. And there are casinos that look like the local shopping mall, the one where half the stores are closed. And then there is the Clown World Casino, thought Dana, which is where bad clowns go where they die. She tried not to look around too much.

"The important thing," Adam said, as he sat on the end of her bed watching her eat her breakfast, "is never to get distracted."

"Hard not to," she said. "Did you see the carpet?" The carpet in the casino was covered with clowns. Clowns juggling, clowns coming out of a tiny car, clowns making balloon animals. She shuddered.

"Hey!" Adam said, smirking. "You've got the easy part. All you have to do is collect a crowd while I go get the thing."

She swallowed a bite of her clown-shaped pancake. "So the plan is—"

"I've got this—well, it looks like a credit card. But if you put it in a slot machine, you'll get a jackpot. Keep doing it, and you'll get a really, really huge jackpot."

"And where and what is this thing you're looking for?"

Adam sighed. "It's a cloak of invisibility."

She snickered. "Not sure we have the caster level for that. We might need to find a wizard."

"The real problem is finding a cloak of invisibility when it's tacked to the ceiling."

"If it's on the ceiling, how are you going to reach it?"

"You know how they have circus acts going on in here? They just leave the equipment up all the time. I'm going to walk the tightrope underneath and grab for it."

"Really?"

"Yeah, you'll be playing the slots, and I'll be walking on a tiny metal rope over certain death three stories up." He grinned at her. "It'll be fun."

THEY TOOK THE ELEVATOR downstairs together but split off before they got to the casino floor. *Don't look up,* Dana reminded herself as she walked into the casino hall, feeling like she was crushing clowns under her feet. The room was enormous. There were something like ten banks of slot machines on either side of the raised central circus stage. A woman in a very small clown suit and full clown makeup was taking a drink order from one of the slot machine players. On stage, a quick change artist, assisted by a woman in a sequin-covered clown costume, was currently switching from an ugly purple suit to an ugly green one.

I kind of want to get on stage and show them what a real change looks like, thought Jay.

Not with all the cameras in here, thought Dana.

But you have to admit, it would be funny.

Suddenly there was a loud clamor of bells. Someone had won a jackpot at the slot machine. But here was the thing, Dana thought—no one but her was paying attention. There weren't even any coins coming out because it all went on a card reader now.

This plan isn't going to work, Adam, she thought. *How can you possibly distract people in a casino? Everything here is a distraction!*

She looked around the room, still careful not to look up. The sides of the room were lined with bars. On the stage, the quick change artist had been joined by a woman singing along with a keyboard player.

There it was, her distraction.

I thought you couldn't sing, said Jay.

No, I said I don't *sing, not that I can't.*

She joined the small crowd applauding the woman and took the warm microphone from her hand. "What the hell," she said. "Play 'Sweet Evelina.'"

"Sweet Evelina" had been Dad's biggest hit. It was a Civil War song—actually it was a big Confederate favorite, which was one of the reasons Dana didn't like singing it. The other reason is that when she sang it, she sounded exactly like Dad. It was uncanny: the pudgy biracial girl and the pot-bellied white man had identical pipes, and it was especially noticeable when she sang the hits. And the effect always brought a crowd.

By the time she was up to the third verse, there were about a hundred people listening, which had to have cheesed off the quick-change artist.

Evelina and I, one fine evening in June,
Took a walk all alone by the light of the moon.
The planets all shone, for the heavens were clear,
And I felt round the heart I would never know fear.

And now the audience was singing the chorus:

Dear Evelina, sweet Evelina,
My love for thee shall never, never die.
Dear Evelina, sweet Evelina,
My love for thee shall, never, never die.

She felt Jay burble with excitement inside her. *Sing Buttercup Time!*

It wasn't a bad idea. In fact, she might skip the last verse, which was kind of depressing, and just repeat the chorus again, and then sing "Buttercup Time."

Then she spotted a woman in the crowd. Most of the people in her audience were dressed for a nice day at the mall. But this woman was in head to toe black leather, and she had long red hair.

She and Jay realized it at the same time: Tanya.

Welcome to our evil corporation, here's your leather jacket, thought Dana. She couldn't let her spot Adam. Instead, she only sang louder, but Tanya was already turning away. Dana sang:

Tanya from Mahler! Tanya from Mahler!
Tanya from Mahler! Hey! Look over here!

There were some murmurings from the crowd. "Sing it with me, folks!" she said.

Tanya from Mahler! Tanya from Mahler!

And now she'd got at least some of them singing along with her. And she'd finally gotten Tanya's attention, to the point that Tanya bulled her way through the crowd, shoving people out of the way.

Dana yelped and jumped off the little stage, running for the exit. An exasperated Tanya pulled free from the tourists and bolted after her.

This is stupid, thought Dana. *She can outrun a car.*

My turn? thought Jay.

Cameras.

Better than dead.

She'd missed a planter in her wild run for freedom and now she was blocked. She turned around and found Tanya right in front of her.

Tanya reached into her open jacket and rested her hand on her gun, just visible in a shoulder holster. "Where's the soda bottle?" she asked.

She'd hoped that the next time she saw someone from Mahler, she could broach the idea of getting Jay out of her. But the secret of being a good negotiator was to wait for the time that the other person was ready to be flexible. And Dana could tell Mahler wasn't ready to negotiate yet. Better to just confuse the issue for now. "What soda bottle?" she said with all the sincerity she could muster.

"The one that was in your rental car in Spokane."

"It was empty! I threw it away! Why are you asking me about a stupid soda bottle, anyway?"

"Empty?" A look of horror spread over Tanya's face. "You're sure?"

"Yes. Are you going to let me go?"

Tanya was still giving her that weird look. "Tell me where Adam is."

Oh my God, thought Dana. *She thinks Adam swallowed your reboot.*

Jay laughed. *We'd still be in the hotel room in Spokane.*

"I know Adam kidnapped you," added Tanya. "If you trust me, I'll help you get away from him."

Dana tried to look confused. "You've got it totally wrong. He's my older brother."

She could tell Tanya didn't believe her. "That's not in his file."

Now Dana was genuinely annoyed. Yes, she was lying, but there was no reason she couldn't be telling the truth, dammit. "Technically he's my half-brother. We have the same father. I ran into him in Spokane, he was between jobs, and we decided to go on a road trip together."

I mean, Jay continued pensively, *a guy could go blind that way.*

Dana tried to ignore Jay. "Besides, he left. He said something about wanting to go to Austin for barbecue?"

"And he left you stranded here?"

Dana grinned. "I kept my car; I don't know what he's driving. We're both happier if I don't ask Adam where he gets his cars. I don't know when I'll see him again. You know Adam. He'll show up again in a few months, and it'll be like, 'Hey Dana, let's go to Montana.'"

"Really," said Tanya. "Well, I bet I know a good way to get him back." She pulled out her gun. "You're coming with me."

Let me take this, said Jay. *I can handle Tanya.*

Instead, Dana screamed, putting all her considerable lungpower into it. Suddenly, something hard slammed into her and knocked her sideways. The gunshot went wild over them both—Dana, and Adam's skinny, invisible body, draped over her.

Tanya looked around as if she didn't quite know where they'd gone. Through the cloak, Dana could see security guards dressed like very angry clowns converging on her.

"Got the cloak," Adam whispered. "Time to go."

CHAPTER 8

THERE WAS SOMETHING REALLY American about bombing down the highway through the Western desert in an old Cadillac, Dana thought. *'Murica!*

They had about half a day until Boise, where they'd pick up some mysterious alien thing in the Old Penitentiary, and then it was back to Spokane for the meeting with Rainbow Daydreams.

That seemed like something that was going to happen to someone else.

How was she going to get Mahler to extract Jay and then let them all go? It was awfully suspicious how badly Tanya wanted Jay back. Dana didn't think Tanya was just trying to cover up her theft; it was something about Jay himself. *What are they planning to do with you, anyway? Weren't you just stuck in a test tube somewhere? And if it's so important to have you around, why did your boss kill the original you?*

Maybe they're going to feed me to Skzzx.

Funny. Yes, she did want Jay out of her at some point—but not if Mahler was just going to kill him. Again.

Any ideas, Jay?

She could feel Jay's internal shrug. Which meant it was pretty much up to her, because Adam was not what you'd call a natural strategic thinker.

"Look, Dana," said Adam, who'd wrapped the cloak of invisibility around his shoulders. "It's the Floating Head!" He put on a goofy face and tilted his head back and forth.

"You know we have to get rid of that thing."

"Yeah," he said. "But it's wicked cool."

"This was the deal—we steal it, we dump it."

Adam sighed. "Okay, sis." He opened the window and flung it out. "Wonder how Mahler's going to find it out there?"

Dana's phone rang.

"You probably should throw that out the window, too."

She ignored him and answered the phone. "Hello?"

"Hello, Dana, this is Peter Elson, your brother."

She had a mental list of all her siblings in order of favorites. Peter was way down there on the list—and the only reason he wasn't at the bottom was that he remembered to take out the trash every time he used the house. "Hi, Peter."

"Did our brother steal Dad's jacket? Tell him we won't have him arrested, we just want the jacket back."

She rolled her eyes. "Adam, did you steal Dad's jacket?" She held the phone up in Adam's general direction.

Adam paused as he rubbed leather conditioner into the jacket. "No, Dana," he said.

"Because Dad's mannequin looks really awful like that, just wearing pants," added Peter.

"Should have laid off the fried peanut-butter-and-banana sandwiches," said Dana.

"And did you really sell the house to some plumbing billionaire?"

A chill ran through her. *No,* she thought. "Peter, you know I wouldn't do something like that. Besides, I only own like one seventy-fifth of it."

"Seventy-eighth," said Peter. "Well, some guy named Greg Mahler showed up at the house like he owns it."

"Greg Mahler?" said Dana. It was getting tough to breathe. "Is he still there?" Out of the corner of her eye, she saw Adam put the jacket down.

"No, he left with Sierra. He was telling us about the Mahler Spa, and she said it sounded very nice and she'd love to see it someday, and he said, 'No time like the present,' and off they went. In a private helicopter, if you can believe that."

"Sierra is at the Mahler Spa with Greg Mahler. And you just let her go?"

"I don't see what you're so angry about. She's a grown woman, even if she is a flaky hippie. And put Adam on, I want to ask him about the jacket."

Dana hung up on him.

"They've got Sierra," said Dana.

"I heard," said Adam, his voice empty of any emotion.

She didn't expect him to be as scared as she was, but she expected at least a little bit of sympathy. "You don't have to care, she's not your sister!" And then, to her embarrassment, she started to cry. She could feel Jay inside her, anxiously warm and fluttering in there, like someone trying to shut all the windows in a house before a thunderstorm.

Adam's bony hand was on her back. "Pull over," he said. "I'll drive. I know where we're going."

She did as she was told, pulling the car to a stop on the shoulder.

He unfastened his seatbelt. "Slide over, I'll go around."

She slid across the bench seat to the passenger side. It took her a few tries to click the seatbelt properly. Even when Adam made a U-turn on the highway, she didn't look up.

"Look, Dana," he said. "Most of the time it feels like I died when Jay did. All this is just extra, like some kind of dream. It's not your fault, and it's not even your problem. I'll get you out of this."

Adam was wrong. Sierra was in danger, and it was all Dana's fault. If only she'd walked away when she had the chance.

DANA STARTLED AT THE sound of the gunshot. They'd come to a stop by the side of the road at a particularly desolate stretch of desert highway. If she concentrated, though, she could see a manhole cover and a post with a shattered camera attached to it, both painted the same color as the dirt, close to where they were parked.

"Did you see that?" said Adam, bringing his arm back into the car. "Did you see that?"

She shook her head.

"Just took out the camera," he said, rolling up the window. "It was a hell of a shot with a handgun. Ask Jay."

She could feel the warm presence of Jay right under her solar plexus, trying vainly to comfort her.

"This is Greg's escape route," he said. "He built it a while ago, and it doesn't get used much, and now they can't see we're here. We're going to go inside, and then we're going to get into the ducts, and I'm going to take you to where Sierra probably is."

She nodded. "How are we going to get out?"

"Back through the ducts. We'll leave the car here. You take the keys, okay?"

His cold fingers brushed her warm palm. He was trying to send some kind of message to her, but she was too numb with fear about what might be happening to Sierra to understand.

The lock on the exit was mechanical and Adam picked it quickly using a set of tools he had in his pocket. Then he pulled her along the wall to the duct, which he opened with a screwdriver. He put a miner's lamp on his forehead and turned it on.

"Hope you're not claustrophobic," he said.

"Not really," she said.

"I'm claustrophobic," he said, smiling a little. "I hate these fucking things."

Inside the duct was a ladder, which she scaled behind Adam. Then she followed him down the narrow, long duct. Soon she realized that adults weren't meant to crawl for long periods of time. Her knees ached and it was incredibly dark, aside from the flickering light that Adam was wearing. As they moved closer to the center of the complex, light began to shine in through the grates. At that point Adam turned his flashlight off.

He stopped short. "Want to see an alien?" he whispered. "That's where they keep Skzzx. Right down there." He backed away from the grate, gesturing her forward.

Even though she was terrified for Sierra, she couldn't help stopping to see. She looked down into the darkened room. Did they really keep the poor thing in the dark? But as her eyes adjusted, she still couldn't see anything.

"He's not in there," she whispered.

Adam looked down. "Huh," he said.

"Do you think he escaped? Wouldn't there be some kind of alarm going off if he escaped?"

Adam thought for a moment. "Not our problem," he said, and started crawling again.

Jay? thought Dana. *What happens if the alien gets out?*

We didn't have a plan for that, said Jay.

Really? thought Dana. That didn't make a lot of sense. If Greg Mahler was the kind of guy who went to the trouble of building an escape route that led out to the middle of the desert, how could he not have a contingency plan if the alien escaped?

Part of her thought, *maybe the alien isn't real.* But that didn't make sense either. She'd definitely seen some weird non-human technology in the past week. Hell, she was carrying around a sample of it inside her body. She was pretty sure that no one on Earth was capable of making something like Jay.

It looked real when I saw it, said Jay. *Right before they made my reboot. I mean, made me.*

She felt Jay's sense of regret and tried to soothe him. Going back to Mahler had him on edge, too.

She was missing something crucial, she was sure of it.

The lights shining through the vents were becoming increasingly bright. She could hear people walking and talking below her. It was hard for her to move as silently as Adam, and she concentrated hard on not bumping into the walls or letting her knees thump against the metal floor.

Adam stopped and sat down. In the dim light through the vent below them, she could see him put his finger to his lips. She nodded, unsure of whether he could see her. He lay down on the bottom of the duct and peered through the grate.

"She's here," he whispered. "She's alone."

Without thinking, she grabbed Adam's hand and squeezed it hard.

"She's fine," he said. "Lean down and take a look."

She put her face up to the grate. There was Sierra, sitting on the floor, meditating in the lotus position. She looked totally uninjured and untroubled. The room itself was less like a jail cell than a small hotel gym. The floor was lined with yoga mats, and there was a big yoga ball. Nothing to climb on, though. Three sides of the room were lined with a mural of a desert scene. On the fourth was a big mirror, which Dana thought might be two-way.

Adam squeezed her shoulder and Dana sat up. He pulled a screwdriver from his pocket and carefully removed the screws holding the grate in place. Patiently and soundlessly, he lifted the grate from the hole and set it inside the duct. Then he removed a coil of rope from his pocket. On one end of the coil was what looked like a metal credit card, which must have been in his wallet. Adam set the card down and flipped a switch on the back. Dana heard the duct warp slightly as the magnet in the card turned on. Then he dropped the other end of the coil down the opening where the grate had been, smacking Sierra on the back of the head with the end of the rope.

Sierra started, then turned and saw them, and broke into a big grin. Dana gestured that she should climb up, but Sierra shook her head. She showed her bicep muscle, pointed at it, and then put her hand in a thumbs-down sign.

Dana pushed Adam aside, pulling her sleeves over her hands, and started climbing down the rope. It brought back some bad memories of junior high gym, but Dana managed to do it with a minimum of slipping and without twisting an ankle. She looked up. The rope looked taller from this direction. Maybe she should have let Adam help Sierra instead, but she'd been too worried about her sister to think straight. And she could always get Jay to scale the rope.

"Are you okay?" she whispered to Sierra.

"I had a very nice cranio-fascial massage," said Sierra. "And I did some yoga. But if you all are leaving, I'm happy to go with you. I mean, they've all been very nice. Greg's been very nice. But you know how sometimes the vibe of a place is just off?"

And that was about as negative as Sierra ever got about anything. "Here," whispered Dana. "Take the car keys. All you need to do is follow the duct to the end, and then take the door to go outside."

Sierra looked puzzled. "Won't you and Adam come with me?"

"I'll be right behind you. I just can't climb when people watch me." *Because I think even Sierra would freak out if she saw me turn into Jay.* She felt Jay's amusement at the prospect.

Above them, Adam was tapping his wrist where most people would wear a wristwatch. Dana made her hands into a basket and gave Sierra a boost. Between Dana's pushing, Sierra holding tightly on to the rope, and Adam pulling the rope upwards, they managed to get her into the duct.

After giving Sierra a minute or two to get started crawling away, Adam stuck his head out the duct. "You've got to move. They can see us."

"I can't do it. I'll have to let the other guy handle it."

A panicked look swept over his face, quickly damped down. "No! Not in here. Dana, let me just—"

But before he could finish the sentence, the mirror suddenly popped like a soap bubble and a very well-armed group of people was standing behind it, watching them.

CHAPTER 9

A WHITE MAN IN AN old-fashioned suit stood in front of the group, Dana imagined how she'd sketch him, then realized there was something off about the way he looked. First of all, the suit was weird; it was like something from an old private-eye movie, with huge lapels and a high waist. He also had his light brown hair slicked back with something greasy, but there was something more to it than that. It was as if he'd been made out of plastic, like he didn't have pores.

Greg Mahler. It had to be.

Adam dropped down through the duct, landing easily on the balls of his feet. He stood next to her, looking again like the terrifying guy she'd met in Spokane. But now she could see that wasn't who he was, it was just the role he played when he was scared. *That makes two of us*, she thought.

"Hi, Greg." Adam's lip curled in a sneer.

"Shoot them," said Greg.

The other people lifted their guns and Dana felt a desperate rush of fear.

"What about the bomb?" said Adam.

"What bomb?"

"The one I'm wearing, asshole. Shoot me and we all die."

You didn't tell me about that, thought Dana. Jay's warmth didn't thaw the chill in her heart.

"Is this when you start threatening me?" said Greg. "That's cute."

"No, this is when I give you a present. This is when I come back and work for you again. You always said I was your favorite. Anything you want. No complaining."

"Anything?" Greg tilted his head, and it seemed to Dana that all his features flowed to the side, as if he were made of something liquid. She shuddered. Whatever the aliens had done to keep him thirty forever, it wasn't working.

"Sure." Adam held out his hands, showing they were empty. "All I want is for you to let my hostage go."

Oh, Adam, she thought. *That's not going to work. You couldn't wait, you tipped your hand too soon—*

"No," said Greg.

Then everything seemed to happen at once. She thought she heard a gunshot. Adam grabbed her roughly by the hand. It felt as if he were on fire. No, it felt as if he were made of needles. She was made of needles. Lots of little needles made of fire, and they were all traveling fast and backwards, as if shot through a tube. Something cold swiped through the space that had been her stomach, but her needles passed through it as if it were nothing.

She had never felt anything so painful before. And then all the little needles were snapping back together, and she and Adam were sitting on a lawn somewhere at the Mahler Spa, their hands still clasped together.

"It worked," said Adam, with a weird croaking laugh.

They were still holding hands. That was because they couldn't pull them apart: thin vermicellis of flesh connected their palms together.

"I can fix that," said Adam, pulling the knife out of his pocket. He sliced through them quickly. Now they both were bleeding. "See? We *are* related. Blood brothers."

"You teleported us," she said. "That hurt." She felt odd, hollowed-out.

"Yes," he said. He looked pale with exhaustion, even for him. "Time for you to run. I can't. I'm done. Maybe if they catch me, they'll let you go. So take this—"

"The bomb?"

"No bomb. Lying." And he pulled something out of Press Elton's jacket pocket. Something invisible that slightly distorted the air.

"The cloak. You didn't throw it out the window."

"Fuck, no. Get out of here. Keep Jay safe for me. And maybe someday—"

"Adam," she said. "Jay's not here. He disappeared when we teleported."

Adam looked at her like he'd just seen the end of the world. "Oh," he said. Then "Oh" again. He let himself fall backwards onto the grass, looking up at the empty sky.

If Dana were smart, she'd take the cloak from Adam's hand and walk away. Why should she stay? She had no obligations here. These people were nothing to her, nothing at all. She was just a woman who drank the wrong soda in a rental car in Spokane...

She didn't want to do that. Adam had taken her back to Mahler to rescue Sierra even though he thought he might never leave again. That's why he'd given her the car keys. She couldn't abandon him.

"Come on, Adam," she said. "You have to get up. We can both fit under the cloak, right?"

He continued to stare up at nothing.

She crouched down next to Adam, looming over him so he was forced to look at her. "I don't know where he went either, but he can't have gone far, and you can't look for him if you just lie there."

"We had our second chance, I think," Adam said, speaking deliberately. "Did I ever thank you? Thank you, Dana." He held the cloak out to her, in his still-bleeding left hand. "You should go."

His right hand had fallen, Dana noticed, across his holster. *Shit.* Because she could see it now: Adam wasn't going to outlive Jay twice.

Dana reflected how best to handle this. Should she remind him that Jay would have wanted Adam to survive, with or without him? No, she had a pretty good idea how Adam thought, and sweet-talking wasn't the way to go here.

"Look, dipshit," she said. "I make the decisions here, not you. Your decisions stink. For one thing, I have no idea where the hell I am, and I'm not about to die of dehydration in the desert because you won't get up off your skinny ass and show me where I'm supposed to go."

A little light kindled in Adam's blue eyes.

Keep talking, she thought. "I've got nothing in my pockets but a clay dog, a pack of peppermint gum, and my wallet. And you stole most of the gum, you thief! Sure, I can make it to Roswell on foot with no compass or water. That's a genius plan. Or, you can find us another car—"

She heard footsteps behind her on the gravel path and turned. It was Greg Mahler. He was alone, and he walked over the grass towards them like he wasn't afraid of anything they could possibly do to him.

Oh, God, thought Dana, and stood up.

Greg stopped ten feet away. "I want to tell you a story," he said. "It's about aliens."

She felt Adam's bony hand grasp hers and yank, as he pulled himself to his feet. He positioned himself between her and Greg even though he was shivering from exhaustion. *She'd been right about Adam, she had.* "No more stories, Greg," he said.

"An apology, then," said Greg. "We chose the wrong human face to add to the gestalt when we came to this planet."

"What?" asked Dana. She looked at the side of Adam's stony expression. It was clear he didn't know what Greg meant, either.

"Greg Mahler was a barbarian," Greg said. "We hope we have chosen more wisely this time."

And then Mahler's face and body melted into something else. Something Dana had only seen in a mirror. He looked exactly like Jay

O'Toole, only a little melted around the edges, like Jello that hadn't quite set. Her stomach twinged with revulsion.

He must have stolen Jay from her somehow when they teleported. How had he done that? And why was Jay blurry? Had something gone wrong?

"Don't you dare look like him," Adam snarled.

"We're sorry that we didn't ask," said the thing with Jay's face and voice. "We needed somebody from this planet, an informant. An interlocutor. Someone to take us down the right path."

With a look of total horror on his face, Adam drew his gun.

Oh hell. Dana clamped her bleeding right hand on his shoulder. "What if that's where Jay went?"

"They just stole the way he looked and the way he talked and it isn't him at all. This is Greg's idea of a joke. His jokes, Dana, you wouldn't believe them." Adam's bony shoulder shook with tension, but his gun hand stayed still.

But that doesn't make sense, thought Dana. *Was Greg the alien all along? No—Greg was the alien's spokeshuman. Aliens. More than one. Sharing one body, with Greg Mahler. The gestalt. That's why the cage had been empty, because Greg was searching for them.*

So who were she and Adam talking to?

The blurred-looking Jay pursed his lips, considering. "It's weird in here. Messier than it was in Dana. More people. But I think—they're not trying to—they want me to be myself." He squinted as if concentrating and his body solidified, like he'd turned the focus knob. He examined one hand, slowly looking at the knuckles, flipping it over to the palm. "There I am."

"But it's not you, Jay," said Adam.

"It's me and a whole bunch of aliens. Four or five? No, four. It's normal to them to share a body, I think. And they want me to—translate? Yes, translate for them. They don't like what Greg's been doing.

They want things to be done differently. They want someone like me, someone...kind? Yes, that's what they're saying."

"Where's Greg?" said Dana.

"He's sleeping," said the thing that looked like Jay. "The aliens have made him sleep."

"Stop fucking with me, Greg," said Adam. He sounded heartbroken and exhausted. "Your jokes aren't funny."

"Wait," said Dana as she squeezed Adam's shoulder. He felt tight enough to snap. "If you're Jay, tell us something Greg wouldn't know."

"Okay," said the thing. It looked down at the ground, then back up again. "The first time I cooked Adam breakfast, I told him that the sausage was made out of turkey, but it was actually pork."

"Jay wouldn't do that." Dana could hear how sincere Adam was.

The thing raised its hands apologetically. "You were so hungry. You'd already eaten three eggs, and you were halfway through your second sausage when you asked me, 'Hey, this isn't pork, is it?' It was only that one time, I promise."

Adam sighed and let the gun drop.

"Rosey, you look so sad—" said the thing, and took a step forward, his arms outstretched. Adam stumbled back a step and collided with Dana. The thing's arms dropped.

Was that story actually meant for her? Was this Jay-creature being— of all things— subtle? Was it asking her to lie to Adam? Because the thing standing there was not the man that Adam had met, fallen in love with, wanted to build a life with. But then, Dana had never met that man either. Jay O'Toole had been dead for almost two months.

How strange it was to look at Jay's duplicate from the outside. She'd known he was a tall, broad man, someone who liked to work out and also loved a good meal. But she hadn't quite realized that he carried himself to look less intimidating. He slouched into himself, one big hand grasping his bare forearm like he was holding himself back from trying to touch Adam again, his beautiful dark eyes never leaving Adam's face.

And she thought, *this thing really wants to be Jay. Maybe it is Jay.* It was certainly the closest to Jay that they could get.

She could see Adam hovering at the moment of decision. He wanted to believe Jay was alive and safe, she could tell, but couldn't quite manage it.

What was the right thing to do?

"That's him," said Dana, suddenly certain. "That's Jay."

Something in Adam's face went soft, and Dana could feel the tension drain from his body. He put the gun back in the holster and held out his hand to Jay.

Dana turned away to give the two of them a little privacy, but she thought she heard Jay whisper, "I knew you'd rescue me." She shivered. Now that it was done, she realized she'd made a mistake. How *could* she know that was Jay?

What if the aliens had planned this all along? What if they were the ones who made Greg murder the original Jay? Maybe this was all about swapping a strong human translator for a weak one, so that the aliens could get back at the humans who'd kept them in a cage for seventy years. God only knew what kind of revenge they were planning.

I fucked up, she thought. *Now what do I do?*

"Dana," said Jay.

She looked up into Jay's dark eyes. She could still feel kindness flowing off him, almost as if she were still carrying him in her body. He smiled at her.

Dana exhaled. She might not know the aliens, but she knew Jay, and she couldn't help liking and trusting him. *You worry too much*, her mother would have said. *You're so sharp you'll cut yourself.*

Anyway, she was done here. Vacation was over and none of this was her responsibility. Time to say goodbye.

Did she have her phone in her pocket? She should call Sierra, because she probably hadn't gotten too far yet. Maybe Sierra could give her a ride back to Dad's house. Because it had been fun, mostly, but they'd reached the end of the road here, and it was time to go back to her normal life. After all, she still had that pitch at Rainbow Daydreams in a couple of days. The pitch that was going to change her life. She felt Mr. March Doge in her jacket pocket. Had she just smeared blood on the sample box? And was it her blood or Adam's?

"Are you okay?" Jay asked.

"I need to call Sierra," said Dana.

"Good idea," Jay said, his expression warm. "I'd like to meet her. After all, I'm dating her brother, right?"

Dana's eyes flicked over to Adam. Had it really been less than a week since she met him in a parking lot in Spokane? Leaning on Jay and huddling in Dad's jacket, he looked like a different person. He flashed her a sweet and unguarded smile.

Oh, what the hell, she thought, and smiled right back at him.

"Besides," Adam said, his smile turning into a smirk, "someone should tell Sierra she's driving a stolen car."

CHAPTER 10

DANA MANAGED TO LOOK like a sober professional all the way from the Rainbow Daydreams conference room, through the lobby, out the front door, and through the parking lot, until she got to the rental car. But when she shut the car door behind her, she started laughing, banging her hands happily against the steering wheel. Was there any better feeling than someone telling you, "Your art is good?" No, there was not.

I actually did it, she thought.

"Hey, Dana," said a voice from the back seat.

"YAAAAA," shouted Dana. She turned around. Adam was sitting in the back seat, his gun disassembled into parts and surrounded by grubby, oily rags.

He snickered at her.

"What are you doing here?" she said.

He ignored the question, attached the long tube at the top of the gun to the handle, slid in the magazine, pointed the gun towards the roof of the car, and pulled the trigger. There was a loud click. He pulled the magazine out. "Did you get the job?'

Excitement bubbled out of her. "They're buying the whole year! All the Doges. It's going to pay my rent for the next nine months. Plus a bonus if I sell enough units. And they want to see anything else I come up with. They said, 'We think you're a real talent.' Those exact words. 'A real talent.'"

He put the smaller tube inside the larger one, put the magazine back in, pointed the gun at the ground, and fired it again. "That sounds good."

"Yes! You don't know. This never happens." She squinted at him. "Why are you here? Where's Jay? Is Jay okay?"

He shrugged. He pulled out the magazine and carefully added the C-shaped piece at the back. He put the empty magazine back in, pointed the gun towards the window, and fired. Click. "You said it was today. Your job interview. Jay's working, but he told me to wish you luck. There a place you can buy a steak dinner in Spokane? Jay always says, good news means steak."

Adam looked down with a strange expression on his face, clutching his gun like a security blanket. He was always a little muted and hard to read, but Dana thought he was feeling shy. *Shy? Adam?*

Dana knew she should be weirded out that Adam had followed her to Spokane and broken into her car. But the truth was, she was happy to see him. After killing it at Rainbow Daydreams, she didn't want to go back to her hotel room alone and get room service. And Adam was good company.

This might be a huge mistake, but it was one she wanted to make.

It was a nice bowling alley, she thought, one that looked unchanged since the seventies, though a little faded. A lot of people had worn her rented shoes before. But the counter clerk had given them a good blast of sanitizing spray and the burgers and onion rings were fresh and hot.

"January's a dog on skis. February's Valentine's Day, right?" asked Adam, talking loudly over the happy drunks two lanes over.

"No," she said. "The Daytona 500. That way we have a potential crossover with the male collectible market."

Adam shrugged. "I'll collect them."

It meant more than she would have thought. Especially if Adam actually paid for the Doges instead of shoplifting them.

Adam gestured with his chin towards the lane. "Aren't you going to go? It's your turn."

"Here's the thing," said Dana. "Every time I get up someone swipes one of my onion rings."

"Big brothers are supposed to do that," he said.

Are we figuring out the rules now? she thought. "I have over thirty big brothers. If that were true, I'd never get any onion rings."

Smirking, he took five onion rings off his plate and put them on hers. "Go bowl," he said.

"There are six onion rings on my plate," she said, lifting her bowling ball from the return. "I counted."

She sighted down the alley. Dana was a strong but erratic bowler, varying unpredictably between strikes and total misses. But tonight she was on fire. Bang. A strike!

She realized that Adam was cheering for her and turned to smile at him. Burgers and bowling, she thought, was a much better idea than steaks. Much more like a celebration.

"You know you're just winning because I'm used to the other kind of pin, right?" he said, getting up from his chair.

"That's bullshit," she said. "What do you mean, the other kind of pin? There's no other kind of pin."

She watched him sight down the alley and lift the ball. She looked down at her plate. Only five onion rings. *Adam, you incorrigible thief.* Dana laughed.

INTERLUDE 1

BEING STUCK ON A cramped spaceship was beginning to get to Allrhl. Back at Home, he'd always meant to do an around-the-world loop, just at the edge of the Fllt Sea where it got too cold to swim without a cover. Of course, he'd planned to go with Hsska, so it was just a whole cairn of regrets, one stacked on another.

He felt his skin purple and mentally forced it towards blue instead. He would not let himself get melancholy, today of all days. Instead, he waited for a gap in the stream of people at the exercise track and dove into it, flicking his tail to force himself to go faster. He snapped his fins all-together, then one-after-another, then cater-corner. Fast, fast, fast. So fast that he could barely think.

Today was his Last Day. Tomorrow was his time in the tank. And he kept hearing Hsska, "Whatever gets out, it won't be you."

But here was the thing, he mentally told her, now that she could no longer answer—he was dead either way. And this way, at least, something of his was going to survive.

Last Day. He supposed he'd better enjoy it.

PART 2

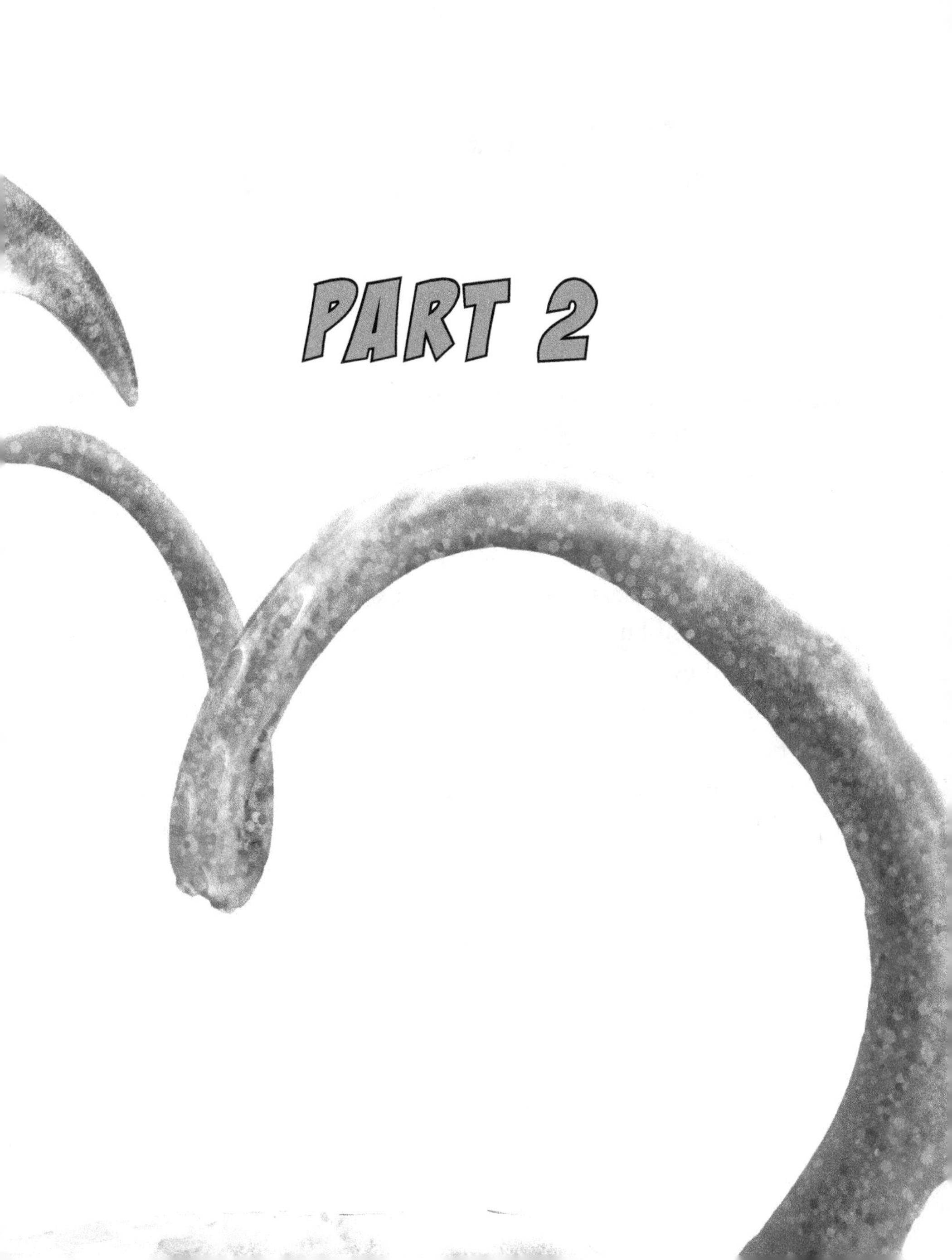

CHAPTER 11

THE IMPORTANT THING, ADAM reminded himself, was that Jay was healthy and safe. It was just fine that keeping him healthy and safe meant that they had to live at Mahler, in Greg's old apartment. They had tossed all of Greg's things in the dumpster, especially the crusty pinup of Ava Gardner tucked under the mattress. They had scrubbed the floors and repainted the walls and moved in their own furniture. They'd hung Jay's beautiful photographs from their camping trips. They'd eviscerated Greg's security system and replaced it with a better one. Adam did most of it because Jay was busy at work, but that wasn't a problem.

Adam agreed with Jay that someone needed to fix what was going on at the Mahler Corporation. And it wasn't going to be Adam. He couldn't even make himself walk inside the building. He was surprised that Jay could, but on the other hand, there were things that he could remember that Jay couldn't. Jay's murder, for one.

Anyway, making the new apartment nice wasn't the problem. Adam had fixed up worse places. No, the problem was that Adam had scrubbed the entire bathroom from top to bottom again, and he could still smell Greg's skunky, old-fashioned cologne. How could this stuff be so strong? Did he need to replace every rubber seal and plastic pipe to get rid of it?

Could Jay smell it too or was it just him?

He thought of calling Jay at work so he could come home and check, but then realized the man himself was standing in the doorway, watching Adam go over the grout for the fourth time with a solution of bleach and an old toothbrush. How long had he been watching?

"Pack your suitcase, Rosey," Jay said. Only Jay called him that now. "I booked us a hotel in San Francisco for the weekend and I'm ready to go when you are."

Adam really liked San Francisco. Jay—who always read guidebooks—took them to something called the Musée Méchanique, a museum of coin-operated games and dioramas, like an old-fashioned penny arcade. Adam spent a happy half-hour watching a little mechanical carnival, feeding in quarter after quarter to make the tiny wire Ferris wheel zoom around, feeling Jay's warm fingers brushing up and down the back of his neck.

And when Adam had finally realized how bored Jay must be with the museum, they'd gone outside onto the pier with the rest of the tourists. The air was so clear it felt like you could see Hawaii. Jay took pictures of the ocean, keeping far back from the water to protect his skin. (Too much salt water was one of the many things that could poison Jay, according to the aliens, but Adam wasn't going to think about that.)

Jay said, "We should come back here on our honeymoon."

If there was a better way for a guy to ask you to marry him, Adam didn't know what it was. "Sure," he'd said, and he'd kissed Jay, not caring if anyone was watching, and then he'd felt how soft Jay's mouth was under his, with Skẓzx's fine little hairs growing over Jay's lips.

Jay was tired—no, why lie? Jay had looked human for as long as he could. Now Jay had to hurry back to the hotel so he could change back to his other body, Skzzx's body, which looked like a big furry coin purse with tentacles.

Adam knew this was harder on Jay. Adam didn't have four aliens in his head, talking to him all the time. He could go out in the sunshine and eat normal food and swim in the ocean. He didn't have to share his body with his own murderer. Even if the aliens were supposedly keeping Greg asleep and harmless. Adam had decided that what Jay needed, most of all, was for Adam to act like Jay was the same man he'd always been. To be kind and sweet and gentle with Jay, just like Jay had always been with him.

But it was hard for Adam to be a nice person. It wasn't natural to him.

So, whenever Adam felt the anger build inside him, he went for a walk. While Jay "napped," a DO NOT DISTURB sign on the door, Adam walked briskly down Powell Street, past a trolley car covered with other tourists. He stopped short in front of the Westin and glared at Union Square. It had palm trees in it. Yes, Adam knew he was in California, but it didn't seem warm enough right now for palm trees. He was wearing a hoodie and Jay's sweater under his leather jacket, and he was still freezing. He bet they were swapping those fuckers out of there every six months or so. Or maybe they were fakes. That was it: fake palm trees. He'd discovered the secret to San Francisco.

"Mister Shapiro?"

Male, twenties or thirties, maybe British. Adam put his hand on his holster, exhaled, and turned. The speaker was an expensively dressed, well-groomed Asian man in his thirties but totally average looking apart from that. Not a guy who'd stand out in a crowd, even with that nice body. More importantly, Adam couldn't see any sign of a gun, and both hands were visible. Adam glared at him but relaxed a little.

"I'm interested in hiring you," said the man.

"I don't need the money," said Adam. Which was true. Greg had paid him well, and most of that money was currently in a safe under the floor of their apartment.

"But I hear you might appreciate a challenge," said the man. "My inheritance has been stolen and I need to get it back."

Adam wondered how much this man actually knew about him, especially with a story like that. Did he think Adam was some kind of treasure hunter? Did this guy know enough to be dangerous to Jay? How did the man know his name? He had to keep him talking long enough so he could figure it out and then deal with it, whatever it was.

"We can talk in the park," Adam said. "After you."

No one else seemed to be following or watching them, as far as Adam could tell. Good. That would make whatever came next easier. They sat on a bench under a palm tree.

"I'm John Chen," said the man.

Which sounded like the Chinese equivalent of John Doe. "How'd you find me?"

"I talked to someone named Tanya at Mahler—"

Adam smirked. That was the great thing about Tanya—you could ask her to do anything, and she'd squint at you for a few seconds then tell you how much it would cost you. That was also the bad thing about Tanya. "How much she get from you?"

"A thousand," said John.

Adam snorted. Tanya had seen a sucker coming.

"But originally I got your name from Dai Hastings."

Dai Hastings! He hadn't heard that name in years. Back before he met Jay, back in his club days, he'd been friends with Dai. Dai's ex-boyfriend had stolen his car and locked it up in a garage where Dai couldn't get to it. And he couldn't go to the police because he'd originally got the car as a gift, and he didn't have any papers. Still, asshole move, right? To take a guy's car like that? And it wasn't like the car belonged to Dai's ex-boyfriend, either.

G-d, that car had been beautiful. A gorgeous McLaren MP4-12C. About the prettiest thing Adam had ever driven. And he'd driven a *lot* of cars.

"I remember Dai," Adam said. "I don't do stuff like that now."

"I think you'd do it for the right reason," said John. "Right now, all I want for you to do is hear me out."

A cold breeze blew through the park and Adam shivered. He stood up. "No, I'm good. Plus I'm freezing out here."

John stood up and rested his hand on the back of the bench. "How about I buy you the best Irish coffee in San Francisco?"

Was he getting picked up? Jay always teased him for being oblivious, but that's because Jay thought he was a lot hotter than he actually was. Besides, Adam was sure this guy was straight.

"If you hear me out, and you aren't interested," said John, "I promise I'll never bother you again."

And that's what he wanted, right? For this guy to give up and go away? Okay, he'd try the "best" Irish coffee in San Francisco. And if it really was that good, he could take Jay there. And then Jay could sit and watch him drink and ask him, "What's it like? Is it good?" And Adam could say, "It's great, I wish you could try it." And it would still be better than Jay being dead, right? Because anything was better than Jay being dead.

Right. He bit back a sigh as he gestured to John to lead the way.

CHAPTER 12

Down at the Buena Vista, the Irish coffee was just the thing to cut through the damp cold that had sunk into Adam's bones. It was sweet and hot, and a lot more alcoholic than Adam had realized at first. *What the hell.* He drank his second one.

Now John was talking again. "Some generations back," John said, "my great-something-grandmother was the Chinese emperor's girlfriend. And he gave her a beautiful sculpture of a mountain carved out of jade."

Adam wondered if he was finally getting warm enough to take off his jacket. Probably not. Plus, he was armed, and people were picky about that out here.

"In the late 80s, my grandmother was living in Hong Kong, which was still under British rule. When it became increasingly clear that the handover was really going to happen, she began to worry that the Chinese government was going to take the jade mountain away from our family. So she shipped it to my parents in London. But it never arrived."

"Yeah, that happens," said Adam, slouching comfortably in his chair. "What she should have done is have someone she trusted carry it."

"It's four foot by three foot by three foot," said John.

"Big rock," said Adam and nodded. There it was: he was drunk. *Hello!*

"Last month," continued John, "we got word that the jade mountain had been found. It's in the home of a wealthy local businessman. We tried approaching him, but he insisted that he had clear title to the sculpture. And we can't prove that we used to own it."

Adam could already tell where this was going, but he wanted John to say it out loud. "So what do you want me to do?"

John leaned in. "I want you to get it back for me."

"You want me to go into some rich guy's house and steal an enormous rock for you? When the rich guy already knows you want it?" Adam laughed. "No, I'm not doing that."

"You did it for Dai."

Adam shrugged. "Dai was a friend. Also, you can drive a car. You can't drive a rock." Had he really said that? *Yeah, let's make him think you're stupid.*

"I can pay you."

"You can't pay me enough." He pointed at the cream-dabbed remnants of his drink. "Thanks for the coffee. But we're done. Find someone else."

"It wasn't just Dai," said John, who sounded irritated. "There was a car theft ring in Worcester, Massachusetts—"

Adam slapped his hand on the table, interrupting John. "I was underage. That was sealed by the judge." And under his old name, too—how had John known his last name used to be Rosen?

John crossed his arms. "I also know some other stories. Like the one about the Roswell Liberators."

The memory came, as it always did, in flashes: *Crowd of shouting people, waving protest signs. Woman in a red hat drops her cardboard sign. And falls to the ground like a doll.* Adam suddenly felt like he might throw up his coffee. "I don't care what you know," he snarled.

"Really? How about this? You have access to a lot of unusual technology. Real out-of-this-world stuff." As that sank in, John flashed him a victorious smile.

How can he know that? Adam had spent all the long years he'd worked for Greg making sure no one knew about Mahler's alien.

If John knew what Mahler really did, did that mean he knew the truth about Jay?

"Moving a sculpture that size shouldn't be a problem for you, Mr. Shapiro. Not if you're properly motivated."

He was drunk, his heart was pounding, he couldn't deal with this. And he was armed. Armed in a bar with a lot of people who probably had one eye on him already, after he'd smacked the table. *Fuck.* How was he supposed to figure this one out? Why the hell had he drunk that second coffee? Strategy was never his strong point.

"Why don't you sleep on it?" said John, his rich-boy accent grating on Adam. "I'll find you tomorrow."

Adam was back at the hotel room right when he said he'd be. He found Jay looking human and resting on top of the neatly made bed, watching baseball. At the side of the room, dinner for one was set up with steak and scotch, his favorite treats. Except he might skip the scotch this time.

"Did you have fun?" asked Jay and smiled at him. He looked beautiful, healthy and strong. His kind, dark eyes shone with love. Jay could have had any man he wanted, but for some reason he wanted Adam.

"I tried Irish coffee," Adam said. "It's good."

Jay grinned. "And I bet you got someone else to pay for it."

"You know me," he said.

Jay nodded towards Adam's dinner. "Eat up, Rosey. I've been thinking about getting my tentacles around you all afternoon."

Adam blushed and looked down at the ground. They were going to be all right. And when he saw John Chen again, who seemed to know everything about him, and everything about Jay, he'd get rid of him. Somehow.

ADAM COULDN'T SLEEP—ANOTHER REASON that second Irish coffee had been a mistake. So after an hour of trying not to jostle Jay, he carefully rolled out from under his fiancé's sprawled body. He'd go down to the bar and have something to drink. Something non-alcoholic, with vitamins in it.

He was so distracted that he managed to sit down and order his drink before he realized the bar looked exactly like a beach club in Hawaii. There were tiki torches and the bar had a grass roof on it. The bartender gave him something iced, with a slice of pineapple, in a glass that looked like one of those heads on Easter Island. Suddenly, there was a sharp hissing noise, like the sprinklers were going off, and water poured from the ceiling into the pool at the center of the room. An indoor rainstorm. Cute.

He wished he could talk to Dana, who loved tourist places. He could picture her little amused smirk on the other side of the table, her acid green-painted fingernails bright against her drink glass. Dana was smart; she'd know what to do about John. How did he know so damn much? It made no sense. *What am I supposed to do, Dana?*

But maybe that didn't matter. All he really needed to do was to tell Jay they'd need to go home in the morning. Back at Mahler, they'd be safe.

He wondered if he'd still smell Greg at the apartment when they got back.

An Asian woman sat down at the other side of the table. She was shorter than Adam, with her hair in two girlish pigtails. "How could you." It didn't sound like a question.

Adam shook his head. "Wrong table."

"I know who you are, Adam," she said, pointing angrily at him. "Why are you helping my cousin? My grandmother left the jade mountain to me. Did you even ask John to prove it was his?"

He was too tired to try to figure out what sort of game she was playing. "It's three a.m., lady," Adam said. "All I want is to have a drink and go back to sleep."

The woman frowned. "So you're not helping him."

"I'm on vacation," Adam said. "Fuck off."

She began to dig around in the giant purse she was carrying. "I've got documents—letters from Grandma—"

Adam stood up and threw some cash down. "Okay," he said. "*I'll* fuck off."

There was a thump as something solid landed on the table. He turned to see what it was. In the woman's hand was an FBI badge. "Corinne Ng," it read.

Adam sighed and sat back down.

"I need you to play along with John," Corinne said. "Pretend he's gotten you to take the job. We'll be tracking you both and building our case against him." She pulled an envelope out of her purse and slid it across the table to Adam. "That's a party invite for tomorrow, from the rich guy that John wants you to rob. You can check out the jade mountain in person and figure out how you'd steal the thing before you actually do it."

Adam took the envelope but didn't open it. Tomorrow, they were supposed to go to the Muir Woods and look at the redwoods. He'd hoped it would be shady enough in the forest for Jay to spend a couple of hours outside, and take some photos like he used to. Now Adam could feel everything tightening around them again, and he had no idea how to fix it. He scraped the side of his foot back and forth on the carpeted floor. When he looked up again, Corinne was gone.

Of course Adam told Jay about all of it. Afterwards, Jay was silent. Thinking it over? Talking to the aliens? Who could tell? Then he suddenly grinned at Adam. "This is great," he said. "This is perfect."

Really? Adam looked dubiously at him.

"Remember when we first started dating, and you broke into my apartment so you could replace my flush valve? I had an Abloy lock. You can't pick an Abloy."

Adam sighed. "I didn't pick it. You told me all about your neighbors and how much you liked them. I figured you'd give them a key and I was right. And they didn't have an Abloy. They had some crap lock I could open with a credit card."

"That's not the point. You're so good at getting into places you aren't supposed to be. And—" he tapped Adam on the chest— "if you steal stuff for the government, it's not a crime."

It dawned on Adam that Jay didn't think that Corrine was just using him to get after John. He thought this was some kind of job interview. For the FBI. *Him?* With his record? *Oh, Jay.*

He was a good thief. That was true. Sometimes it seemed like everything good in his life was something he'd stolen. His name, his pretend sister, even Jay. Things he had no right to own. And the only way he could earn them was to take care of them better than the people who they should have belonged to.

And there was something else: Adam had spent the last ten years doing what Greg wanted, even though the thought of it tasted sour in Adam's mouth. What was Adam going to do, if no one was telling him what he was supposed to do? He was going to fuck everything up. Jay was right, Adam needed a job.

Jay wrapped his arm around him, pulled him closer, and kissed the side of his head. "Besides, if we're going to a rich guy party, I get to dress you up."

CHAPTER 13

Adam had to admit, he liked the rich guy's house. It was modern and bright and clean, with huge windows and a lot of light. There was black leather furniture. Good, uncomplicated art. Not a lot of stuff to trip over. Very nice.

But he didn't like the party much. It was just people talking—no dancing, as far as he could tell—and Adam could never figure out how to break into little circles of strangers. Usually he just followed Jay around, eating and drinking too much, while Jay made friends for them both. But tonight he was working, checking out the place before the real robbery. So he gave Jay's hand a squeeze and headed deeper into the house.

He passed through the entryway to a room with a giant dining table and several black leather couches. It was an enormous space, and the noise of the chattering partygoers was unpleasantly loud. A long table was covered in all kinds of fancy appetizers. He swiped some kind of salmon sushi thing and continued onward.

At the end of the living room was a hallway was lined with glass French doors, opening on an interior patio. And inside the patio was an enormous jade sculpture, sitting exposed to the elements, which seemed like a good way to ruin it. There was a couple snuggling close together on a metal bench in the patio, but Adam ignored them, put on his gloves, and opened the door.

Outside the air was cool and clear, pleasant with Press Elson's leather jacket, speaking of things he'd stolen. It seemed unusually quiet after the noise of the party. He felt his head clear as he took an inventory of the patio. Black slate flooring. One metal bench, with a metal coffee table. Four productive lemon trees, one in each corner. Glass doors on the side opposite him, opening onto a kitchen that was currently full of caterers. Glass windows on each end of the patio, one opening on to the living room/dining room, the other opening onto what looked like the master bedroom, though he'd have to check that for certain.

Two cameras, both pointed so they'd capture both the jade sculpture and half of the French doors. Probably there was a house alarm, too. Pretty standard for this kind of house. Adam didn't see any motion detectors, but that wasn't surprising on a patio. No one wanted to be woken up every time a squirrel ran by. He wondered if there was something under the sculpture, but he'd have to take a closer look. He took a glance at the people at on the bench. They were deep into it, so he risked ducking under the sculpture.

It was a huge rock—maybe six or seven hundred pounds, if he had to guess—and it was on a stand that looked like it was made to support it. It was supposed to be like one of those dark-wood Chinese stands, but it was made out of metal. He couldn't see any wiring connected under the sculpture, so maybe there wasn't any kind of pressure sensor in there. If he was lucky, they were just trusting that the weight and bulk of the statue would keep it from being stolen. And the fact that it was inside the house with an alarm in a neighborhood that was probably well-protected by the police.

Adam looked over at the couple. Still no sign they'd noticed him.

So now he had one problem: how did you steal an enormous rock?

He walked back into the house and made for the bathroom, making sure to get lost on the way and wander into the bedroom. It was so neat it looked like a hotel, and featured an impressively large mattress. And it had a window overlooking the patio, just like he'd figured.

He doubled back to the bathroom off the main part of the party. Once inside, he opened the window. Good, there was an alarm sensor in there, and it was a brand he recognized. Still wearing his gloves, he swiftly removed the sensor, replaced it with one of the ones in his jacket pocket, and shut the window again. Hopefully that would be enough to kill the alarm system for a few days. But he still had to figure out how to get into the patio of a well-guarded house. And how to get out with a gigantic rock. Even if he could get into the house, how was he supposed to get the rock out? So many windows, so many risks of being spotted.

He stopped short with the realization. What if he could get in by climbing the roof? It shouldn't be too dangerous. The house was only a story high, after all. All he'd have to do was get on the roof and walk across until he reached the patio. He'd be pretty hard to see that way. He could cover up the cameras.

Okay, that's how he'd get in. But how would he get the rock out?

He thought about it while he retrieved Jay from his circle of new friends, and while he and Jay took a taxi back to their hotel. Back in the hotel room, Adam took notes on the house with his own shorthand. The more he thought about it, the more he liked the idea of going over the roof. He'd spotted a utility pole in the backyard—he'd stash a ladder there in advance. No one would notice that it made no sense to have a ladder there. Then he'd wait for a night that the rich guy was out, lean the ladder against the house, climb on to the roof, spray-paint the cameras, and use a rope ladder to get down to the patio.

"You seem happy," Jay said, looking up from his guidebook.

Huh. Had he been whistling again? "Mostly just thinking about how to do this the right way."

"No," said Jay. "I'm glad this happened. I want you to impress the FBI agent. I mean, I know you were trying to get away from Mahler.

You've got too many bad memories there. And thanks to me, you're stuck there for good. But you don't have to work there, too."

Adam felt uncomfortable. He'd never had conversations like this with anyone besides Jay. And how did he explain that yes, he had bad memories of Mahler, but he had bad memories from everywhere? If he'd never come to work at Mahler, he never would have met Jay, and that was the worst thought of all because he'd seen his world without Jay in it.

The night after Jay died, he came back to their apartment, alone, and tried to sleep in their bed and spent the whole night shivering, unable to get warm, wondering why he didn't just get his gun and follow Jay to wherever he'd gone. And then he'd remembered the reboot. At first he'd told himself that it wouldn't be Jay, not really, but then he thought, *What if it's awake? What if it knows it's stuck in a cold freezer and it can't see or hear or move? What if it's suffering in there?* As soon as it was light outside, he'd called Tanya.

How did he explain all that? "I don't care, Jay," he mumbled, his voice coming out rough in his own ears.

Jay leaned over and kissed him, first on the lips, then on the forehead. Adam felt a peaceful, calm feeling descend upon him. Maybe he hadn't been able to save Jay the first time. But the man next to him was Jay, too. And the best part of Adam would always come to life for Jay's sake.

"I know you think I'm unhappy," said Jay, "But I'm not. It's kind of like living with your great aunts. They love me, even though they don't always get me."

Maybe Jay's great aunts. Adam's great aunts were mean, skinny chain smokers, always fighting with each other or his mother about some damn thing. Nope.

"I couldn't take it. Never being alone."

"I never liked being alone," said Jay.

This was true. When Jay was a security guard at Mahler, watching the front gate, he'd always get in trouble because he was so chatty with everyone who came in. So Adam would come out and keep him company. That way Jay didn't get lonely, and the people stuck in line didn't get angry and honk at him.

It was a good memory.

Had Adam made this all harder on himself than he had to? What if he didn't have to pretend that nothing had changed? Then he and Jay could learn to be happy with the way things actually were. He could do that, if Jay could.

"And the aliens love you too," said Jay.

"Why?" said Adam. He could have bitten his tongue the minute he said it.

"They think you're the man who saved them from Greg. And you make me happy."

Adam exhaled. "You are such a dumbass."

"No, you are," said Jay, and without warning, rolled over onto Adam, crushing him to the mattress.

Adam laughed, dropped his pen and notebook to the floor, and slid his legs out from under Jay, ready to go on counterattack. Jay had wrestled in high school, but Adam was skinny, strong, and mean, so all things considered, they were evenly matched.

CHAPTER 14

IT WAS COOL AND clear, a great night for a burglary. Adam shouldered the ladder and walked towards the house, suppressing the urge to whistle. He was surprised to see Corrine standing silently in front of the shrubbery. She put her finger to her lips, and then waved at him, a big grin on her face. He stopped short, but she gestured that he should continue, and then mimed climbing a ladder.

Okay, he had an audience from the FBI. All part of the interview, maybe. Better do this right.

He'd considered wearing the cloak of invisibility but it tended to tangle around his legs. Speed and dark clothing were going to be his best friends. He carefully planted the ladder in the dirt and began to scale it. The further he climbed, the windier it was and the more of the city lights he could see, then the sudden darkness of the Pacific Ocean beyond. He paused, pretty sure that he'd found the Golden Gate Bridge. Which made the little clump of lights in the middle of the bay Alcatraz. Jay had been pushing him to go see it, but Adam had no interest in visiting a prison.

He walked swiftly across the sloping roof, circling the camera's range, took the spray can from his pocket, and sprayed the camera's lens until it was covered. Quickly, he crossed to the other side and repeated the action.

Now came the one part of this that made him feel a little guilty. He shoved the ice tool, with the rope already attached, deep into a roof tile. Water damage was no joke, but he hoped the homeowner would figure it out before things got too bad. He slowly lowered the knotted rope to the ground, listened for a moment, and then climbed down the rope to the patio.

There it was: the jade mountain. Adam opened his backpack and carefully removed a gun-shaped object from its metal case. He aimed it at the mountain and fired. The mountain, and its supporting frame, shrank down to the size of a brick. Adam didn't really understand how Skzzx's technology worked, but it was good stuff. He carefully put the safety back on his shrink ray, checked it, and put it back in the protective box. There were a lot of things he didn't want to accidentally shoot with it. He lifted the jade anthill and put it in his backpack on top of his shrink ray. It was less heavy than he'd anticipated—about the weight of a brick, actually.

He climbed up the rope as quickly as possible, then drew up the rope behind him and dropped it on the roof. Corinne caught his eye and waved to him again. He turned around to go down the ladder—he knew guys who could go down a ladder facing front, but he also knew a guy who'd broken his leg that way.

Then he heard Corinne gasp and knew that something had gone terribly wrong.

He turned around. John Chen was standing in the garden, his gun pointed at Corinne. Corinne had her empty hands raised in the air. "Who's the girl, Adam?" John asked.

"She's my lookout," Adam lied. "I met her at the hotel bar."

"Useless," said John and shot Corinne. She fell to the ground with a little cry. "Where's the sculpture?"

"Where's my money?" said Adam. Corinne wasn't moving. *Shit.* This neighborhood was going to notice, right? Gunshots weren't normal here?

"New plan," said John. "Give me the sculpture and you get to leave."

Somehow, Adam doubted that. Nope, what was going to happen is that he was going to tell John where the sculpture was, and then John was going to kill him, too. So his best bet, his absolute best bet, was to shoot John first.

He could keep telling himself that, but he didn't want to do it, and part of that was because something was off. What was it?

He looked down at Corrine lying there, like a sprawled doll, her eyes shut. Like she was dead. No, like she was playing dead. Because that cute little gulp had not been the noise a person made when she was shot. Because your eyes didn't close when you died.

Because she was working together with John. Of course. That's how she'd found him in the first place.

They could have their stupid rock, but he wasn't going to let them think they'd tricked him. He kicked her in the side. Her eyes flew open, she let out a terrific yelp, and her arms and legs curled up and retracted into her torso. Like she was a turtle.

Adam gasped and backed up a step. His gun was in his hand—how it had gotten there, he couldn't say. "What the hell!"

"Mr. Shapiro—" said John.

"Don't fuck around!" said Adam, holding the gun on John. "What's going on?"

John slowly holstered his gun. "Mr. Shapiro—Adam," he said. The British accent was gone. "I'm Ben Nakamura from the Committee on Alien Contact. It's part of the FBI. Corrine and I work together."

"You kicked me in the junk, you jerk!" shouted Corrine.

John—no, Ben—ignored her. "Skzzx isn't the only alien on Earth. They're not even the only alien in America. By a lot. And our organization, well, we're America's experts on aliens."

Adam almost laughed, but managed to choke it back. So much of this whole thing had been lies and he and Jay had been so wrong about most of it, but at the end of the day, Jay had nailed it exactly. They'd been testing him, all along. It had all been a really fucked-up job interview. Because he might be a murderer, he might be a thief, but he was also an expert on aliens. Or alien, at least. How many Americans could say they'd had their dick inside an alien?

He holstered his gun. "So," he said, and grinned at Ben. "Did I get the job?"

CHAPTER 15

VACATION WAS OVER AND they were back in Roswell in their apartment at the Mahler Corporation. Adam looked over at Jay, who was sitting at their dining room table with a notepad and pen. Jay's lips would move silently and then he'd stop, as if listening, and then he'd write something on the notepad. Which meant he was having a discussion with the aliens.

Skzzx had big changes planned for the Mahler Corporation, now that they'd made "Greg" resign and installed Jay as the new CEO. As Jay explained it, they were going to secretly help the people of Earth by using alien technology and then they were going to reveal that aliens were real. Skzzx thought that this would mean that everyone would love them.

Jay was sure this was a great idea, but Adam thought it showed how much Jay's aliens still had to learn about humans. But at the end of the day, Adam didn't care what Skzzx got up to, as long as Jay was happy and safe. And Skzzx had given Adam an assignment, too: he was supposed to be in charge of security for them. "We trust you to take care of us," one of the aliens had said, smiling at Adam with Jay's face.

Of course he'd take care of them. Whether he trusted them, he wasn't sure.

Jay had told Adam once that there were no predators at all on the Rzzln's homeworld. No tigers, no wolves, nothing like that. Just the Rzzln grabbing the plants that floated by in the heavy, watery air. The Rzzln only had teeth because the plants were so hard to chew. "So they never learned how to be afraid like humans did," Jay had explained and Adam had turned that over and over in his mind ever since.

Adam remembered the first time he'd seen Skzzx. He'd been seventeen years old, and he'd been working at Mahler for six months when his boss had taken him and the rest of the young meatheads down to Area 51. First, they'd had to go through decontamination. They'd all joked around with each other in the shower and the locker room. He remembered giving that one guy from Tucson grief about his hairy back. Then they'd walked into the dark concrete room with the big glass case and the lights had flicked on and Skzzx had been there, hissing and flinging their tentacles against the glass. All the guys had been dead quiet going back through decontamination and sat there in total silence in the auditorium afterwards when Greg Mahler had gotten on stage and told them that this was their chance to be heroes.

Looking back, of course, that was Greg looking like Skzzx, and the only reason they'd gone through decontamination was to give Greg time to change. It was kind of funny, and maybe someday Adam would be able to see the humor in it. At least Adam knew now that anyone who talked about heroes, glory, or saving the world was lying to you.

That was his goal now: every year he was going to be a little less of a dumbass.

Adam looked at Jay again. Jay had his head tilted at a weird angle, and his pen was clenched in his hand like a gearshift. One of the aliens was borrowing Jay's body to write something down. Alien Jay jerkily turned his head towards Adam and then his posture shifted and relaxed. Jay himself gave Adam a little smile. "Hi, Rosey," he said. Then whichever alien it had been, Captain maybe, took over again and got back to work.

Adam sighed. He'd already worked out today. He could drive to Albuquerque and go bug Dana. The last time he'd been over, he heard a wobble in her kitchen fan that he needed to fix. But it was a weekday so she'd be carving one of her little dog sculptures. She said she didn't mind if he watched, but even he could tell she was just being polite.

So he was stuck watching golf on television. How could he have this many channels and the only sport on was golf?

Something hit the window and Adam jumped. Ben Nakamura was outside, waving at him.

"DO YOU KNOW WHY we recruited you?" Ben asked, once they were inside the bubble.

Adam shrugged. Because he knew Skzzx, right? And Jay, if they knew about Jay? They probably did.

"We've got a big problem coming," said Ben. "There's a fleet of alien spaceships headed towards Earth. They should be here in a month or so."

"And we're flying out to stop them?" Why would Ben ask him to do that? Wouldn't you hire an astronaut? Though if Ben wanted to train him to be an astronaut, he wouldn't say no. Flying a spaceship sounded amazing. Those things were *fast.* And in space, there wasn't much you could hit. What could go wrong?

"Oh, God no," said Ben. "No, we just need people in place before they get here so we're ready to handle the situation. Today we're dealing with a different problem. Much more in line with your skill set."

Ben's story was this: there was once a weird old rich man who gave money to a bunch of museums, which they liked, and some paintings and sculptures, which they didn't. Because they took the money, they had to put the rich guy's collection on display once in a while. Which is why one of Ben's co-workers had spotted a silver, egg-shaped alien spaceship on display in the Minneapolis Institute of Art. No one at the museum knew what it was, luckily, but Ben really wanted it out of there before it hatched. So he and Adam were going to steal it.

Stealing for the government! Adam found himself smiling at the thought of it.

Even though Ben was able to get him a good set of blueprints, Adam liked to walk through a place before a job. For one thing, he needed to know where the cameras and sensors were, and that sometimes changed from the original blueprint. He and Ben took a bubble up to Minneapolis and were in a park across the street from the art museum within the hour. The plan was to tour the museum, kill a few hours in Minneapolis, steal the egg once the museum closed, and be home by morning.

The museum was part of a cluster of buildings and was attached to a theater for kids. The museum part was basically L-shaped, and the entrance was at the top of the L. Adam and Ben passed the ticket booth, then two security guards. The guards, wearing jackets that didn't fit, were quickly pawing through people's bags, giving most of their attention to their discussion of the leftover birthday cake in the break room. Chatty, gentle security guards always reminded Adam of Jay. Adam and Ben hadn't brought bags so they went directly through a set of glass doors to a three-story atrium. On the left was a gift shop and a coffeeshop. On the right, a small exhibit room, which contained several ugly paintings, a statue of a woman reaching up in the air while standing on one leg, and an alien spaceship.

Adam and Ben walked into the exhibit room. Up close, the spaceship looked like a metal egg that had been covered, here and there, with extra lumps of metal. But when he looked really closely, he could see the lines where the thing could open. It was not a pretty thing, and he couldn't figure out why anyone would buy it as a sculpture, but what did he know about art?

Adam looked up. There were two cameras on the ceiling, a couple of motion sensors, a fire alarm, and a locator for the visitor's guide. It was a respectable level of security, but not like stealing the crown jewels or something. Just like he'd thought, the biggest concern was going to be the cameras, which is why he'd brought the cloak of invisibility.

Three sides of the room were solid walls, so the only obvious entrance was the big door he'd just come through. Of course, there was a dropped ceiling covered with ceiling tiles, so there might be a less-obvious route from above. He hated crawling through ceilings, though. It always made him feel like the walls were closing in on him and he'd never forget the time he fell through an old, rusted-out duct, crashing down on to the floor. He'd been so glad his ankle was only sprained, not broken. Absolute last choice, even for a thrill-seeker like him.

Adam went back to the entrance of the exhibit room and scanned the rest of the atrium. There were two stairs, one at either end of the atrium. One stair only went up to the second floor; the other went up to the third. Across the atrium was the gift shop, the entrance to the museum's offices, and the coffeeshop. Next to that was a windowless wall. When Adam turned the corner, he could see the brick wall was one side of a playroom for kids and their parents. One little guy, just about old enough to walk, had his mouth fixed to the glass like a remora. Adam waved at him and the baby continued to slide his mouth back and forth across the glass.

Adam needed to figure out how to disable the burglar alarm and how to get in and out of the museum without being spotted. Even if he wore the cloak, someone could still see the door opening and closing. The front entrance, where they'd come in, was far too visible from the street. There was a set of doors at the end of the atrium, but they'd been blocked off with a thick glass wall. The less well-guarded entrance on the short, lower side of the L was too far from the spaceship.

While Adam checked out all the entrances, Ben had followed him silently. But as they left the second story entrance, Ben said he wanted to show Adam something interesting.

Might as well pretend to be real museum guests.

On the third floor was a silver car from, of all places, Czechoslovakia. A 1930s Tatra. Adam had heard of them before, but he'd never seen one in person. They were good sports cars, for their day, with a maximum speed of a hundred miles an hour. And this particular one was in perfect condition, like a silver teardrop. "Why are you showing me this?" he asked.

"I heard you like cars," said Ben.

Was Ben yanking his chain? Ben knew about the little auto parts business he'd had going back in Worcester, even though the judge had promised his record was sealed, and he'd changed his name since then. That was the government for you, never to be trusted.

Better pretend he didn't notice.

They walked back down to the first floor and Adam put on his gloves. "Does this mean you're about to do something I shouldn't see?" asked Ben.

Really? "Just getting our exit ready."

"I'll wait in the gift shop."

The first floor of the art museum was mostly offices. Adam thought that was a mistake—people could get awfully careless about security in a place they worked every day. He stood in the hallway next to the gift shop fiddling with what looked like a phone (he didn't have a real phone, it made you too easy to track) until someone walked by and used his ID to unlock the door to the offices. Then Adam followed the man in and politely thanked him.

He strolled over to the side door that he'd marked on the blueprint. Not only was it in a courtyard, which meant it couldn't be seen from the street, it was blocked from public view by a giant wall. Between that and the cloak, he was in business. He opened the door, quickly switched out the real alarm sensor with one of Skzzx's fakes and jammed the deadbolt with aerosol glue. The other lock looked easy to pick.

They'd probably fix that after tonight, though.

He went back in through the main entrance. The happy, excited feeling that had followed him ever since they left Roswell had worn off. This was too simple. He wanted to do something a little stupid, to make this all trickier. But no, he had to be reasonable. This was a job, right?

At least he could swipe something from the gift shop. That would make him feel better.

Behind him, Ben cleared his throat. "Adam," he said softly. "See those guys looking at the egg? Do you know them?"

"Mmm," he said, looking up and moving towards the gift shop entrance, careful to stay out of view of the people Ben had indicated. He recognized one of them. With that natural bleached-out streak on the back of his dark hair, he was hard to miss. "They work for—"

Ben put his hand up like a traffic cop: *stop*.

Okay, he wouldn't say it out loud. They worked for Fred Laskin, who'd made a ton of money as the owner of the Laskin Ice Cream Factory chain, which was the chain where all the ice cream was custom-scooped to order by robots you programmed by pushing buttons. Literal buttons, not a touch pad. Adam had loved the place as a kid. But Laskin didn't care about ice cream, all his profits went directly into his real love, which was aliens. Laskin was convinced that aliens were walking the Earth (which was true) and he was going to prove it by showing the world a real-life alien artifact.

Most of what he owned was movie props and garbage, but he'd told the world he'd acquired part of the Roswell spaceship. So Greg had sent Adam to reclaim it. Which was how he met Bleach Guy. Not met, exactly. How he'd punched Bleach Guy in the stomach and gotten out of Laskin's storage facility with small chunk of burned-looking metal.

"Would they recognize you?" asked Ben.

"Probably not," said Adam. "I was wearing a ski mask."

Ben gave him a weird look. "I don't want to know, do I?"

Adam shrugged. "It was a fake, anyway. That guy will buy anything." Outside the world of ice cream robots, Laskin was kind of a meathead.

"You think they're stealing it now?" asked Ben. "In broad daylight?"

"They're not the brightest guys," said Adam.

Ben's face froze. "Oh shit. They're not going to steal it. They're going to open it."

Makes sense, thought Adam. *They need a crowd, and the museum is open.* "If we pull the fire alarm, we can get everyone out."

"I'll pull it," said Ben. "They won't know me. So you'll need to—"

Adam pointed towards the playroom around the corner. "Get the kids out."

Ben gave him a weird look again. Had Ben forgotten the kids were there?

Or maybe Ben didn't think Adam was the kind of guy who'd care about kids in danger. That was kind of a nasty thought.

Adam left the gift shop before Ben could say whatever was on his mind. He opened the glass doors of the playroom. "Excuse me," he said. A few of the moms looked up at the strange man. "The fire alarm's about to go off. I'm going to need you to leave the museum from the second floor entrance."

One mom looked up from her phone. "How do you know—"

And then the sirens went off.

The mom hrrumphed at him, scooped up her door-licking baby, and headed away from Laskin's men. Adam grinned at the little guy and the baby gave him a suspicious glare. His kind of kid.

Adam doubled back to the atrium, where Ben had his badge out and was trying to talk reasonably to the Laskin guys, who were arguing back. And here came the security guards, who were trying to get them all to leave because of the fire alarm, and were not prepared to have Bleach Guy draw his gun and start screaming at them.

No one in particular was paying attention to Adam, so he tried hard to look like another museum guest leaving the place, then at the last minute swerved towards Bleach Guy and got him with his Taser. Bleach Guy was down!

Ben was explaining to Bleach Guy's partner that she was now under arrest when a strange creaking noise came from the egg. A purplish, gooey club extended from it, like living Jello. The security guards bolted for the front door. Smart, but not brave. "Not good," said Ben. "Did you—"

But whatever he was planning to say to the woman was lost as suddenly the rest of the creature pulled out of the egg. It was huge and sticky looking, like a big, purple ball of mucus.

"Adam, remember where the Tatra was?" asked Ben.

"What?" Adam said. *Now?*

The woman held out an orange crystal, like a kid feeding an elephant at the zoo. A long strand of goo reached out off the ball and walloped her. She fell to the ground, hitting her head, and lay still.

Was he supposed to shoot this thing? How did you shoot mucus?

"Run!" said Ben, and took off towards the front door, but instead of going outside, he headed up the stairs. Adam followed him. So did the angry purple alien.

They ran up the hard concrete stairs. Adam tried to keep in shape, but Ben was a freaking jackrabbit, and Adam's legs were beginning to burn. *Ignore it.*

"It's got to follow us," said Ben, between gasps. "If you get there first, start the car."

What? thought Adam, but didn't have time to think much more. Past the old paintings. Through a narrow doorway he didn't know if the purple alien could fit through, but it did, glooping purple snail-trails on the wall. *Don't look back! Run!*

Ben was fast and Adam could not have said anything if he tried. Hell, he could barely breathe. He was going to have to spend more time on the treadmill when he got back home, that was clear. Past a couple of suits of armor, and then a room of Jewish stuff, and then a big ugly ceramic dog thing on a tiny suitcase.

Adam didn't understand art. And he really didn't understand art museums. He liked them though, generally, as long as he wasn't being chased by a giant purple angry snot alien. Then he thought that museums were too damn big for their own good.

Ben skidded around a corner and Adam followed him. Behind them there was a crash as the giant ceramic dog thing went down hard. He got closer to Ben on the straightaway. Then he spotted the Tatra, shining like mercury. Was he going to have to hot-wire the thing while dodging the Blob? He hoped not. He wrestled the door up to open it—a suicide door, he'd never seen one up close before—and jumped in the driver's seat. And the keys were there. He turned on the ignition and the engine caught and purred. Beautiful, beautiful.

He looked in the rearview mirror. He could barely see out, because it was a tiny opening, with three sheets of glass. Everything back there looked purple.

Ben got into the passenger seat and sat down. "Drive forward," he said. "Fast as you can."

"Where?"

"Hit the accelerator, Adam!"

Damn it. He was going to hit the glass case across from it at speed and ruin the car, and probably break his neck. *Fuck it.* The engine roared—it might be old, but that engine still had all the power it needed—and as he accelerated, something blurry formed ahead of him, like a heat haze. He shifted into second with a clonk, then up and to the right into third. He zoomed, aiming for the blur, and as he struck it, the air changed. *Foomp.* He was in a hallway, and there were a bunch of people running towards the car, firing laser guns above them.

"Stop!" yelled Ben, right in his ear. *Ouch.*

Adam hit the brakes hard, which was a fucking mistake with a rear wheel drive car. The car began to fishtail and Adam steered into the skid, the wall of the hallway coming up fast, and at the last minute, he yanked the wheel away. He shifted into park and turned around. Next to him, Ben was breathing hard. Behind the car, the purple snotwad was frozen stiff and there were a bunch of people pointing laser guns at it. Or freeze rays. Alien space guns for sure, though.

He turned off the car and got out. He was no longer in the museum. It smelled like he was in an underground tunnel that had been converted to office space. Dingy white paint. Nasty carpet that had seen better days, even before the tire marks.

"Welcome to CAC headquarters," said Ben. "We're under Denver Airport."

One of the people with laser guns looked kind of familiar. Corrine turned around and waved.

Adam could tell that Ben wanted him to start asking questions. How had they gotten there? What was the purple thing? Where did they get freeze rays? The answer to all three: aliens. Obviously. Then there was going to be a tour. Maybe he'd even get to see the cafeteria and break room.

Or to put it another way: at a certain point all this secret society stuff reminded him of Greg, and he was done with it.

Adam stooped down and checked the side of the Tatra. Smooth and perfect as ever. He hadn't even smeared it. What a beautiful thing it was! They called them "Nazi Killers," he remembered, a name you had to love. He reflected: Denver to Roswell was a comfortable two days' drive. And then he could show it to Jay, like he wanted to do with every beautiful thing he found.

"Let me do you a favor, Ben," said Adam. "Why don't I drive this thing back for you?'

INTERLUDE 2

ALLRHL—*OLIVER*, HE REMINDED HIMSELF—BRACED his hands against the window and looked at Earth. They were close enough now that he could differentiate the water from the land, and he felt the muscles of his face tighten. He took a moment to mentally decode what that meant; he was smiling, a sign that he felt good, friendly, open to new experiences. Blue-tinted.

He did feel happy, he realized. First of all, because the leaders hadn't been lying. He did feel like himself, only in a new body. He'd been so afraid that this wouldn't be true, that they'd decided to make a Strategic and Considered Lie to get them all in the tanks. But no, everything inside the hard brainshield seemed to work normally. That was a tremendous relief. Oliver could handle being in an alien body, as long as he got to bring his own mind along with him.

Granted, the new body was ridiculous. Like everyone else who'd been through the process, he'd spent an uncomfortable few days tripping over things and falling. It was weird not to be able to swim over a minor obstacle. It made Oliver realize that human floors must be so empty because they needed to walk on them. Of course! It explained so much of the way their buildings were designed. He'd have to write a paper on it, when the University was re-established.

The best part of his body was the skin. This body craved being touched. Just a brush of his own hand along the hairless inside of his arm could cheer him up. Not to mention the disproportionately large genitals. The first time he'd touched them, it had felt so good that it seemed like his heart was stopping. How strange it was to be in a body that welcomed direct contact!

It was annoying that he could only display one color—though if he did have to pick one, blue was the one he would have chosen—but then he'd discovered clothing. Right now, he was wearing a stretchy jumpsuit with speckles of determined red, new-growth orange, and pensive brown. When he looked at his reflection, he felt like his outside was finally approximating his inside.

Tomorrow he'd add something yellow, for curiosity. His people still didn't have enough knowledge to duplicate *tastes* and *smells* as they would be on Earth. He'd sat amongst his friends in the classroom (and that was another thing he liked—it was like being back in the crèche, or the university) watching cooking shows and wondering. What did "sweet" mean? Did things that were the same color taste the same? How was a tomato like and unlike a cherry?

All in all, Oliver reflected, he was ready to get off the *fsst* ship and finally see Earth. He hoped he could find a way to love their new home; he was going to be there a long time.

PART 3

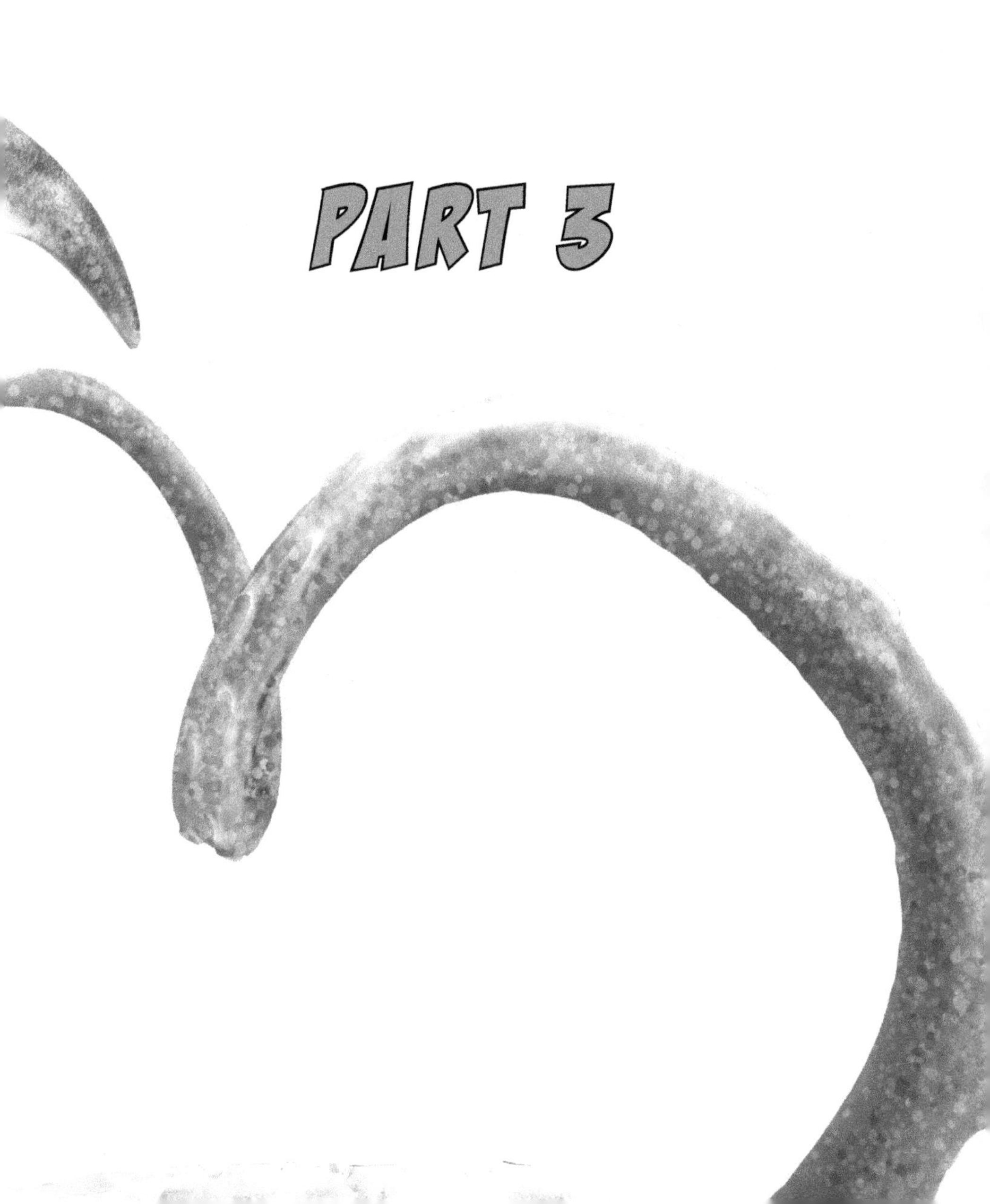

CHAPTER 16

ADAM WAS STANDING IN his apartment kitchen up to his elbows in flour. He'd never been much of a cook before meeting Jay, even though he'd always been good with his hands. He'd never really seen the point, especially since keeping fit was important for his work. But these little beef pies were going to be for his wedding. He felt warm at the thought. Every weekend Jay told him what they were going to make and how they were going to make it, and when they were finished, they'd put the food in the freezer. So far there had been little spinach things and mushroom things and chicken and apple things and now these beef pies. And soon they'd be done and it would be time to get married.

Sometimes he thought about all the things that had had to happen for him to get married to the man he loved and he still couldn't believe it was real.

He felt Jay's warm hand on his upper back. "Those look good," Jay said.

"Still a little lumpy," he said.

"You want them to look homemade."

"Not that homemade."

Jay laughed and took the tray from him, moving to where he was painting the pies with scrambled eggs. It made them shinier, which was apparently something you wanted in a pie.

He turned to watch Jay close the oven door and set the timer. Then Adam heard the living room window shatter, and then the alarm went off. On the grass outside, Adam could see men running out of a small vehicle. Adam reached for his gun, but he wasn't wearing it—he'd left it on the dinner table behind him. Stupid, stupid.

"Get in the safe room!" he shouted to Jay while he bolted the few steps to the table to grab his gun. He could hear that the men, all four of them, had already stepped off the grass onto the hardwood floor of their apartment. He picked up the gun and turned, arms braced, safety off, and aimed at the man in the lead.

He only got off one shot before one of the men in back shot Adam in the face. He figured out that it wasn't a bullet a moment later as some kind of putty spread from his forehead to his chin, covering his eyes, nose, and mouth. He clawed at it with his left hand, still holding his gun in his right. He managed to punch a hole over his nostril, but as soon as he pulled his finger away, the stuff grew back again.

He could still hear. Could he at least shoot one of them before he passed out? He had no idea where they were. They were silent, the siren was blaring and the only one he could hear was Jay, telling them to get out. Then he heard one of the men yelp. He bet Jay had a knife from the block, but what was that going to do against four men? He had to get this stuff off because until he did, he was totally useless.

He heard the vehicle take off, and the putty on his face disappeared. He bent over, gasping desperately for air. He could see the shattered window and the depression on the lawn where the vehicle had been. *I don't want to know what happened. Jay can't be*—Adam couldn't even think it. His left fist clenched tight as he forced himself to look at the spot where Jay had been standing. There was a knife on the floor, coated with purple blood on the tip. Not Jay's. Jay's blood looked like cream. There were footprints in the scattered flour and tracks where something heavy got dragged through it to the living room window.

The door to the apartment opened and two of his best people came in. He could see five more out on the lawn. Just like they'd planned in all their drills, ever since Skzzx had asked Adam to protect them. He thought that he'd done enough, he thought they were ready.

But it was too late. Jay was gone.

CHAPTER 17

Raj Singh gently kissed Dana on the back of her neck and she felt every hair on her body stand on end. *Wow, he's good at that,* she thought, as he circled her sofa and sat down next to her. He smiled and gave her hand a little squeeze.

Could she call Raj her boyfriend yet? She wasn't sure—they'd only been dating a few weeks. She'd been leaving her apartment when she'd spotted a tall, handsome man in the courtyard, hitting tennis balls to his corgi. And she hadn't been able to resist ducking back inside to get her own racket, and then running down the stairs to join him.

So, reflected Dana, it was really beyond time they took this thing beyond some handholding and enthusiastic kissing. But Raj had shown up at her apartment with his corgi in tow, and there were some things Dana didn't like to do with an audience. Even a canine one. "Hey, Raj?" she said. "Do you mind if we put your dog somewhere else? She keeps staring at me."

"She's probably just jealous," said Raj.

Sadie, the corgi, sneezed. One ear flopped over adorably.

"I'm kidding, Sadie. Dana's probably jealous of *you*."

Yes, thought Dana. *Because only one of us has seen you naked, and it's the dog.* "Raj," she said, "why don't you put your dog in the bathroom and shut the door?"

She had hoped—heck, she'd expected—to see more enthusiasm in Raj's eyes than that. In fact, the look he was giving her was more like the look you'd give someone just before you told her about your other girlfriend.

WHAM WHAM WHAM WHAM WHAM WHAM WHAM

Dana's door shook. "Dana!" called a man's voice. "Are you in there?" Only one person in Dana's life was that rude.

Adam always showed up without warning because he didn't like phones, but usually he was a lot quieter than this. She opened the door. "What the hell?" she said, about to tell him to turn around and head back to Roswell, she was having a relationship crisis, until she saw the stricken look on his face.

"They've got Jay," he said, the words tumbling out of his mouth. "I need you. You have to come back with me." Then Adam's pale, bony face abruptly turned hard and cold and absolutely unreadable. "Raj."

Raj put his hand on Dana's shoulder. *Now, he's interested.* "What were you saying, Adam?" asked Raj.

She could see Adam thinking. "You should come with us," he said, after a moment. "Hell, bring the dog."

"I can't," said Raj.

"James Bond would do it," said Adam. "What's wrong with you?"

James Bond? "I'm missing something," said Dana.

"Your boyfriend works for MI-6," said Adam, crossing his arms in front of himself.

"You know I'm only here as an observer—" started Raj. "Why are you bringing Dana with you?"

"Fuck this," said Adam. "Dana?"

"Wait, he's a spy?" said Dana. "You're a spy? You're spying on me?"

He was a spy, and he'd spent the last six weeks pretending to be her boyfriend. No wonder she could never get him to make a move on her. What an asshole! She was going to tell Raj exactly what she thought of the way he'd treated her, when Adam's cold hand grabbed her forearm.

Oh yeah. Jay. Raj would have to wait.

"Come on, Dana," Adam said.

ADAM AND DANA SAT on the floor of the bubble, the American West passing by through smoked glass. Dana was still angry. Raj was a spy. And he was spying on *her*. No, that didn't make sense. There was no reason British intelligence would be interested in her.

But Jay, on the other hand, Jay would be pretty interesting for anybody.

She didn't deserve to be treated like this. And if Adam knew that Raj was a spy, why hadn't he told her? She scowled at Adam, who had a set of paper blueprints strewn across the floor, and was tracing a path with his index finger. She could tell he was nearly vibrating with misery and shock and felt guilty about blaming him for Raj. She sighed. She was too softhearted to yell at him as much as he deserved.

She'd thought that after their previous adventures, there was a pretty good chance she'd never see Adam or Jay again. Like your BFFs from summer camp. And that if someone did reach out, it would be Jay. Yet here they were.

At least once a week, Adam kept showing up at her apartment. If she was home, he'd join in whatever activity she had planned, no matter how boring it was. If she wasn't, he'd pick the lock, and she'd find him with his feet up on the sofa, watching sports. And even though she never caught him doing it, he'd fixed a lot of little things around her apartment. The window in the bathroom wasn't painted shut any more. The kitchen drawer next to the fridge opened all the way.

Neither of them ever mentioned it.

She was always happy to see him, but the whole thing was kind of hard to explain.

"There are some things I haven't told you," Adam said, without looking up.

"Like about Raj," she said, tartly.

"Jay thought—" he paused, then let out a deep breath. "Jay thought if we waited, he might tell you himself. But there's more than that. I've been doing some consulting. There's a group, part of the FBI, called the Committee on Alien Contact. And they wanted me to do some stuff for them. Mostly stealing things, right? Which I'm good at."

This was true. Adam was currently wearing Dad's leather jacket, which she knew he'd swiped from a locked case at the Elson house. Dana wasn't totally sure exactly what else Adam had been doing for the Mahler Corporation in the bad old days when it was run by Greg Mahler, and she liked it that way.

Adam continued. "Jay thought it would be a good idea if I worked for the Committee because then we could control what they heard about Skzzx. But it turned out that they wanted to pass information the other way. Like that Skzzx isn't the only alien on the planet. Not by a long shot." He looked up at her, watching her face as that sunk in.

Aliens? thought Dana. *Plural? Not just Skzzx?* She was less surprised by this than she would have thought. Maybe once you knew one secret alien existed, it wasn't a surprise that more than one secret alien existed. Still: more secret aliens. Really kind of cool.

Adam continued. "There's a cruise ship called the *Mercury* anchored in place three hundred miles off San Francisco. It used to be owned by a bunch of libertarians who wanted to start their own country, but then that kind of went to hell, and then a big section was bought by SoftFruit. Which is run by aliens."

"Wait a minute," said Dana. "SoftFruit, the phone company? My phone was made by aliens?"

Adam shrugged.

At this point, her curiosity could no longer be contained. "You're saying, there's a libertarian island near San Francisco, made out of an old cruise ship—"

"The *Mercury*."

"Filled with aliens making cell phones?"

"I don't think it's *just* aliens."

"But why, Adam? Why would a bunch of aliens come to Earth to make cell phones?"

"I don't know." He ran his finger up and down the sole of his shoe. It looked like Dad's jacket was swallowing him up.

Now was not the time to pester Adam for more information, not when he was panicked about what might be happening to Jay. "So you think the SoftFruit aliens kidnapped Jay? And we're going looking for him?"

Adam nodded. "We're going to take the bubble to SFO and then take the ferry across. I need to take your phone so they can't track us."

She pulled the phone out of her pocket and Adam slipped it into his jacket. *Why would that work?* "I think Jay's okay. I think I would have known otherwise." She wasn't totally sure she was right, but she knew how Adam operated, and she was worried about him.

He smiled dimly at her but didn't ask why she thought she knew. "You're missing dinner. Want an apple?" He pulled two from his jacket pocket.

They were Granny Smith, her favorite. "Look," she said. "I know you're a lot skinnier than Dad, but how did you fit those in there? And the blueprints?"

Adam relaxed, back on more comfortable ground now that they were talking about gadgetry. He pulled a small green bag from inside his jacket pocket. "I never showed you this thing? It's one of Skzzx's toys. Check it out." He stuck his hand inside, and kept going. And going. His arm disappeared steadily into the bag, but the bag stayed small and apparently empty. He pulled his arm out. "It's totally safe. See?" He pulled it over his head, letting the bag drop down to his shoulders. It looked like his head had disappeared. Then he pulled the bag off and held it out to Dana.

"That was freaky looking." She reached out for the bag and stuck her head inside. She was looking at the floor of a large, metal-lined room, lit with LED lights. On the floor around her were organized stacks of various supplies, including about five dozen apples and her phone. She pulled her head out again. "Where's the room?"

"It's its own universe, and it's just that room," said Adam. He shrugged. "That's what they told me. We put oxygen and lights in there. You could even spend a couple of days inside, if you had to."

"Which is why it has a porta-potty."

"Did you see the Xbox?"

"Must have been behind the recliner." She smiled at him. "It's a Bag of Holding. You've got a Bag of Holding."

He put the bag back in his jacket and shook his head, smirking faintly. "Nerd."

CHAPTER 18

DANA REFLECTED THAT UNTIL six months ago, she'd had a pretty average life, if you didn't count the daughter-of-a-dead-rock-star thing. She worked as a commercial artist. She hung out with her friends, went to the movies, and drank too much coffee. Sometimes she sat on her sofa at night and ate cookies straight from the box.

And then she'd accidentally drunk the wrong soda on a business trip to Spokane and everything had changed. Her life was a whole lot weirder, for one thing. For example, Jay had left something of himself inside of her (wow, there was no way not to make that sound like a double-entrendre). Now, when they were close to each other she could tell where he was and what he was feeling. She was like Counselor Troi, but only for Jay.

And now, instead of going to outer space, she was going to use her goofy little superpower to try to find Jay on the permanently anchored cruise ship *Mercury*.

The ferry Dana and Adam were riding docked at the *Mercury*, which felt almost like dry land after a miserably bouncy couple of hours from SFO. The ferry had been designed so passengers could cross easily from deck to deck and people were already pressed against the exit rope. Dana could see the SoftFruit sign a quarter of a mile or so away. She started to move towards the exit but then felt Adam's bony hand tighten gently around her upper arm.

"Wait," he said.

And then she saw the crowd of people on the *Mercury* waiting for the ferry to dock. None of them looked like aliens, at least not obviously. Some were holding trays of food or what looked like drugs, some of them had rickshaws, and some of them seemed to just be looking to make new friends. *Come visit the* Mercury, *where nothing is illegal!* And she was about to get between the libertarian entrepreneurs and their customers. "Well, crap," she said.

"Get ready," Adam said, cracking his neck.

The dock attendants checked the ramp and opened the rope. One of them stood there holding his semi-automatic rifle and looking at the swarm of people on the dock in a meaningful way. They seemed to have formed some kind of detente—as long as the Mercurians stayed off the ferry, everything was cool. But the first people off the ferry were getting engulfed. The speed of the crowd had slowed down a lot.

It gave Dana time to get a good look at the *Mercury*. Like a lot of cruise ships, it had probably started out looking like a mall in the rich part of town, but now the part that she could see had definitely been through better days. The luxury shops had been subdivided into tiny stalls, for one thing. She could smell the aroma of charred meat over the scent of bad toilets, industrial disinfectant, and ocean. The section that belonged to SoftFruit looked much cleaner, and more like it had been designed rather than accumulated. But the design was slightly off, not like humans would have done it. The building looked squat, and the windows too small and far apart. Now that she'd seen how wrong it was, she couldn't stop seeing it.

My cell phone was made by aliens.

She and Adam crossed over the ramp to the *Mercury* and were instantly mobbed. No, she didn't want to buy meat on a stick, or an open bottle of water. She shoved past a woman holding up an old copy of *The Fountainhead* and suddenly felt a big hairy arm go around her neck. "Not that way," said a gruff voice. "Come on, cutie."

He was very strong and he was dragging her away from the SoftFruit entrance. She tried to kick him in the kneecap, or to elbow him in the stomach, but it turned out that was pretty tough to do when someone had his arm around your neck and was keeping you from breathing.

"Yeah, cutie," he said. "Go ahead and fight."

So she zapped him with the Taser she'd been carrying up her sleeve. He yelped, dropped her and fell backwards. She landed on top of his twitching body, but managed to get up before anyone stepped on her by grabbing onto someone's backpack. None of the people around them paid any attention to her or the man on the ground. By the time she caught up to Adam, who was standing still and grinning at her, she realized that she'd never gotten a clear view of her assailant.

"You said a Taser was a weird birthday present," Adam said. "But they work great, right?"

Dana reminded herself that Adam actually enjoyed getting in fights. By his standards, he'd just given her a treat: the chance to smack down someone who deserved it. "I think he peed on my leg," Dana said.

"They do that," he nodded.

Somehow Adam had gotten them both jobs in housekeeping at SoftFruit—or, more accurately, had gotten Adam Kornbluth and Dana Smithson jobs at SoftFruit. Dressed in the ugliest uniforms ever, they were walking the hallways of the SoftFruit section within an hour. Adam pushed the cart while she leaned against the stateroom doors trying to figure out where Jay was.

Adam seemed less panicked now that they had a plan to get Jay back. No, that wasn't it. She knew the exact moment that he'd started to calm down. It was when she'd told him that she thought Jay was okay. Adam had apparently believed her.

She was going to have to be more careful about what she said to Adam.

Suddenly he broke the silence. "Jay and I are getting married. You should come."

She smiled. "When?"

He shrugged. "Not sure. It's not going to be a big deal. We'll probably just have it at home. We'd have done it by now, but I had to get my name changed first to make it legal."

"Are you taking Jay's last name or something?" she said.

He knelt down on the carpet, pulled a socket wrench from his pocket, and started tightening the squeaky wheel of the cart without looking at her. "When I started working at Mahler, I was kind of underage. I didn't want anyone to find me. So I picked a new name."

What was your name? she thought, but she wasn't going to ask that. "How did you get a bank account? Or a driver's license?"

He shrugged and stood up. The socket wrench disappeared into his pocket. "I didn't. Hasn't been a problem so far."

She put her hand on his arm. "How did you pay your taxes?"

"I didn't," he said, looking straight at her and grinning.

"It's been like ten years! Adam, they send people to prison for that!"

"You sound just like Jay. Anyway, I fixed it."

Every so often, she realized Adam was just a little nuts.

But their conversation was distracting them from the faint noise she was hearing. She held up a hand. *There it is,* she thought.

Adam raised his eyebrows at her.

Jay's signal was usually a sweet, high-pitched noise that she somehow associated with the color yellow. But something was wrong with it. She could sense a crackling overlay, like static, or an electrical storm. *What the hell does that mean?*

"Is he hurt?" Adam mouthed.

She shrugged and probably looked confused.

Adam pointed at himself and she backed up to give him room. He took the skeleton key from his pocket and the gun from its holster. Holding the gun trained into the room, he opened the door.

Jay O'Toole sat on the desk, watching the door. He was wearing a suit, which was unusual, and it was the first time she'd ever seen him scowl at Adam. "What the hell are you two doing here?"

"We're rescuing you," said Dana.

Jay laughed. "Rescue? I'm here working on a strategic partnership with SoftFruit."

Adam seemed to be struck dumb.

Strategic partnership? That was a phrase she didn't think she'd ever heard come out of Jay's mouth. Had he picked it up from the SoftFruit people? "That's a weird way to say 'SoftFruit kidnapped me,'" said Dana.

Jay shook his head, a melancholy look on his face. "Dana, I don't know what Adam's been telling you, but if you come with me, I'll make sure you get back home safely." He held out his hand to her.

Adam grabbed her by the arm and suddenly the world turned into needles.

ADAM RIPPED HIS HAND from her arm and Dana thought that this was what it would sound like if masking tape were made out of meat. Also, her arm hurt. A lot. She looked at the bloody streaks on her forearm. She was going to end up with four weird marzipan-white stripes, the exact color of Adam's pasty hand, melded to her own brown skin. She still had some pale speckles on the palm of her hand from the last time this had happened.

Gah, teleporting was the absolute worst.

"What the hell is going on?" said Dana. "Why is Jay acting like he hates you? And talking about strategic partnerships? And wearing a suit?"

"You couldn't tell?" said Adam. "That wasn't Jay. That was Greg Mahler, borrowing Jay's body. He's awake."

What? thought Dana. *Not Jay?* And then she thought—*he didn't act much like Jay.* She was a little angry at herself for not spotting it, but she hadn't known it was a possibility—as far as she knew the aliens were keeping Greg in some kind of coma.

Adam sat down on the bed like he'd like to sleep for days, which was pretty much what happened every time he teleported, at least from what Dana had seen. He pulled what looked like an epipen from his bag of holding and jammed it into his thigh, wincing as the needle shot home.

"Are you sure that was Greg? Weren't the aliens supposed to be keeping him asleep? And how come he looks like Jay now?"

"Give me a minute." He held up the empty epipen. Or whatever it was. "You want one?"

She shook her head. *No, Adam, I don't want your mystery energy drugs.*

"They can't kill him. They can't kick him out. And they can't keep him asleep forever." Adam grinned like a wolf as whatever he'd injected kicked in. "I never met anyone else who lied like Greg. He got you, didn't he?"

Yes, he had, and she didn't feel great about it.

"There's one good thing," he said. "Jay's not going to get hurt. Greg always takes care of Greg."

"But how are we going to get Jay back if Greg's awake?" she asked as she took the bandage Adam handed her.

"Can you talk to Jay without Greg knowing?" Adam covered his bleeding palm in some kind of plastic sealant.

Dana shrugged. "I don't know how. He can't read my mind anymore."

"Okay," Adam said. "We had a plan for this. There's a second team following us out of SFO. We're going to have to raid SoftFruit, knock Greg out, get him back to Roswell, and deal with him when we get home."

"Great. What do I do?"

Adam exhaled. "Stay in this room. When we've got Jay, I'll come get you."

Dana tried not to feel disappointed. "You're saying, you don't want me to be a commando."

He snorted. "Cheer up. I've got a present for you," and he reached into his bag.

"I'm just going to be sitting here, you don't need to get me anything. Unless it's a sandwich."

"Uh, no." Adam's arm nearly disappeared into the bag and he pulled out a gigantic semiautomatic rifle. "Do you remember how to use this?"

She nodded, thinking about her last visit to Jay and Adam's place, when she'd ended up on their private indoor range, proving she couldn't hit a target even by accident. "What am I supposed to do with it?"

"If anyone tries to open the door who isn't me, scare him with it. If that doesn't work, shoot at him and hope you hit something."

Dana awkwardly balanced the gun across her lap. *No way I'm doing that. He's right, I'd be a shitty commando.*

Adam put Dad's leather jacket on and stuffed the bag back in his pocket. He banged on a panel in the ceiling until it opened, revealing a duct with a ladder inside. He climbed easily up to the upper bunk bed and started to scale the ladder.

"Hey!" said Dana. "What am I supposed to do while I wait? Can I have my phone back?"

She knew Adam must have heard her, but he didn't respond.

WISH I HAD MY phone, thought Dana. She'd been in the stateroom for at least an hour, and the only thing that had happened was a big storm had gone by, rocking the boat sharply for a few minutes. She'd found a copy of *The Fountainhead* in the bedside table drawer, but it was not her idea of a good read.

She'd just gotten to the worst sex scene she'd ever read that wasn't by Jonathan Franzen when the door opened. There was an old man in a

Hawaiian shirt with his equally frail-looking wife standing in the doorway. "What are you doing in our cabin, missy?" he asked.

"I'm sure there must be a misunderstanding," said Dana, standing up. She was pretty sure she'd been assigned this stateroom—or at least her alter ego had.

"I need to rest my feet," said the old woman. She sat down on the bed where Dana had been resting. "Getting off the cruise ship was awful." Dana was embarrassed to realize that her rifle was still sitting on the bed, but the old woman rested her hand on it. "Can't be too careful, can you?"

It was at this moment that Dana realized two things: that she'd let the old man fall out of her line of sight, and that Jay—no, make that Greg—was standing outside the door. She heard a faint electrical hum behind her and bolted towards the exit. "Adam!" she yelled, at the closed door of the empty bathroom. "They've got a blaster!"

The old man believed that Adam was in there or at least, he believed her enough so that he shot at the empty bathroom, rather than at her, as she ran past. Which left a second problem—Greg—who grabbed her by the upper arms.

He still looked like Jay, but she wasn't going to let that trick her this time. She reached out for Jay, using whatever trace of himself he'd left inside her. But she could feel Greg's energy buzz between them, blocking her. Meanwhile, Greg was trying to slam her head into the wall. *Sorry, Jay,* she thought, letting the Taser drop from her sleeve to her hand, and zapping Greg with it.

For a moment, she was looking at Jay's stricken face, then he melted and shifted into Skzzx's tentacle-covered body. And now he was really pissed off at her. A tentacle wrapped around her neck and squeezed. *Nope, definitely not Jay. Jay would never do that.* The room seemed to be going dark, and it was harder and harder to think, but she could still see what she was looking for.

She'd seen Jay look like Skzzx before—he liked to relax into his other shape when he was watching football, even though it meant he took up most of the sofa. Alien Jay was like a big chrysanthemum with tentacles rather than petals. He was covered in soft, pearlescent fur, and he had a long, toothy mouth bisecting his body. Skzzx's people didn't wear clothing, probably because no one wanted to sew pants with that many legs, which had led to a very embarrassing moment when she'd asked Jay, "Why's that tentacle rolled up like a kielbasa?"

Ignoring Greg's snapping slit of a mouth, Dana reached down, grabbed that unmentionable tentacle, and gave it a good, hard twist. Greg let out a horrible shriek made entirely of consonants, dropped her, and rolled over onto his longer-tentacled side, hissing in distress. But his enormous alien body still blocked most of the hallway behind her. Even though the old man had finally figured out that Adam wasn't hiding in the bathroom, he couldn't chase her. With blaster fire and bullets erupting around her, Dana zigzagged down the hallway and out the doorway onto the deck of the ship where the evening crowd hid her from view.

CHAPTER 19

THERE WAS A WILD party mixed with a street market on the deck of the *Mercury*. Ordinarily, it would be little chilly this far out at sea, but the heavy crowd kept it warm enough for shirtsleeves. Dana stripped off her SoftFruit uniform shirt and dropped it onto a sheet where a woman was selling pirated phones and handbags. Underneath Dana was wearing the Star Wars T-shirt she'd had on when they docked and her favorite pair of orange-colored jeans. She pulled a hair tie from her pocket and turned her hair into a puffy ponytail.

There. At least she'd be a little less easy to recognize when the SoftFruit people came looking for her.

Dana ambled along past the arcade of shops, ignoring the touts outside. The more she thought about it, the stranger it was that Greg was working with SoftFruit. He'd devoted most of his life to keeping America safe from knowing the truth about Roswell. So what was he doing having an apparently amicable relationship with the aliens of SoftFruit?

Dana stopped in front of a folk singer with a guitar, keeping her hands jammed in her pockets to protect their contents.

So here was what she knew about SoftFruit: they made fantastic phones. Probably they had other excellent alien technology they'd be happy to share with Greg, but Skzzx's people were no slouches in the tech department. Greg wasn't doing this just because he wanted a new phone. So what did he want?

And given how he felt about aliens, why was he willing to sell himself out to get it?

But while thinking about this, Dana had lost track of the crowd. "Hi, cutie," a voice said. It was the man who had grabbed her at the dock.

She pulled her hand out of her pocket, Taser at the ready. "Stay back," she said.

And then someone behind her had her arm twisted behind her back in a way that nearly made her yelp with pain. "Drop the Taser or I break your arm," he said.

Oh fuck, she thought, and dropped the Taser. The second man handcuffed both hands behind her.

"We're going this way," said the man from the dock. His companion backed this up with a sharp knifepoint held against her lower back. *Come with us or lose a kidney.*

They walked her away from the crowd towards a quieter side street. The locals had a New York-level ability to ignore the bad stuff happening near them. Where were they taking her? Did it matter? Even if it was to see their kitten collection, she didn't want to go.

Luckily, she'd inherited something else from her father: fantastic lungpower. She inhaled as much as she could, and screamed.

It was so loud that the man behind her twitched his knife away from her back for a moment. She stomped on his foot and ran as fast as she could towards the crowd. Not like they'd help her, but maybe she could find a place to hide.

But the man from the dock was coming up on her fast, and it was weirdly hard to run with her arms handcuffed behind her. *Crap,* she thought. *Wish I had my Taser.* Then it was too late to wish for much of anything. She could feel the man grab her by the chain of the handcuffs.

Abruptly, he let her go with a gasp. "Get off me! Get off me!" he yelled.

She turned around. There was a corgi hanging off the man's leg by her teeth. And behind the corgi, holding his gun pointed at Dana's assailant, was Raj Singh.

RAJ TOOK HER TO the closest thing the *Mercury* had to a French sidewalk cafe. A trio of heavily armed guards separated the diners from the crowds. *Classy,* thought Dana, and slipped Sadie, who was sitting on the ground between her and Raj, a French fry.

Did rescuing her from a pair of creeps, and buying her dinner, make up for all Raj's lies? No, it did not. "You should have told me, Raj."

"I couldn't," he said. "You know that."

"Okay, then. If you couldn't tell me about your job, you shouldn't have dated me." She squinted at him "Were you ever actually interested?"

"I wasn't uninterested," said Raj.

Just like that—poof—all of Dana's attraction to Raj disappeared. It didn't matter how good looking he was. He was just the jerk who tried to date her to spy on Jay.

Was it just her, or did Sadie look disgusted too? The dog shook her head and started eating something under the table.

Raj leaned towards her. "Try to see this from our perspective, Dana. Anyone who was paying any attention at all noticed there was something up with Greg. Over seventy years, he never aged a day. He wasn't a good guy, and we could never work with him, but he was a known quantity. And then, suddenly, he's gone, and he's replaced by a security guard who barely graduated high school. I mean, honestly, Jay's last job at Mahler was checking IDs at the front gate. And then he's suddenly the CEO. Wouldn't you send someone to take a look?"

"That's not what I object to." How did you explain to someone that you didn't like being used as a tool? Why didn't Raj understand?

Raj looked down at his coffee "Tell me what you want, Dana."

She sighed, and looked down at Sadie's little tush, which was all that she could see at the moment. "Are all dogs from outer space, or just corgis?"

A jingling came from under the table. "Help me up," said a woman's voice.

Okay, the alien dog talks. Let's hope she's more helpful than Raj.

Raj lifted Sadie and set her in the chair next to him. Even knowing what she knew, Dana thought she was about the cutest thing she'd ever seen, with her big brown eyes and ridiculously large ears. "Glad that's over," said Sadie. "Raj, I'm dying for a beer. Be a sweetheart and get me one? In a bowl, if you wouldn't mind."

While Raj attempted to signal the waiter, Sadie leaned her head confidingly towards Dana. "Let's see, what will you want to know? Yes, this is my natural shape; no, this isn't my home planet. And yes, all corgis are aliens. We just happen to resemble dogs."

"So when you always see the Queen with a pair of corgis—"

"They're advisors from my home planet, Sirius."

"Sirius?"

"No, I'm joking," said Sadie, and let out a barking laugh.

Dana smiled, because she couldn't help it. Stupid puns were her Kryptonite. She moved closer to Sadie, ignoring the urge to scratch her behind the ears. "You know what I'm trying to do here. I'm trying to rescue Jay from SoftFruit."

"Thought you were a bit of an unusual choice to bring on a rescue mission," said Sadie, tilting her head slightly, as if she'd spotted a squirrel.

Dana ignored Sadie's fishing expedition and simply nodded. "But what I don't know is why you and Raj are here."

"Observation only," said Sadie, primly.

"Then thank you for rescuing me," said Dana.

"You have to understand," said Raj, sliding the bowl of beer towards Sadie. "We're not at cross-purposes here. The Rzzln, Skzzx's people, have no real interest in Earth. The corgis have been providing helpful advice to my country for a very long time. And neither the corgis, or the Rzzln, as far as we can tell, have any intention of working with SoftFruit. We'd all be perfectly happy for you to extract Jay in whatever manner you like."

Sadie paused in noisily lapping up her beer. "Have you ever asked Skzzx why they came to this planet?"

And here was something that Dana could give her. "Pilot always says it was to meet hot aliens. But I think they're joking. Captain says they're here for scientific research."

"Pilot? Captain?" asked Raj.

"Four aliens are in the Skzzx collective," said Dana. "Their names are a little hard to say. So we call them Captain, Teacher, Mom, and Pilot."

"And two humans," said Sadie. "Greg Mahler and Jay O'Toole."

Dana looked at her. Despite herself, she was beginning to enjoy fencing with Sadie. "Am I supposed to be confirming something here?"

Sadie winked and lapped up a little more beer.

"What we're trying to explain," said Raj, "is that the Rzzln are like Switzerland. They don't get involved. Skzzx came here to study Earth, and it's their own fault they got stuck here when they crashed their ship. It was an accident, not the start of a larger Rzzln plan. We'd just like to know how O'Toole took over from Mahler as their human representative, given his total lack of qualifications."

Dana shook her head. "Raj, you really can't be as much of a snob as you're pretending. And it's not going to work."

Some dogs looked like they could smile, and that was what Sadie was doing. "Can't fault us for trying. Tell you what, I'll give you a present. Go on, ask me about SoftFruit."

"Tell me about SoftFruit, Sadie."

"Did you know that they created their phones to collect data on the humans who use them? Data that is then shipped back to their homeworld? What do you think they use that data for?"

"Creating lucrative targeted advertising?"

"You're a funny woman, Dana," said Sadie. "I can see why Raj likes you so much."

Dana lifted a French fry and then felt someone's eyes on her. It was Adam, standing nearby with a man she didn't recognize. Adam vaulted over the guard rope, leaving the other man to say something mollifying to the guard. He picked up an empty chair from one of the other tables, without asking the people already sitting there. Setting it down with its back towards the table, he sat down backwards, straddling it.

"Hey, Dana," said Adam. "Hey, bitch. Hey, other bitch."

"Oh, come on, Adam," said Dana.

"These assholes bothering you?" he asked.

"They rescued me," said Dana, feeling a little embarrassed.

"We *were* having a polite conversation," said Raj.

"I lost my Taser though," continued Dana, as if Raj hadn't spoken.

"I can fix that," said Adam. He pulled a new Taser out of his jacket pocket. "Charged up and everything. You know there was an earthquake in San Francisco?"

Sadie lapped up the last of her beer. "You humans are slow. I could have told you that was going to happen yesterday."

"Yep," said Adam, not reacting to the talking dog. "Nothing's going in or out of SFO. Not for at least a day. What are you doing up here, anyway, Dana? I thought I told you to stay put."

"I tried," she said. "Guess what works both ways?"

He looked confused for a moment, and then his eyes widened as he realized what she'd meant. If she could sense Greg, Greg could sense her. He quickly regained his poker face. "How come I didn't figure that out?"

Adam, you really don't want me to answer that. "Don't worry about it. I'm fine."

Adam smiled, a brief flicker.

The other man brought a chair over and sat down next to Adam. "That guy sure didn't like it when you jumped the fence."

"Ben Nakamura, Dana Elson," said Adam. "I work with Ben sometimes. I assume the rest of you all know each other, because you're all spies."

"You're not supposed to say that out loud, Adam," said Ben, sounding amused.

Adam shrugged and stole one of Dana's fries. "These are cold," he said.

"Get your own," said Dana. So there they were. Adam had just told her that backup wasn't coming. They were on their own. And she might be able to track down Jay, but Greg was just as capable of tracking her down. And given that she'd just about twisted off his kielbasa last time they'd met, he wasn't going to be happy to see her.

What did she have to work with? Everything she saw at this table.

"Sadie?" she said. "You're right. Jay O'Toole is part of the Skzzx Collective. He's being held against his will by SoftFruit. We need to get him back."

"Are you expecting us to go in armed to the teeth?" asked Sadie. "That isn't going to happen."

"Here's the thing," said Dana. "You want Jay back in charge. Do you know what he's been doing at Mahler? He's been hiring artists to make nice pictures of aliens with tentacles so the first thing people think when they see him isn't Cthulhu. He wants to tell people about Roswell, but he's not rushing things. Compare that to the kind of things Greg got up to."

"We can't," said Sadie. Before Dana could say anything, she held up a paw. "We can only give you information. Did you meet anyone from SoftFruit?"

"An old man and woman. They looked like humans. Earth people."

"SoftFruit—they don't actually look like that. But they're pretty close, we think, to being able to create simulacra of individual humans." Sadie looked seriously at Dana, one ear flopping over. "You've met Mahler. What would he like most of all?"

His own body back. "I think there would be no objection in giving him what he wants, from Jay's perspective. There have certainly been some disagreements in management decisions…"

Beside her, Adam made a strangled noise, like a sock getting caught in a vacuum cleaner.

Dana continued, "But my understanding is that it isn't physically possible."

"Mahler would disagree with you," said Sadie. "And I think he's offering to pay SoftFruit by giving them the rest of the collective."

Dana exhaled. "Are you sure that you and Raj—"

"I'm sorry," said Sadie. She licked Dana on the arm. *Ick. Alien dog spit.* "I do wish you good luck." She looked up at Raj. "Would you mind paying the check, darling? You're the one with the wallet."

"HOW MUCH OF THAT should we believe?" asked Dana, once Sadie and Raj had left the table.

"I believe that Sadie and Raj aren't going to help you get Jay back," said Ben.

"You think he's fucking the dog?" asked Adam.

"Oh, there's a mental image I needed," said Dana, rubbing her face. Adam gingerly patted her on the back, like there was a small risk she'd explode on contact.

"I'd better check in," said Ben. "Dana, it's nice to meet you."

He disappeared through the crowd. Poof. Like a spy. "Speaking of no help," said Dana. "Do you think Sadie was right? That Greg's doing all this to get a new robot body?"

"It wouldn't work," said Adam. "Teacher explained it to me. Greg's part of Skzzx for good. It's like mixing paint—you can't unmix it afterward. So even if they made him a new body..."

"There's no way to get Greg into it." She sighed. It would have been nice if it would have worked, if they really could have gotten rid of Greg.

Sadie had seemed so sure of herself; it was too bad she was totally wrong. "So what are we going to do?"

"We're going to have to get into the SoftFruit section through the ducts," said Adam. "Your job is to stick close to me and sense Greg. If we get close enough, I can tranq him. Then we'll stuff him in the bag and take a bubble back to Roswell."

"I don't know, Adam. Greg'll sense me as soon as I sense him. This seems like a bad idea."

He put his cold hand on her forearm. "I'm not going to get you hurt, Dana."

That wasn't what worried her. "But what if he has guards?"

"It'll be my job to take them out."

You mean shoot them? Dana bit her lip and shook her head. She cared about Adam, but there was a side to him she was never going to understand. She didn't want to understand it, either, and she certainly didn't want to see it in action.

He looked at her, puzzled, like she'd suddenly started speaking a foreign language. "It's okay. I'm good at this."

"But, if Sadie's wrong, we still don't know why Greg's working with SoftFruit."

He gripped the table and leaned forward. "Because Greg Mahler is the kind of guy who won't be happy until he's shit in everyone else's punchbowl."

She looked down at the remnants of her fries, away from Adam's bright blue eyes. "I can't do it, Adam. I can't."

He stood up and squeezed her gently on the shoulder. He didn't seem angry, which made her feel worse. "Don't worry, Dana. I can handle it myself." He took a small smoked-glass disk out of his pocket. "It's not safe for you to stay here alone. This bubble's programmed to go back to Roswell. I'll meet you there after I get Jay."

And then he was gone, leaving her alone with her cold French fries.

CHAPTER 20

DANA COVERED HER FACE with her hands and sat at the table. She felt like a failure. There had to be a way out of this. There had to be a reason for what Greg was doing. Adam didn't deserve any more blood on his hands, damn it, he was retired from all that.

She'd been a bad friend to Adam. She should have kept him from making the same old mistakes.

She knew, from the outside, her relationship with Adam made no sense. No algorithm would have matched them together. What did they have in common, after all? Their personalities were different, they didn't see the world the same way and yet, he'd been a really good friend to her. He'd even helped her clean out Mom's house to get it ready for the realtor. When she stood in the entryway of Mom's home, paralyzed by all the things she had to deal with, Adam had been the one who rented the dumpster, and driven the UHaul to take away the furniture she couldn't use.

And now it was her turn to be his friend.

Her Adam was the man who couldn't see a broken thing without taking out his tool kit, not the one who carried his gun around like a security blanket. And whether he knew it or not, he kept showing up in her life because the man she saw was the man he wanted to be.

What did their friendship say about her? She dismissed the thought.

Fix this, she told herself. *You're smarter than Adam. You can see things he's missed.*

She would start by thinking about Greg Mahler. He hated aliens, even though he was part of the Skzzx collective now. So why would he want to come and work with the SoftFruit aliens? What could they possibly offer him? That whole robot body thing made no sense—Adam had been right about that.

Gah, this was getting her nowhere.

Okay, SoftFruit. What did she know about them? What could they offer that Greg could want?

She knew they had a small research outfit on this floating libertarian island-ship. This was where they were designing the phones that they sold at tiny, elegant stores all over the country. She knew that a lot of the researchers were secretly aliens, though, obviously, not everyone working for SoftFruit was an alien. The cleaning staff wasn't, which is why she and Adam had been able to sneak in. And probably not manufacturing either—which reminded her of a weird thing she'd heard about SoftFruit. What was it? Now she remembered: it was that their manufacturing process was so top-secret that no one knew where their phones were made. No journalist had been able to trace them back further than container ships landing in the port of San Francisco.

Which was pretty weird, now that she stopped to think about it. The *Mercury* wasn't big enough to hold a manufacturing plant. Where were they making the phones? Back on their home world?

Maybe Adam was right to be so suspicious of phones.

Why would a group of aliens want to land on Earth, just to sell cell phones anyway? Spy Dog had told her that SoftFruit building on the *Mercury* housed researcher aliens, studying humans through the data they collected from their phones. For science, maybe, or maybe they lived on Tenure Planet, where you published or got thrown into a volcano...

And then, all of a sudden, she understood what she'd been doing wrong. Bam. She'd been looking at it the wrong way the whole time. It wasn't about what Greg wanted. It was about what *SoftFruit* wanted. And what they thought they could get out of Greg Mahler.

Okay, she didn't know all the details yet, though she knew she had to get back into SoftFruit. Adam was probably crawling through a duct right now, but that wasn't her style. Dana was going to have to charm her way in. She knew she could do it—after all, she'd survived five years as a freelance artist. And how had she done that? By persuading companies that what she offered was exactly what they needed. By persuading them that they could trust her. Charming was her business.

But there was one big problem. She looked down at the cold bowl of French fry fragments. Was she really going to do this? Was she really going to break into SoftFruit? She'd helped Adam before, in ways that skirted the bounds of legality. Or not even skirted, because Adam didn't seem to consider car theft a crime. But he'd always been right next to her when they'd done it. Now he'd told her to go home and given her the bubble that would take her there safely. If she found a way to sneak into SoftFruit, she was making her own choice to break the law. She had no one else to blame.

Once Adam had turned up when she was hosting her book club, and she'd introduced him to everyone as her brother, and he'd given them all the sweetest, shyest smile. He'd sat down with her friends and eaten some wine and cake, and told Mari why her car was making that noise, before disappearing into the bedroom to watch sports. And when she said goodbye to everyone and went to the kitchen to clean up, all the dishes were done and put away in the cabinet. She hadn't even noticed when he'd done it.

Was it just a joke when she called Adam her brother? It didn't feel like a joke, not anymore. And now, she was going to make this right.

Dana stood in the SoftFruit lobby, dressed in costume as a commercial artist. Which was like what she wore as an actual commercial artist, only more so. Her outfit consisted of a hot pink suit jacket, neatly buttoned over her Star Wars T-shirt, her favorite bright orange jeans, an artist's portfolio, and most importantly, an enormous pair of lime green glasses with parrots on each side of the frames. She had purchased the additional accouterments at the *Mercury* market in exchange for her Taser. The glasses had originally belonged to someone a bit more nearsighted than Dana, but she could still see through them. She was willing to take the discomfort of miscorrected lenses in case Greg had put her face into the SoftFruit computers to be detained on sight. Hopefully if she kept the glasses on, the system wouldn't recognize her.

It worked for Superman, right? And Clark Kent's glasses didn't even have magenta, sequin-covered parrots on them.

She watched the line of business-suit clad people walk through the entry gate and briefly considered joining them, but then she realized that they were all wearing electronic badges and using them so she approached the receptionist instead.

The receptionist, at twenty steps away, looked like a pretty young woman, but as she moved closer, Dana could tell something was off. The receptionist was wearing a lot of makeup. Her foundation looked like it had been sprayed on with an airbrush. "Can I help you?" she asked when Dana got to the desk. When she smiled, Dana could see that the makeup was wearing off around her mouth and the skin underneath looked green.

Alien! thought Dana. It was still cool to realize she was in the same room as someone from a totally different planet. She hoped that the bit of social engineering she was about to engage in would work on someone who wasn't human. "I have a 9:30 with Sara in the Art Department?" she said.

"Which Sara?" asked the receptionist.

"I don't know," said Dana, widening her eyes and letting them water a little. "My name is Felice Smithson. She just told me to ask for Sara. In the Art Department."

"We have five Saras in the Art Department."

"Look," said Dana, sniffling. "It's a job interview. I really need this job. Can you just call whichever Sara you think it might be?"

The receptionist sighed.

Dana allowed one small tear to fall out of her eye, then wiped it off with her finger without removing her glasses, embarrassment written all over her face.

"Wait there," said the receptionist, nodding towards a comfortable-looking set of chairs.

"Can I just use the ladies' room?" asked Dana, with a self-deprecating laugh. "I need to clean myself up a little."

The receptionist got out of her chair. "We need to take your picture first, okay, honey? Could you stand on the X?"

Dana couldn't see any way out of it. She stood on the X.

"One-two-three, say cheese!" said the receptionist.

Dana sneezed. It was a perfectly credible, believable sneeze, and it just happened to shake her head backwards, ruining the picture. She held up her jacket sleeve to her nose, a panicked look in her eyes.

"Did something come out of your nose?" asked the receptionist.

"I think so," said Dana.

"That happens to me, too!" said the receptionist. "I think it's really bad engineering on someone's part. But I shouldn't complain." She reached behind the desk and handed Dana her pass. It said FELIZ SMITHSON and featured a blurry, unrecognizable picture. "Go get yourself cleaned up. By the time you come back," she said reassuringly, "we'll have figured this out."

Dana went into the ladies' room, considered splashing water on her face, wondered if aliens washed their faces with water or, say, a solution of hydrochloric acid, and then reemerged, walking down the hallway swinging the artist's portfolio like she was meant to be there. She felt a little guilty about lying to the receptionist, who had been a sweetie. So she'd better move quickly before the woman, or whatever she was, could get in trouble.

This was the tricky part. Now she had to find Adam before he did anything he was going to regret. She figured the best way to do that was to head towards where Jay was using her handy-dandy internal Jay-focused compass.

Her plan paid off when someone dressed completely in black dropped through the ceiling and landed right in front of her. Adam grabbed her by the arm and yanked her into the stairwell. Blocking her into the corner—presumably he was avoiding cameras she hadn't spotted—he pulled up his ski mask. She hadn't seen him so pissed off at her for a while. "What the hell are you doing?" he whispered hoarsely.

Well, he didn't scare her. "I know why SoftFruit wanted Jay. I mean, Greg."

"I don't care."

She sniffed carefully. She didn't smell gunpowder residue, just clean gun oil and Ivory soap. That meant she still had time to talk him out of whatever mayhem he was planning. "Because from the outside," she said, "it looks like he's successfully negotiated with the US government. For like seventy years."

"So what?" said Adam, but she could see the little wheels inside his head were turning. Good.

"Do you have some kind of ID card from the Committee on Alien Contact? Something really official-looking? With a gold seal on it?"

He looked suspiciously at her.

"Here's what we do. We set up a meeting for you with SoftFruit. As, you know, a representative from the Committee on Alien Contact. We find out what SoftFruit wants from the government, because it's got to be something huge. You tell them you'll report positively to your superiors. And then they don't need Greg anymore, so we offer him a ride back to Mahler. Because he's such a good friend of the US government, right? And Greg will go along with it, because he won't have any choice."

Adam stared at her for a moment. Then he laughed his weird, choked laugh. "What the hell," he said. "Let's give it a shot."

CHAPTER 21

DANA SAT NEXT TO Adam in the conference room. A receptionist, not the same one she had tricked, was circling the room, setting down cups of coffee. He looked like he'd gotten ready in a hurry: he'd totally forgotten to cover the back of his neck in makeup, and it was bright-Smurf-blue above his shirt collar.

Wonder what alien coffee tastes like, though Dana. She took a sip. It tasted like cheap office coffee: toasted socks.

Two suited SoftFruit types, who called themselves Mr. Smith and Ms. Williams, stood nervously in front of a crooked projector screen. "We apologize," said Mr. Smith, "We haven't had time to complete the PowerPoint deck. Your visit comes as something of a surprise to us—"

"Mr. Shapiro prefers it that way," said Dana. "He feels you get a more authentic presentation."

Adam leaned back in his chair, crossed his arms, and smirked.

"Yes, all right," said Mr. Smith, fumbling with the remote. "Let's get started."

The image on the screen was so clear that Dana nearly gasped. It was a streetscape of San Francisco, focusing on the Transamerica Pyramid.

"San Francisco," said Ms. Williams, unnecessarily. "The Transamerica Pyramid. This is a real-time image of the city. We felt that such a striking landmark was an appropriate site for our gift to the American government. Mr. Smith, can you begin the countdown?"

"Wait!" said Dana. "Countdown?"

"I hate to spoil the surprise," said Ms. Williams.

"We've been assured that the American government loves surprises," said Mr. Smith, clutching the remote.

Adam squinted suspiciously. "Are you people about to blow up the Transamerica Pyramid?"

"Actually, we were about to trigger an earthquake strong enough to topple the pyramid," said Ms. Williams.

"It will be very impressive," said Mr. Smith.

"Shall we start the countdown?"

"No!" said Adam and Dana together.

Oh dear Lord, thought Dana. *Greg, what the hell is wrong with you? Are you trying to get the SoftFruit people killed?*

Well, yes. That was exactly what he was trying to do, even if he had to destroy San Francisco to do it. He was trying to make the SoftFruit aliens look totally toxic. But why?

Maybe just because they were aliens and he hated them? Or maybe because he was an asshole.

"Perhaps we'll start with the PowerPoint," said Ms. Williams. "We can always do the demonstration afterwards."

Was it time for Dana to suggest that maybe Greg hadn't been the best consultant to hire? She could see that Mr. Smith and Ms. Williams were beginning to have some doubts, now that they were seeing Adam and Dana's reaction to their proposed demonstration. But if she pushed too hard at this point, there was the risk that the aliens would double down on trusting Greg, and decide that Adam and Dana were offering more than they could deliver. Or they could decide to trust *neither* party.

No, better listen to the presentation first and then figure out how to keep these people from destroying San Francisco.

Mr. Smith nodded, and the screen switched to a PowerPoint slide. It was an image of a planet, mostly covered with what looked like water. A huge block of white text began to roll over the image.

"I don't think I can read that," said Dana.

"I'll summarize," said Ms. Williams. "That's an image of our homeworld, which was in many ways much like Earth."

Was? thought Dana, as the image of the planet exploded. She gasped, and looked over at Adam. His face was blank, unreadable. What was he thinking? Adam had the best poker face of anyone she knew.

"The American government has made contact with the first scout ship. We were permitted to settle here as the company SoftFruit, after adapting ourselves to a more human appearance. However..." and here Mr. Smith clicked the Powerpoint forward.

On the screen appeared one bulleted line of text: "There are eight other ships."

"There are eight other ships," said Ms. Williams. "Larger ones. They contain all the survivors of our planet."

The screen clicked forward again. On the slide, in all caps, it read: "WE REQUEST SANCTUARY."

"We request sanctuary from the American government," said Ms. Williams. "We are willing to pay any fee." San Francisco reappeared on the screen. "For example, because our technology is far superior to yours, we are willing to provide many useful weapons, weapons that will make your country more powerful than any other. Let me demonstrate—"

"Stop!" said Adam. "You want to bring your people to Earth? How many people?"

Mr. Smith and Ms. Williams looked at each other as if packets of data were being slowly transmitted between them. Was that actually what was happening?

"About three million," said Ms. Williams. The two SoftFruit executives turned and smiled nervously at Adam.

How Dana wanted to interject! This was a tricky bit of negotiation here. They had to give the SoftFruit people enough hope to get them to release Greg, but not actually commit to anything. After all, they didn't actually have the authority to act. Still, it was very sad—

"Sure," said Adam. "Land 'em right now. Why not? Aim for Iowa, there's no one there."

Dana's eyes widened. Adam grinned at her.

Mr. Smith gave an involuntary gasp.

"What's the price?" said Ms. Williams.

"It's free," said Adam. "Oh, and don't blow up San Francisco. I'm going back there on my honeymoon." He looked at Dana. "There's a really great museum on Fisherman's Wharf."

Dana had no idea what Adam was talking about. Also, she might be in shock. *Three million aliens?*

Mr. Smith grabbed and hugged Ms. Williams. She started to cry, and her tears looked like blue ink.

Adam stood up. "One more thing," he said. "I hear you've been working with Greg Mahler? We can give him a ride back to Roswell. No problem at all." He slid his hand into his jacket pocket.

DANA, ADAM, AND JAY sat on the floor of the bubble, Jay leaning his head against Adam's shoulder. Through its smoky walls, Dana could see the Transamerica Pyramid rising proudly over San Francisco, still in one piece.

At least one thing had gone right today.

"I can't believe you did that," said Dana. "I cannot believe you did that." And *why* had he done it? To rescue Jay? Or did he feel sorry for the aliens?

Adam shrugged, displacing Jay slightly.

It didn't matter what Adam had been thinking—the problem was that, once again, he'd been unable to see the big picture. He'd just invited eight alien spaceships to land in Iowa. What kind of aliens were they? John Hurt chestbuster aliens? Adam didn't know.

She wondered which laws she'd broken when she and Adam had pretended to be from the government. Adam was only a freelancer, and she wasn't even that. *People go to prison for this, Adam!* she thought. *Not even regular prison, top-secret spy prison!* How had all of this gotten so far out of control? She was supposed to be smart! She wasn't the kind of person who did this kind of thing!

"We're going to be in such deep shit," said Dana.

"Who cares?" said Adam. "Jay, you okay?"

"A little tired," admitted Jay, rubbing his face. His skin slid around limply as he did it.

"Dana doesn't care what you look like. Go ahead and change."

I've got other things to worry about, Jay. He smiled weakly at her and melted into his alien form. Adam rested his head on Jay's fuzzy side like he was a pillow. "I'm going to take a nap."

Nap! You can nap? Knowing what the government's going to do to us?

This was the Elson in her, she was sure of it. She'd tried to tamp it down and lead a quiet, blameless life, but it had snuck up on her just the same. It was like her sister Irene, who'd been an accountant for thirty-five years and one day had just dropped her pencil, stood up from her desk, and left her office forever. Now Irene was working as a rodeo clown in Colorado. Not one of the Elson children was normal, and they could only fake it for so long before they ended up heading out to Roswell with an alien and his fiancé, the law fast on their heels.

Speaking of which, she should probably check the news. "Can I have my phone back?"

Adam reached into his pocket, his eyes shut, and handed her the phone. It rang once and then connected the call, a feature Dana had not been aware it possessed. On the screen was an extremely angry Ben Nakamura.

"How did you get this number?" she said.

"Don't ask stupid questions," said Ben. "What the hell did you just do?"

Might as well just brazen it out. "We rescued Jay. All by ourselves, with no help from the U.S. Government."

"We've just had eight spaceships land in Iowa! Filled with aliens! I'm flying to the White House right now! What do you have to say about that?"

"Congratulations on the promotion," said Dana.

Ben growled and hung up.

Dana looked over at Adam. His eyes were still shut and he had a peaceful, contented look on his face. Was it just because he'd rescued Jay? Or was he listening to her call with Ben?

Then again, it wasn't every day that a man saved three million souls. If Adam hadn't told the aliens they could land on Earth, where would they have gone?

Maybe they were nice aliens.

She lay down and set her head on Jay's side. He was warm, and his fur was chinchilla-soft. One of his tentacles curled around her in a friendly way. She could tell he was in a really good mood. In fact—was he laughing at her?

"You worry too much, Dana," said Adam.

INTERLUDE 3

OLIVER STOOD IN LINE at the coffee shop. Every day he introduced himself to some new human thing, and today, it was coffee. His lessons on the ship had taught him that humans liked it a lot.

There was so much for him to examine in the coffeehouse, and so much of it was confusing. Why, for example, did they have so many empty mugs for sale? Wasn't the point of a coffeehouse to get a *filled* mug? Did people actually come to these places and say, "I've decided I don't want coffee, I just want the container it comes in?"

Mugs were weird in general. Liquids that stayed inside an open-topped container were still kind of unnerving to him. Mugs on his planet looked a lot more like what the humans called bowling balls, the little indentations intended for claws to grasp, with a skin easy to pierce with a mouthpart. Drinks were a special treat on Home, anyway—who needed to drink, when they all absorbed moisture through the skin?

Finally, he made it to the front of the line, and there it was. The little note of recognition in the cashier's eyes as she took in his bright blue skin and realized that she was talking to an alien. It was beginning to wear Oliver down a little. Especially since, as he'd been reminded, he had to look happy. He had to look grateful. He squeezed his forearm with his warm hand to comfort himself. *It will be all right,* he told himself. *It will get easier.*

"Can I help you, sir?" she said.

"I'd like a small black coffee, please." He remembered to exchange the valuable pieces of paper in his wallet for the service he'd requested, and to put the metal disks the cashier handed to him in the tip jar. The cashier handed him a warm mug. "Remember," she said. "It's hot. Blow on it, and let it cool a little, or it'll burn your mouth."

Did she say that to everyone? Or just to aliens? Did it matter, if she was trying to be kind? It was hard and tiring to have to analyze everything around him.

He took his mug to the table and set it in front of him. How was he supposed to tell if it was too hot? Carefully, he dipped his smallest finger into the liquid, feeling the odd sensation of the border between the coffee and the air against his skin. The temperature of the coffee seemed pleasant enough, but now he had coffee on his finger. He let his lips close around it, and when he tasted the coffee, he laughed.

Back on Home, he used to love to go lllk-bug-charming with his friends. There was a trick to it. You had to whistle in just the right way to lure them out from under the rocks and then—pounce! Crunch! They were so delicious, and they were something he never thought he'd enjoy again.

Somehow, coffee tasted exactly like a fresh lllk.

"You must really like coffee," said the cashier.

"Tastes like Home," said Oliver, and smiled.

PART 4

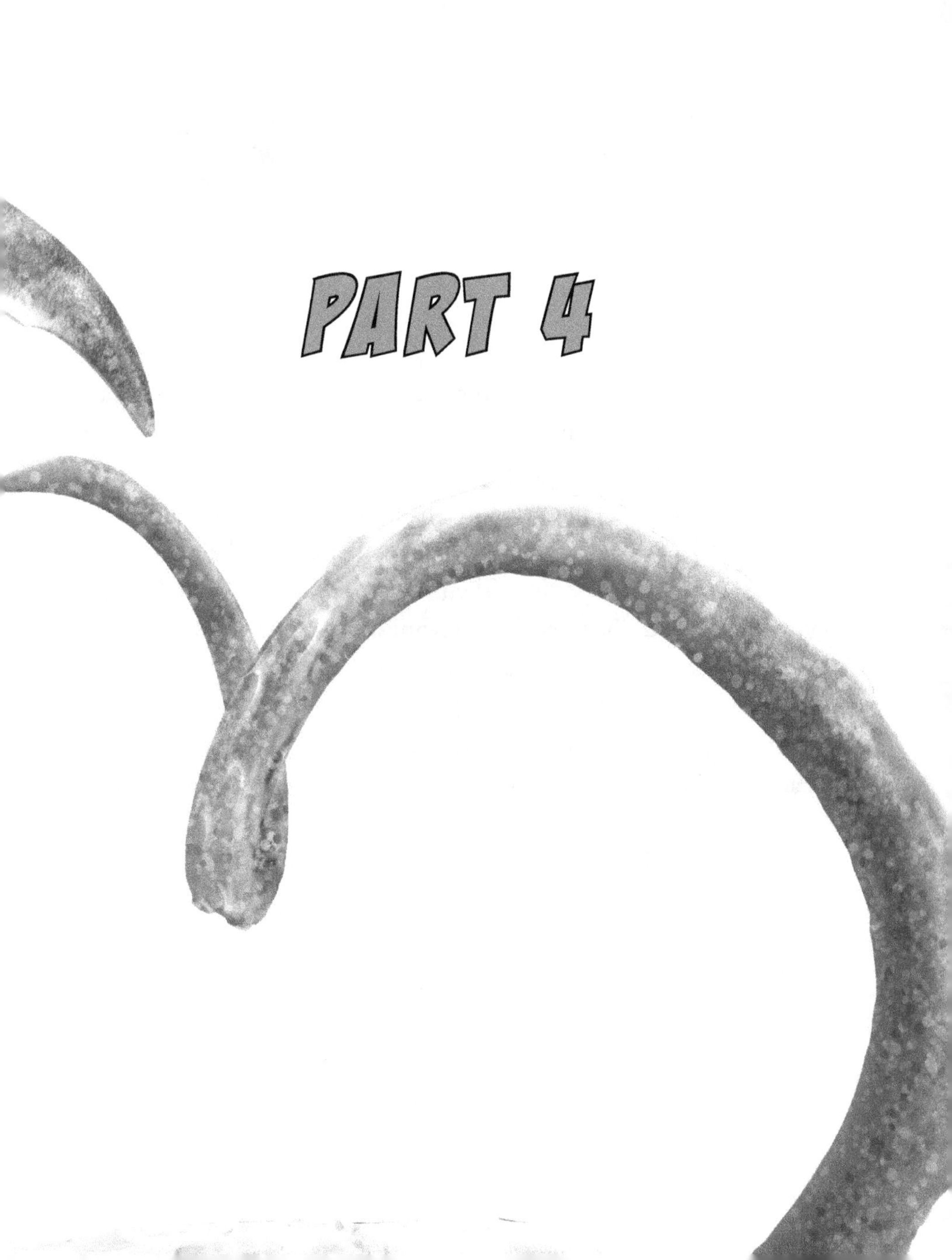

CHAPTER 22

Dana stood in her mother's empty house for the last time. It was times like this that she wished that she had—not another sibling, she had plenty of those—but another full sibling. In a lot of ways, it had been just her and Mom, and now it was just her.

She stood in the kitchen, resting her hands on the counter and thought *this is for the last time.* Then she crossed through to the family room, where she'd done her first drawings. *This is for the last time.* She inhaled the scent of the front hall. *For the last time.*

She couldn't stand it. It was like watching by Mom's hospital bed again so she got in her car and drove and drove and didn't stop until she was at Dad's house in the desert.

By the time she arrived, the sky was pitch black, and it seemed like every star in the sky was visible. She stepped outside and stopped for a moment. Standing out here always made her feel how big the universe was, and how empty. But here was Dad's house, which always comforted her. How many times had she been here, first with her mother, and then by herself? How often had she run here with all her little heartbreaks?

She hadn't even packed a bag. Well, her siblings had left plenty of clothes behind, and there was a stash of toothbrushes somewhere. And

Dana was an artist, and an Elson, and she had the right to be flaky every once in a while.

She opened the door, and only then realized that the lights were on inside.

"Dana?" a voice called. "Is that you?"

Sierra was sitting on one of the stools at the kitchen counter. There were two bottles of beer in front of her, and a chip & dip with hummus and vegetables in it, and two cloth napkins. She hopped down from the stool and held out her arms.

"I had a feeling," she said, "that you'd want me to be here."

Dana didn't believe in ESP or telepathy or any of that stuff but she saw Sierra's face blur, and she realized that she'd started to cry. *Yes,* she thought, *that's exactly what I want.*

She woke up at six the next morning to barking outside her window. Vigorous barking, not a coyote or a wolf, the sort of noise that would come from a small dog. Say, a corgi-sized dog.

"Sadie?" she whispered out the window.

"Yes," Sadie said. "I need to speak with you. It's urgent."

"Wnnf," said Dana and rolled over, pulling the stale, saggy pillow over her head. Could she sleep through Sadie's barking? She wasn't sure, but she was tired enough to try.

Was Sadie here to arrest her? She figured it would be Ben with the handcuffs, but maybe she'd been wrong. Maybe the CAC was going to let Sadie's people deal with her. What would it be like in a jail run by corgis? She pictured sweet, fluffy dogs, wearing tiny prison guard uniforms, yipping at her ankles...

"Dana?" said Sadie. "Dana?" She waited a moment, and then started to bark again. She was amazingly loud for such a small animal.

Dana heard the front door open, and then Sierra's voice. "Look at you! Hello, you sweet girl! Are you lost?"

There was a tiny bark as Sadie obviously got caught.

"I've got you," said Sierra. "Let's take you inside. How about some water, hey good girl? And I might even have a nice can of dog food for you."

Dana considered staying in bed and letting Sierra deal with Spy Dog. If Sadie arrived alone, the odds she was planning to arrest Dana were pretty small. So there must be something else Sadie wanted. As far as Dana was concerned, Sadie had blown her off when she needed help, and she was perfectly all right about returning the favor. But then again, what would Sadie do to Sierra?

Grumbling and yanking down her brother Ace's ZZ Top T-shirt over her sister Mina's University of Arizona sweatpants, Dana trudged angrily to the kitchen.

Sadie was slurping water out of the dish but raised her lip when Sierra offered her a can of Alpo.

"I don't recognize this dog," said Sierra. "And she's obviously someone's pet. Her fur looks really soft and fluffy."

Sadie preened.

"Do you think one of our family left her behind?" continued Sierra.

"No," said Dana. "I'm pretty sure she's my neighbor's dog."

"Back in Albuquerque? So how did she get out here?" Sierra bent down and scratched Sadie behind the ears. Despite herself, Sadie looked pleased. "I wish she could tell us."

Yes, that would be interesting. But then Dana realized she could hear something, a sort of a high-pitched whistling noise. Sadie whimpered and ducked under the kitchen table. Dana followed her and so did Sierra.

"What is that?" said Dana.

"I don't know," said Sierra, "but I've heard that dogs can detect all kinds of—"

Suddenly, there was a gigantic crash outside. Barking excitedly, Sadie ran towards the front door. She scratched the door with her paws, leaving marks on the wood. Dana opened the door and Sadie bolted out, followed by Dana and Sierra. Stopping only to pull on the sneakers she'd left by the front door, Dana chased Sadie across the sand, Sierra pounding behind.

The three followed a long, burned streak across the desert. Sadie stopped suddenly, and Dana did the same, catching her breath, as she realized they'd come to a halt near the edge of a charred-looking crater. Half-buried at the bottom of the crater was a small silver egg-shaped craft. It looked like an escape pod from a spaceship, Dana thought, as Sierra caught up to her and Sadie.

Dana wondered what Skzzx's little spaceship had looked like, and how angry the rest of the Rzzln were with the way Skzzx had been treated for the past seventy years. "This isn't safe. Maybe we should get back to the house," said Dana.

"The dog's not afraid," said Sierra. "Animals are very wise about this kind of thing."

"What do dogs know about alien spaceships?" asked Dana. "Come on, Sierra, before it notices—"

The door in the spaceship opened and a pale human hand, sticking out of the end of a dark sleeve, emerged. A head of dark hair followed. The thing in the spaceship looked up, and Dana saw its bright blue eyes and handsome-devil smile.

"Oh my God," she said. "It's Dad."

Sierra raised her hands in the air and waved them back and forth. "Dad!" she called. "Over here!"

Standing next to her, Sadie let out a small whimper.

CHAPTER 23

It was just sad, thought Dana. When Dad was alive, he'd barely spent any time with her, and then he'd died when she was still a toddler. And here she was with this creature from a spaceship—she'd bet her left kidney he wasn't really her father—and something in the back of her mind kept calling *Dad! Dad! I drew you a picture, want to see?*

"Twenty-five years," said Dad. "I can't believe it."

"What do you remember?" said Sierra, patting Dad's arm as they scaled the hill walking back towards the house.

He graced Sierra with a smile. "The last thing I remember, I was in a hotel in Denver."

A bathroom in a hotel in Denver, thought Dana. *On the toilet.* Dad's death had not been dignified.

"I must have passed out," Dad continued, "and when I came to, I was in a spaceship. And these grey creatures with enormous eyes and tiny mouths had me on a thing like a metal doctor's table. They helped me to my feet and they gave me these clothes and they put me in that little spaceship over there. And it just rocketed back home to Earth! I thought I was dead for sure when I saw the ground coming up so fast."

"What did the aliens want, do you think?" asked Dana.

Dad looked at her and smiled. "I remember you! You're Gwen's daughter, aren't you? The little smart one from Albuquerque. Still as bright as can be, I'll bet!"

Why was Dana so flattered? This wasn't Dad. And even if it had been, what good could flattery do her now?

Every so often, Mom would get in a mood and then she would start playing Dad's old love songs and take out the scrapbook she'd made about Dad. Then she'd look at her concert ticket. The pictures carefully trimmed from the concert program. A blurry selfie backstage. And then, extensively documented photographs of her, Dad, and Dana in her prettiest little dresses, on the few visits they'd had together.

She was still angry at both of them, she realized: Mom for never moving on from the one central night of her life. Dad for being a profligate, wandering soul. How could she be so angry about the qualities in them that had resulted in her?

Sierra opened the door. Dad walked inside and froze. He'd caught sight of himself in one of the gold-frosted mirrors. Not a geriatric rocker still trying to hold on to greatness, but back to being a handsome young man, the one who'd first become a star.

Lucky you, thought Dana. *Play your cards right, you've got another fifty years of breaking hearts ahead of you.*

Why was she so angry at something that wasn't really her father?

While Sierra took Dad into the kitchen to ply him with hummus and pita chips, Dana brought Sadie back to her room, under the pretext of calling her neighbor to pick up his lost dog.

"What the hell is that thing?" said Dana. "When Dad died, he sure didn't look like that. He was forty years older, for one thing."

"It's a present," said Sadie.

Dana raised her eyebrows.

"Not from us," Sadie held a paw to her chest. "From a different group. They've been sending similar emissaries to the UK as well. Not all clones of your father, to be clear."

"Does he know what he is?"

"The other clones claim not to, and they turn evasive when asked." Sadie sighed. "Have you ever heard of the Greys? The big-eyed, big headed aliens in the movies?"

"So they're real?"

"Well, the movies aren't totally accurate, but they did spend a good twenty years kidnapping humans to experiment on. Usually they'd return them unharmed, but the humans generally didn't enjoy the experience. The Greys have recently had a change of leadership, and they've decided gifts like your father are the way to make recompense to Earth. All the Greys' presents are based on popular and well-documented humans. Like your father."

Popular and well-documented. That was true. Dana had spent too much time over the years watching recordings of Dad's old movies and concerts. "So you're saying that there's some kind of alien robot in my house talking to my sister who thinks he's my Dad."

Sadie licked her lips, considering. "More of a humanoid than a robot, I think. I'm going to arrange to have him picked up."

Dana wasn't sure she liked that. It looked and acted like Dad, after all. She didn't want to think of him being experimented on by a bunch of corgis.

"It's lovely, actually," said Sadie, anticipating her unhappiness. "We've been housing them on a private island. James Bond and Queen Elizabeth the First are fast friends—"

"James Bond is fictional," said Dana.

"Whoops," said Sadie, with an embarrassed grin. "Pretend I didn't say that. But the ladies do seem to like him."

Dana sighed. She didn't want Fake Dad to end up on North Brother Island. Still, she didn't know exactly how she could stop Sadie, who apparently had a whole Spy Dog infrastructure behind her.

That would be something to see. She could picture the leader corgi walking down the hallway, barking out instructions, assistants scrambling behind her with folders flapping damply in their mouths. Dana wondered if everything was dog-sized or human-sized. What did their desks look like? How did they work the elevators?

Focus, Dana.

She might be able to call Adam's spy friend Ben and see if he could help her negotiate a better outcome for Fake Dad. Of course, Ben seemed pretty angry about three million aliens landing in Iowa. Maybe he'd gotten past it by now? Or maybe if she called him, arresting her would rise to the top of his to-do list.

"Do you hear something?" asked Sadie. "No, of course you don't."

Dana did hear something, actually. Sort of a low rumble. She walked to the window and looked outside, where she saw a long line of cars, like a giant snake, headed towards the house. Or like all of her siblings were en route for the chance to see Dad.

Sadie whimpered. "Oh dear," she said.

CHAPTER 24

ADAM WAS DOWN IN the musty basement of the Press Elson house, looking at Press's gun collection. It always made him a little sad; it was a wonderful collection, but it was so dusty, he suspected he was the only one who ever came down here.

Wearing his gloves, he took a beautiful Henry rifle—a real one—out of the glass cabinet and set it down on the table. It just killed him to see that no one was maintaining these. If you didn't take care of the stock, the wood was going to dry out and split, and there was no coming back from that.

The room was silent, except for the hum of the florescent lights and the humidifiers, but he could hear the family walking around and chatting upstairs. That was another reason to be in the basement. He was a good thief but a terrible liar, and if anyone started asking him questions about how Dana had found him, and when he'd learned who his father was, he'd be in trouble.

Coming here had been a bad idea in general. But Jay was a huge Press Elson fan, and there was no way he was going to miss the chance to meet Press in person. Adam had been at the receiving end of more than one lecture of how central Press was to the history of country music, though at this point in their marriage he tended to nod and smile rather than try to remember all the details about how Press Elson had influenced Conway Twitty (or was it George Jones? Or Glen Campbell?). All Jay's favorite singers looked alike, middle-aged white men in cowboy suits and shirts with huge, pointed collars, and Adam had no idea how Jay could tell them apart. As far as Adam was concerned, Press was the only one of them who was any good, because he was the only one who made music you could dance to, instead of stuff for moping in your truck. But Adam had enough good sense not to say this to Jay, because if he did, Jay would get a look in his eye, and take out his old cruddy portable LP player with the cowboy on it and his scratched-up records—

The door opened, and Press Elson himself walked in. *Oh, shit.*

"What are you doing down here, son?" said Press.

"Looking at the Henry," said Adam. "Thinking what I need to bring next time to fix it up."

"Glad someone's thinking about that," said Press. He was silent, looking Adam over.

Adam found himself hunching into Press's old leather jacket, the one he'd stolen from upstairs. Up close, Press looked like a rock star. Not just because he was handsome, but because he looked like someone important.

"I don't think I ever met you before," Press continued. "But I can just about imagine what your mama might look like. Pretty little Jewish girl, about that big around. From somewhere near Boston, I guess, from the way you talk. Dark black hair, bright blue eyes."

That was pretty close to true. It left out the batshit crazy part, the next-boyfriend's-going-to-save-me part. "Her eyes are brown," said Adam.

"Son, I hate to tell you this. You do look like me. And if you were twenty years older, I might not be able to say for sure. But a man loses a step or two over time, if you catch my meaning. I never even met your mama. You're not my son."

Adam exhaled, and looked Press right in the eye. Bright blue, just like his own. Sierra had been right about that. "I knew that."

"Do I have this backwards?" said Press. "Excuse an old man. Are you saying you're here with one of my boys?"

Jay would like that, or maybe he wouldn't, because Jay had loved his dad. "No," he said. "It was kind of a joke. Dana told Sierra I was her brother. And Sierra believed her. And then it just…kept going."

Press's face cracked into a smile. "Little Miss Dana? Smartest baby I ever saw. You know Dana?"

Hadn't he just said he knew her? "Sure."

Press gave him a suspicious look. "You're not a singer, are you?"

Adam laughed. Press might be a rock star, but his brain bounced around like a cat on a trampoline. "No."

"Well, hell," said Press. "Little Miss Dana! Son, you're too damn skinny. Come on upstairs, and I'll make you a fried peanut butter and banana sandwich." Press patted him on the shoulder. "Nice jacket."

DANA FELT LUCKY THAT she'd snagged a bedroom before Dad got there because now that Sierra had called every sibling she could reach, the house was filling fast. Casseroles were streaming into the kitchen, sleeping bags into the Island Pit, amplifiers onto the backyard stage. It was going to be a blowout of a family party. A really unforgettable one. Like they'd all been waiting for a special guest who none of them had really expected to show up.

Faced with her siblings' unfeigned enthusiasm, Dana felt lonely. It didn't help that she was one of the youngest of the family. Dad plainly remembered some of them very well. For the oldest, he'd probably been something close to a regular father, as opposed to a special guest star.

It was always a disappointment to Mom that Dana didn't remember having met Dad. Mom seemed to think that if she just told Dana the stories and looked at the pictures one more time, something would spark in the back of Dana's mind. Hadn't Dad been a star, after all? But there was nothing there to remember. Dana had just been too young when Dad died for anything to stick. Usually Mom had been patient with her, but Dana had never forgotten the time when she pinched her lips together and sighed, "You're so smart, Dana, you ought to remember *something.*" Dana had felt guilty about it, even though she knew it wasn't in any way her fault. How she'd hated letting Mom down!

There was a knock on the door. "Can I come in?"

It was Jay. "Sure," she said, and slid over on the bed. She'd picked the smallest, coziest bedroom and there was really nowhere else to sit but on the saggy mattress, unless you wanted to try to balance on the bedside table. It was still her favorite room, though, because it was near the front door, and there was a beautiful view of the desert outside the window.

Up close, Jay was looking healthy and happy. He'd never developed Greg's weird rubber-doll skin. Alien possession agreed with him, she guessed. "What are you doing hiding in here?" he asked. "Don't you want to see Press?"

He's not really my dad, just an alien duplicate, she thought. Yes, that would go over well. "Peter's already tried to swipe the room," she said.

Jay shrugged. "We've got an extra bed in the RV. If someone takes this room, you can bunk with Adam and me. I'll even make you pancakes."

She looked away from Jay's warm brown eyes. "All right, that's not the reason. But I'd like to think I'm a smart person. When someone lets you down enough times, you stop letting them have the chance to do it again."

Jay leaned back on the bed, balancing on his elbows. "You're right. He's not going to be a good dad to you. It's too late for that. You've already grown up without him. But he is a great musician. And I think we both want to be able to tell our kids that we saw him play."

She'd always thought of Jay as sweet but kind of dim. But that wasn't really fair to him, was it? Jay was really smart about people, and in this case, he was dead right.

"Okay," she sighed. "I'm getting up."

DESPITE HERSELF, DANA WAS excited to see that the backyard stage was already set up for a concert. One of her oldest siblings, Vern, a bassist who'd been in a bunch of country bands, was on stage with Dad, along with a drummer who she thought was one of Fiona's youngest. And there were two guitar players, the identical twins, Sally and Molly, and Peter was playing keyboards.

Jay steered her over to a wooden platform by the old, sturdy pine tree she used to climb as a girl. Sierra and Adam had already used a blanket to stake out a space next to Marguerite, who owned a children's dance studio in rural Texas. Marguerite had a husband and five children, all of whom were redheaded and bucktoothed. They looked like a family of Easter Bunnies.

Even in the days when he was wearing white, spangled jumpsuits, Dad had never been much for formality in a concert. His shows always felt like a backyard barbecue party. Dad would sweat freely under the hot stage lights. He'd have rambling conversations with other people on stage. He'd interrupt a song and start fresh if he didn't like the way it sounded. So it was no surprise the concert started with no particular fanfare, just ambling into being.

"I'm so glad to be here," Dad said, leaning on the mike stand.

"I bet you're glad to be anywhere!" said Vern.

"That too," said Dad. "It's good to see all your smiling faces. What do you think, kids? Let's start with an oldie. How about 'Buttercup Time?'"

Jay gasped and raised his arms above his head. "Whoo-hoo!"

"Hey, Vern!" said Dad. "I've got a fan!" Sally—or maybe Molly—strummed the three A chords that started the song, and then Dad began to sing. "Well, it's buttercup time and the air is sweet..."

Holy shit, thought Dana. *I'm at a Press Elson concert.* But then it she had no time to think, because everyone, including her, started to dance.

Dana did not like to get a swelled head about it, but she was an excellent dancer. Most of the Elson kids were, with the big exception of Sierra, who always looked like she was tossing cabers, or possibly wrestling a bear. But Dana danced with her anyway. And then she danced to "Prison Party" with Adam, who seemed to have seen Dad's movies just as many times as she had. They both had the tilted hip-straight leg thing *down.*

About an hour into it, Dad pointed directly at Dana. "Little Miss Dana!" Dad called. "I hear you singing back there!"

Dana shook her head.

Dad paused. "Who else wants to hear Miss Dana sing?"

Her siblings applauded. *Traitors.* Dana skulked to the stage and took the proffered microphone from Peter.

"What would you like to sing, Miss Dana?"

I wouldn't, she thought. Then she caught the eye of one of the people in the crowd: a small, fuzzy, adorable spy, waiting for her chance to get Dad alone. Sadie was sitting between two blankets gnawing on a deer antler. "How about 'Dirty Old Dog'?"

Dad looked conspiratorial. "That's one of my favorites, Little Girl. I'll start, then I'll pass it over to you." He nodded to Vern and then he started to sing. "Well, you're a dirty old dog, mister, always running round the yard..."

She'd picked the right song, reflected Dana. Okay, maybe the dog thing was a little literal. But the meaning hit her—you cheat, you lie, I can't trust you, but I can't stop loving you either.

Dad looked right at her and winked.

After the song was over, Dad shooed her back into the audience, but so nicely that she couldn't complain. She didn't want to dance, or to talk to her siblings, so she climbed the old pine tree, like she used to when she was a kid. The sturdy branch that was her favorite still felt smooth next to the trunk from all the times she'd climbed up there with a book.

Down on the stage, Dad was shifting things up, switching to his ballads. He'd played all the biggest hits, like "Sweet Evelina," and the ones that weren't as well known but just as loved. The mood was changing down below, the couples increasingly entwined in each other's arms.

Finally, Dad sighed. "This is been a beautiful night. I'll never forget it, seeing all your wonderful faces. I have been so blessed, children, and I love you all. But I think it's time to say goodnight now."

There were answering groans in the audience as everyone recognized the opening from "Foolish, Foolish Heart," Dana's personal favorite.

"I think it's time to say goodnight now," sang Dad, "I see the sun has fallen low. So easy to lose track of time, so hard to let you go."

What Dana had always liked about that song is that at first it sounded like the singer is just saying goodnight to his lover. And it was only about two-thirds of the way through the song that you realized that "you" has left the singer and moved on, that the singer is bravely trying to hide that he's still in love. And Dad could still nail it. The little break in his voice made her silently sing along with the last two lines, mouthing her father's words: "You leave the two of us alone, me, and my foolish, foolish heart."

Down from her tree, Dana could see it all: the tears pouring down Sierra's face, the intense look on the drummer's face as he worked the brushes and watched Dad for his cues, Jay and Adam wrapped in each other. The little wistful smile on Dad's face. Then Dad finished the song and stepped back from the mike, and the whole crowd roared its applause for Press Elson.

CHAPTER 25

MOST OF THE FAMILY was still whooping it up on the patio or in the Island Pit, but Dana was ready for bed. She paused briefly at the kitchen, where Dad was holding court. Even if she wanted to talk to him, it seemed too hard to breach the crowd of siblings surrounding him. She was passing the living room when she heard someone call out to her.

"Hey, Dana," said Adam. He was stretched out on one of the white leather sofas, his socks up on the armrest, drinking from a reusable water bottle. He was all by himself. He'd managed to find the only quiet space in the whole house.

"Hey, Adam," she said. "Not talking to Dad? I think I saw Jay in there."

He shrugged. "Too many people."

Dana had to agree. She stepped down into the living room and stretched out on the other white leather sofa. She'd never really liked this room. The white sofas, the mirrored walls, and the glass-topped coffee tables reminded her of being stuck in an ice cube. She had vague memories of being yelled at as a child for leaving fingerprints on the table. Maybe everyone did—maybe that's why none of her siblings liked the living room. But it turned out the big, white sofa was actually really comfortable if you lay down on it instead of sitting on it. There was a big, sparkling, crystal chandelier above it with a lot of little light bulbs, like stars in the sky. Someone had dusted it recently and changed all the broken light bulbs.

"Yesterday was your last day in your mom's house, right?" Adam said.

It always surprised her that Adam remembered things like that. You wouldn't think he was that kind of person. "Yeah," she said. "I don't think I could have gotten it cleared out without you."

He was silent for a moment. "My mom had this boyfriend," he said, looking at the crystal chandelier, not at her. "My mom had a *lot* of boyfriends, but my favorite was a guy named Dave. He was a good guy. He used to take me to the gun range, and he was a real hard-ass about ear protection. He used to say, 'Adam, you only get one set of ears.' Anyway, I helped him clean out his aunt's house after she died. That woman kept everything. Dave used to say, 'You know, Adam, you bring something into your house, someone's got to take it out of your house.'"

"It's just hard," said Dana. "Throwing out all the drawings you did when you were a kid, you know? The spoon Mom used to make brownies. It all seems really important."

"I'm not a 'stuff' guy. I figure it's all up in here." Adam tapped his temple. "Or if I forget, that's okay, too. You don't have to remember everything."

"Dave tell you that?" asked Dana.

"Ah, probably." He sounded amused.

This sofa was really comfortable. If Dana wasn't careful, she was going to fall asleep on it. "No one bothered you today, did they?" she asked. "I mean, about Dad being your father." Surely Dad would know which of them were and weren't his. Or maybe he wouldn't. Maybe you could have picked any eighty-nine people of the right age and Dad would have accepted them as his own.

Adam snorted. "I talked to Press. He knew."

She rolled over on the sofa, facing Adam. "Are we in trouble?"

He looked at her. "I don't think so. He made me a fried peanut butter and banana sandwich."

"Those things are famous."

Adam looked up at the chandelier again. "I think he liked me."

Hanging out with Adam always made Dana feel like she was getting away with something. "Well, that's good," she said.

SOFTLY SINGING "FOOLISH, FOOLISH Heart," she walked down the hallway to her little room, hoping Peter hadn't chucked all her stuff onto the floor and stolen the bed for himself. *Ugh, Peter.*

A shadow loomed at the end of the hallway. A very small and adorable shadow. Sadie the Spy Dog was waiting for her.

"Dana," said Sadie. "You can't put this off forever. I need your help to reclaim your father without incident."

"And what if I refuse?" said Dana.

"I call Westminster."

And they send out the whole Dog Show. Then Dana realized something. Why would an *American* alien be *Sadie's* problem? Yes, she understood that Sadie had tried to gather intelligence on Skzzx, but this wasn't the same kind of situation. *She's out of her jurisdiction. She's looking for an easy win after the thing on the* Mercury. "So you're saying they don't know you're out here?"

Sadie's mouth opened, then shut again.

"Here's what I think," said Dana, crouching down. "I think if I were going to call anyone, it would be Ben Nakamura. I'll bet Adam knows his number. And I wonder how pleased he'd be to see you pissing on his hydrant."

"You wouldn't," said Sadie. "You wouldn't put Press's welfare at risk by calling the CAC. You have no idea what they'd do. Oh, Ben's friendly enough, but the CAC has a history."

Dana resisted the impulse to ask Sadie for more details. "Exactly," said Dana. "I'd only take the risk of calling the CAC if you called your people first."

Sadie's ears sagged. She whimpered, softly. *Bluff called.*

Dana couldn't help feeling sorry for her. Sadie might be a hardboiled alien spy on the inside, but on the outside, she was a small, fuzzy dog. She was just too cute to stay mad at. "Tell you what," Dana said. "Why don't you and I keep watch on each other. Then we can make sure neither of us calls in outside help."

"Some guacamole wouldn't go amiss, either," added Sadie, perking up.

DANA WOKE UP THE next morning to find Sadie asleep at the end of the bed. She was adorable lying on her side, like she'd been rotated ninety degrees off plumb, and she was making little snuffling snores. Outside, Dana heard a heavy metallic clatter. Without jostling Sadie, she sat up and looked out the window. It was Dad, rolling a motorcycle into position.

Quickly Dana pulled on her shoes and ran outside. "You're leaving," she said. "Without saying goodbye to everyone."

Dad flashed that charismatic smile at her. It was quite the thing so early in the morning. "I think I already said goodbye."

Dana sighed.

Dad took her hand. "Let me tell you a story, Dana. Once upon a time—"

"Really?" she said.

"Bear with your old Dad. Once upon a time, there was a king and queen, and they wanted a little baby very much. And when at last their child was born to them, they asked all the fairy godmothers in the land to give their son a present. But they forgot to invite one of them, and fairy godmothers hold a grudge."

I think I've heard this one before, thought Dana. It was cold in the early desert morning, and she shivered.

"So the little boy was given every gift. And the second to last fairy gave him the best one of all. He'd make everyone who met him happy, and they'd love him. But then came the last fairy godmother, the forgotten one, and she turned that last blessing into a curse. She said, 'It's true, but it'll only last for a night.'"

She got it. She didn't like it, but she got it. *What if you're wrong? What if you're better than that?* But she knew that he was too set in his ways to believe her.

He let go of her hand and patted her cheek. "You are my smart one, Dana. Don't forget that."

And suddenly she remembered something. She remembered why she'd always loved the little room by the front door. She'd been there the last time she'd seen her dad before he died. She'd been bouncing up and down in her crib—just tall enough to stand and hold the rail. And Dad had been standing with Mom in the doorway, her head on his shoulder, his arm around her waist.

She'd been only a baby. How could she remember? But it was a real, true memory of the three of them together, not something from a photograph. Something that was really hers.

"Look, Dad," she said. "I can't explain, but I need you to know something."

"All right, Miss Dana."

She wanted to tell him about her memory, but that's not what slipped out of her mouth. "Watch out for corgis, all right?"

Disappointment flickered in Dad's eyes. "Bye, Dana," he said, and started up his motorcycle. She backed up, and off Dad went, scattering gravel behind him.

It was only then that Dana realized exactly what she'd said to Dad. *Watch out for corgis. Hah!* She was going to relive that moment for sure.

And she turned around and went back inside her home.

PART 5

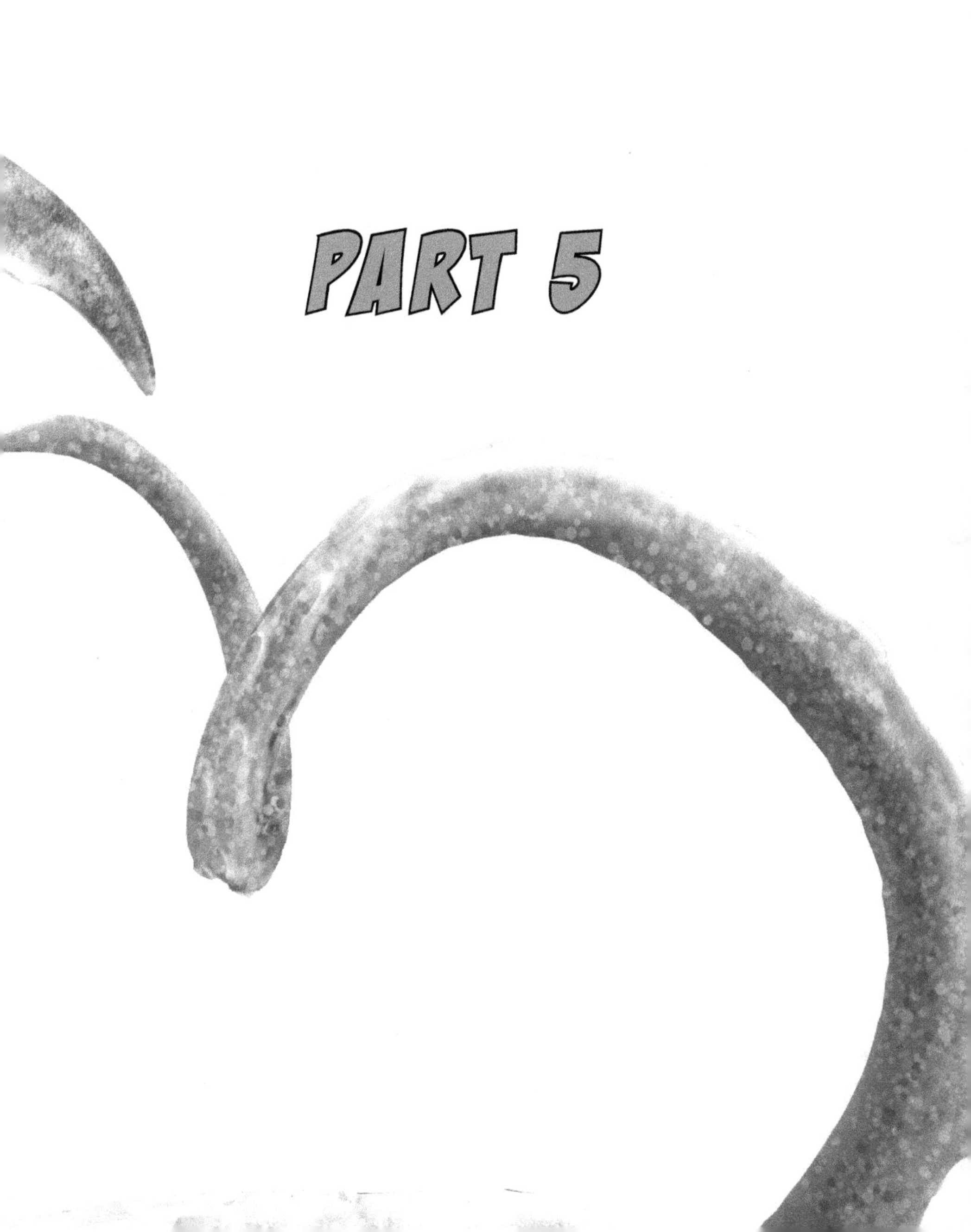

CHAPTER 26

ADAM STRETCHED OUT COMFORTABLY on the sofa, his feet on the armrest, his head resting on Jay's lap, watching the ceiling fan slowly spin overhead. Jay was gently stroking his hair. So far, Adam had to say being married was pretty great.

"I've been thinking about something," Jay said.

"I'll write the damn thank you notes," Adam said. "Don't we have a year? I have eleven and a half months to go."

"It's about the Poseidons," said Jay.

Adam sighed. For some reason, Jay felt responsible for taking care of the SoftFruit aliens, who wanted to be called the "Poseidons." Adam was sure they didn't need any help, though. He had watched the footage of their spaceships landing in Iowa a month earlier, crushing acres of corn under them. Giant slides had emerged from the sides of the spaceships, and the aliens had come streaming out with their luggage like clowns from a car, too fast for anyone to stop. As soon as they touched ground, they'd slung their luggage on their backs, and it had been clear that they were actually jetpacks, because *fooshŧ*, off they flew. Scattered to the winds. Then the empty spaceships took off, too. The spaceships were all parked on the moon now.

By the time the government had shown up, everyone was gone but the aliens' leaders and a neatly-stacked pile of gifts. The aliens had left enormous gold statues, shaped like a man with a fish tail and a fish spear for the farmers whose crops they'd flattened. This seemed to go over well, as far as the farmers were concerned. They also left a mysterious suitcase for the U.S. Government. Adam was kind of curious to know what was in it, but not curious enough to talk to Ben about it. Ben seemed a little pissy at the moment.

Obviously the Poseidons had planned the whole thing out in advance. Good for them.

"I'm worried about them," said Jay. "You know they closed all the phone stores?"

There had been some really angry SoftFruit phone owners out there—and most of them seemed mad that their phones didn't work any more, as opposed to being mad that aliens were spying on them. This is why Adam didn't own a cell phone. Nothing good would come of it.

"They're buying new buildings," said Jay. "No one knows what they're putting in there. I was kind of hoping you'd go over to the one in Albuquerque and check it out."

"Is this your idea?" Adam said.

Jay's face crumpled.

Oh shit. Adam suddenly felt sick. He knew what Jay thought. Greg, whispering in Jay's ear, still ordering them around. "I meant Ben," he said. "I wondered if he called."

"No," Jay said. "The rest of Skzzx, they feel like they made a lot of mistakes when they landed, because they didn't understand humans. And they're afraid the Poseidons are going to make the same kind of mistakes. We all talked it out, and it seems like a good idea to get some more information."

He could see Jay was still troubled. He reached up his hand and stroked Jay's cheek. "I think your aliens have some pretty good ideas. Sure, I'll do it."

"It's not critical. Don't do anything dangerous."

Adam stretched. "Maybe you'll owe me a favor if I do."

Jay looked more cheerful. "Maybe I'll pay you in advance."

ADAM SAT ON THE front steps of the apartment across the street from the Poseidons' new building. He was holding one of his favorite gadgets—it looked like a smartphone, but was actually a set of electronic binoculars. It was great. You could spy on people for hours with this thing, and no one would notice because you were just a guy screwing around with your phone.

Adam had figured that once he was married, he was going to calm down, but so far it didn't seem to have happened. He still liked breaking into places he wasn't supposed to be. That didn't mean he was going to be stupid about it though. He'd tried to track down the blueprints for the Poseidons' building, but they were so out of date, he didn't think it was worth using them to plan his route. His other trick for getting inside a strange place to get some kind of schlepper job, saying he'd work for less if paid in cash. He'd give a fake name, work for long enough to figure out the security weak points, then he'd break in the same night. That wasn't going to work here either because no one was even going into or out of the building. It was kind of weird. So his current plan was to watch for an hour, see if there were signs of life, and if the building was still empty, he'd just improvise.

A little old man came down the steps then stopped, turned around, and stared at Adam. He was a tiny, stooped man, and either he'd shrunk since he bought his clothes, or he liked to buy clothes that were way too big on him. Or he was wearing someone else's clothes, how would Adam know? The old man's hair was fluffed up in the back like he hadn't brushed it right. With put his hands on his hips, he reminded Adam of an angry blue jay. "I don't recognize you, kid. You don't live here."

What was Adam going to do, fight with the guy? He'd break the man in half. He'd just have to scare him off.

Adam glared at the man, pretended to dial and put his fake phone to his ear. "Yeah. So, I've got the package. Where's the delivery?" He paused as if listening to the person at the other end. "No, a Toyota Camry. No, fuck you. Most popular car in America. What do you want with a Ford? I'll get you a Ford tomorrow."

Most people, when confronted by an apparent criminal on their front steps, would walk away like they hadn't seen anything. But the little old man was not most people. He stuck his index finger out at Adam. "You don't live here! You don't do that garbage here! You get off my steps or I'm calling the cops!"

Adam had to admit he liked this guy. Adam had to be less than half his age and was at least six inches taller, but he still wasn't backing down. "Hey," Adam said. "I'm just messing with you." He set the fake phone down on the step. "Let me show you my badge."

"*You're* a cop."

Adam grinned. "Better." He took out his CAC id. The sunlight gleamed off the gold FBI seal. This thing was so useful, Ben was never getting it back.

"What are you doing here?" asked the old guy.

"That building across the street?" Adam said. "Aliens bought it."

"Humph," said the old guy.

"You don't like aliens?"

The old guy shrugged and sat down next to Adam on the step. He introduced himself as Bob Cooper and added that he'd owned his unit in the building for thirty years. He was very clear on this next part: the landlords hated him because *his* unit wasn't an apartment, because it was a *condo*, because he owned it. And they were taking him out of his *condo* in a *box*. Adam got the sense that ever since Mr. Cooper retired, he'd been keeping a close eye on the neighborhood, and getting angry at all of it.

"What's going on with that building?" asked Adam.

"Nothing's going on with that building," said Mr. Cooper. "It used to be a garden supply store, but it closed five years ago. Ever since then, it's just been falling apart. I heard the two kids who inherited it couldn't decide what to do with the place. One of them wanted to sell, one wanted to reopen, and neither of them had enough money to buy the other out."

"Shame," said Adam. "And nothing changed recently?"

Mr. Cooper shook his head. "No. I wouldn't have known aliens bought it unless you told me." Adam could tell that Mr. Cooper was angry that this piece of gossip had passed him by.

"Have you seen anyone go in or out? Anyone at all?"

"No. I would have noticed."

"Do me a favor," said Adam. He took a notepad and pencil out of his pocket. "Keep an eye on the place for me, and if anything weird happens, call this number." He wrote down the number for his apartment. They had a land-line phone, constantly scanned for bugs by the Mahler tech guys, which was really the best you could do.

Mr. Cooper took the paper and nodded. Adam could tell he took it seriously.

Adam stood up. "And I'm just going to see if they left the door unlocked."

From the parking lot, Adam looked over the aliens' building with his IR glasses, which looked exactly like sunglasses. Nothing, even after he circled the whole building to be certain. As Mr. Cooper had said, it was deserted.

A chain-link fence surrounded the building. When it was new, it had probably been very sturdy, but now it was sagging at the top in several places, and the door hung slightly askew. The building's windows had all been boarded over to protect the place from passing young hoodlums.

Five years later, the boards were all peeling at the edges. They looked as if Adam could break them off with his bare hands.

Adam sighed. Whatever the Poseidons were planning for this building, they hadn't done anything about it. Going inside was a total waste of time. Still, he'd promised Jay.

He thought for a moment. Did he want to wait for nightfall? No—the place appeared totally quiet. He might as well have the benefit of seeing what he was looking at. Before he climbed the fence, he thought he'd try the door. The lock on the door was a piece of garbage, easy to pick. When the door swung open, he could see the boarded-up building and the cracked asphalt of the parking lot, riddled with weeds, and that was it.

He carefully looked both ways along the fence, as far as he could see, just in case he'd somehow missed something. Then he walked inside. It was just as it looked like from the outside: a run-down, abandoned building, which for some reason was owned by aliens.

And then he took one more step, and he felt something like the skin on the surface of water brush over him—only there was air on both sides—and he nearly gasped in shock. There was a new store in front of him, freshly painted, with big glass windows, and a big sign on the front: POSEIDON GROCERY.

Oh, and there were about ten aliens in workers' jumpsuits staring at him.

The shitty training he'd gotten from Greg always crept back on him when he was startled. Adam's hand reflexively twitched for his gun, but he wasn't going to use it. What would that get him, right? A couple of dead aliens and a bunch of angry ones. *Use your brain*, Adam reminded himself. *Watch and see.*

"Mr. Shapiro!" said one of the workers. "Do you remember me? I'm Ava Williams!"

"Yeah," he said, after a minute. She was one of the two aliens she'd met on the *Mercury*, the ones he'd said could land in Iowa. Back then she'd been wearing really heavy foundation, the kind you wore if you needed to cover your beard stubble. Without it, she was the color of a cherry Life Savers, all red and shiny.

"Would you like to see what we're working on?"

"I'm guessing it's a grocery store?" he said.

"Yes, it is!" she said, beaming. "Come and see!"

She walked through the sliding glass doors and Adam followed her, trailed by the rest of the aliens. Having them following him made him uneasy. He kept his hand away from his gun, but not that far away.

It was, as promised, a grocery store. One of those really nice ones, the kind that always made Adam mentally start tallying up his purchases before he got anywhere near the register, even though he didn't need to anymore. A lot of the shelves were still empty, though.

"We're opening next week!" said Ms. Williams. "That's why not everything is here yet."

Why were the aliens opening a grocery store? He squinted at Ms. Williams. "Do you eat special food or something?"

"Oh no," she laughed. "We've all been adapted. This is a gift for the humans. And—wait—-here is a gift for you." They had stopped at the candy aisle, which was already well-stocked. "Am I correct that you've just been married?"

He looked at her dubiously.

"You're wearing a wedding ring," she said. "And in any case, the truth is, Mr. Shapiro, we do keep up with your activities. You see, we all owe you a debt. We're still trying to determine the best way to repay it. But until then, perhaps a small wedding gift?"

She handed him a package of maple sugar candy. There were some Yankee foods that Adam still loved, even after ten years away from home. He ate lobster once or twice a year, even though he felt really guilty about it. Although he didn't have much of a sweet tooth, he loved Necco wafers, and he loved maple sugar candies shaped like Pilgrims. For some reason, they tasted better than the ones like maple leaves. (He liked biting the heads off first, growling like Godzilla.) But he'd never seen a package with two boy Pilgrims before; before this, it had always been one boy, one girl.

At first glance, it seemed like a nice gift. But then he started wondering how they knew to give him this. How did they know he liked weird Yankee candy? How did they know he was coming? Did they have this candy box stashed aside for him, just in case he showed up?

There was no way this box of candy was what it appeared to be. Once he got a few blocks away, it was going right in the trash.

Besides, Jay couldn't eat his Pilgrim, anyway.

Ms. Williams was talking again. "And of course, we want to get something for Ms. Elson. What do you think she'd like?"

"A nice boyfriend," he said, distracted.

Then he realized what he'd said, and could have bitten his tongue.

"Ha ha ha," said Ms. Williams.

ADAM WAS DREAMING OF being in the jungle, toasty-warm and covered in vines, when the ringing phone woke him up. He slid out from under Jay's tentacles and grabbed the receiver. "Hello?" he mumbled. What time was it? 3 AM? Adam stretched his neck to the side. One of Jay's tentacles started rubbing the place in Adam's neck that always got stiff when he slept.

"Mr. Shapiro," said the voice on the other end. It was the little old guy from Albuquerque, Bob Cooper. "You told me to call you if something happened to the aliens' building?"

Instantly Adam was awake. "Yeah?"

"It's on fire. And someone shut off the water to the neighborhood. Thought you'd want to know."

Adam took a bubble up to Albuquerque, which made it a fifteen-minute trip. But by the time he got there, there was nothing there but a brick shell, a big fire, and a lot of angry firemen. Mr. Cooper was sitting on the front steps of his apartment, glaring at the fire. Adam sat down next to him. "Thanks for calling," he said.

"That's it?" said Mr. Cooper. "That's all you're going to do—watch it burn?"

"Wait a sec," said Adam. "There's only so fast Tanya can fly Big Bird."

Mr. Cooper opened his mouth like he was going to say something, but then they both could hear the engine of Tanya's airplane, zooming overhead, and Mr. Cooper looked up. As Tanya flew over the burning building, a hatch in the base of the airplane opened up, and thousands of gallons of water dumped down on the fire. The fire was extinguished and the firemen got soaked. *Oops.* Adam didn't think that they looked like they minded, though. Tanya circled and headed back the way she had come.

With the fire out, Adam took out his night-vision goggles to see what was left. The building looked like a lost cause. "We got here too late," he said.

"That's a shame," said Mr. Cooper.

Adam couldn't help but agree. He'd understand if some kid wanted to put some graffiti on the Poseidon Grocery—nice fresh paint just called for graffiti, right? And he knew as well as anyone that some people were going to hate you, just for who you were. But starting a fire and shutting off the water so no one could put it out was a real jerk move. "Hope they all got out okay."

"There were people in there?" asked Mr. Cooper.

Adam nodded.

Mr. Cooper sighed. "This used to be a nice neighborhood."

Adam doubted that. People didn't change much, as far as he could tell, but a certain kind of old person remembered everyone as nicer when they were younger. Or maybe they started wishing they'd done more to make the world a nicer place.

Sometimes Jay knew how Adam felt before Adam did, and he did feel responsible for the welfare of the Poseidons. He'd invited them, so they were his problem. Well, he was taking care of a lot of people, right? He'd just add them to the list. First, he'd need to help whoever made it out of the fire rebuild this grocery. He'd have to find a good contractor in Albuquerque...

Suddenly, there was a strange noise from the site of the grocery. It sounded like a small avalanche, and the ground swelled slightly. And then there was an inflating noise, like the world's largest balloon was being filled. Then a large, white thing swelled from the burned zone, filling and filling. Finally a duplicate of the original Poseidon Grocery was inflated in place of the old one. *How did they do that?* Adam wondered. *How did you inflate glass?* But it wasn't just the glass. He swore he could see the fixtures inside, just like before. And was that Ava Williams waving at him, the other aliens standing behind her?

The lights inside went on with a loud click. He winced and took off his glasses. The Poseidon Grocery looked good as new. It might have been the best *screw you, we're not going anywhere* he'd seen in a while. You had to admire it.

Next to him, Mr. Cooper whistled, two fingers in his mouth. "Yeah, aliens!" he said and applauded.

CHAPTER 27

EVER SINCE DANA HAD made her first sale to Rainbow Daydreams, she'd been bubbling with artistic ideas. Take the silvery, tentacle-covered stuffie she'd designed, inspired by Skzzx. You could use it as a pillow, or as a bolster, or you could pull open the zippered mouth to hide your treasures inside it. Jay thought it was really funny, but of all the projects she'd done for Rainbow Daydreams, the Alien Cuddle Pal had sold the most units. Who wouldn't want a soft, squishy alien to love?

She'd gotten even more productive after the whole thing on the *Mercury*. Just knowing aliens were out there had set her imagination firing. She took a sketchbook everywhere to illustrate little things she remembered: dark blue alien tears, the peeling makeup around the receptionist's mouth. Right now it was just realistic details, but she was going to figure out how to turn what she'd seen into an adorable collectible for Rainbow Daydreams. Maybe a snuggly, purple alien baby in a shiny, space-suit-styled onesie? She still hadn't sold Rainbow Daydreams a baby doll, and baby dolls were *huge*. One of those suckers could pay her rent for months. She pulled her sketchbook out of her purse and wrote down a quick note: SHINY PURPLE ALIEN BABY.

Now there was a note that was going to make no sense to Future Dana.

She hadn't actually met any more aliens after leaving the *Mercury*. With over three hundred million people living in the United States, three million aliens slipped into the crowd like pebbles tossed into a pond. Dana reflected that the SoftFruit aliens—freshly renamed the Poseidons—seemed to have intentionally placed themselves far apart from each other. You'd see a bright-red woman at the bus stop, a green man riding his bike through the park, but never a clump of them together.

But even if Poseidons themselves were hard to find, you could go to their supermarkets. They'd closed the old SoftFruit stores, where they'd sold the phones they'd used to track human behavior, aggregating the data that would enable the Poseidons to understand life on Earth. In retrospect, Dana reflected, those stores had been really oddly designed, and there was a simple, obvious explanation: aliens. Low slung ceilings, lots of white paint, glass boxes to hold the devices on top of scratched-metal pillars. Those things all looked normal if you were a gigantic centipede-fishlike creature in your original form.

Now the Poseidons were building supermarkets. No one knew what their goal was, but Dana liked visiting the Poseidon Grocery near her house. Poseidon aesthetics meant that there was plenty of space in the aisles, and the low-slung ceiling was cozy. And sometimes you could find Poseidon fruits there. Nothing the Poseidons ate had much of a flavor, other than saltiness, but the fruits were covered in brightly colored patterns, like natural Ukrainian Easter eggs. She liked to buy a half-dozen of them, put them in a bowl on her coffee table, and sketch them.

Just walking into the Poseidon Grocery and thinking "aliens built this place" cheered her up. Maybe Press Elson's daughter wasn't meant to live a normal life. Maybe she needed a little dash of weird to keep her head together. Or maybe she was just happy because, like Adam had predicted, they'd gotten away with it. She was glad the Poseidons were safe. She was glad that Adam was the type of person who didn't let the rules get in the way of doing what was right. Sometimes she wished she had that kind of daring, too.

And she was *really* glad that she and Adam weren't in prison for impersonating government agents.

Dana stood in the produce section of the Poseidon Grocery, listening to the weird alien music, which sounded kind of like whalesong, trying to decide if she wanted the local tomatoes or the organic tomatoes for her dinner. *Which one makes me a better person?*

She went with the local tomatoes, which were three cents cheaper per pound, and realized there was someone looming over her cart. Ben Nakamura, who still looked pissed off, was staring down at her.

"I've got a car outside," he said.

"Me too!" she said. She smiled cheerfully up at him.

He looked amused, despite himself. "I'd like to talk with you. Would you please join me in my car?"

Curious, she abandoned her cart and followed Ben. It obviously wasn't his car—it was a late model sedan that gave off the floral aroma of a rental. When was the last time she'd rented a car? When she accidentally drank Jay's reboot?

Dana shut the door, and Ben turned towards her. How would she sketch him, if she had to? He'd intentionally made himself as average-looking as possible. A dull Mr. Rogers-style haircut. A gray t-shirt and jeans. No jewelry, just an old Timex watch, which looked like a beat-up timepiece, rather than James Bond paraphernalia. No cologne, and unobtrusive soap and deodorant. There was nothing about Ben that called attention in any way, except for a pair of unusually expressive eyebrows. And though he was pleasant enough, he was making himself very hard to read.

Well, she liked a challenge.

"I'm here to offer you a job," he said.

"You need an artist?"

"I need people, period. Suddenly my area of responsibility expanded dramatically."

And they kept you in charge, thought Dana. *Someone must think well of you.*

Ben continued. "And the Poseidons wanted you on the team."

She guessed this was her reward, so to speak, for helping to save the Poseidons. Though that was really more Adam than her, honestly. "You haven't told me what you expect me to do."

He looked seriously at her. "Negotiate, essentially. Translate. Get all the pieces moving together."

"I'm not interested. If I wanted to work for someone else, I wouldn't have gone to art school." She put her hand on the handle of the car door. The door was locked.

When had Ben locked the door? She'd missed it. She hadn't been afraid to follow Ben to the car, but that's because Adam hadn't been afraid of him. But there were a lot of things that would frighten normal people that didn't frighten Adam.

Ben was a spy. She shouldn't trust him, by definition, and she didn't. Would the door unlock if she tried that, she wondered?

Don't show he's made you nervous, she told herself. *He'll use it against you.*

"Speaking of that," said Ben. "You're a freelance artist. I've never met a freelance artist whose taxes were totally in order. Maybe I should talk to the IRS about you."

She crossed her arms. "Go ahead. Audit me. That won't get you what you want—it'll just annoy me. Besides, that's a weak-ass threat. You really want to hurt me? Go ahead, spit out whatever you're really thinking about."

He looked soberly at her. "Jay O'Toole requires a small amount of plutonium in his diet for his continued health and well-being. Work for me, and I'll make sure that supply doesn't get cut off."

Dana felt her heart rate speed up and fought to control her breathing. "That far? You'll risk pissing off the Rzzln—a species with spaceflight capabilities and nothing in particular they need from Earth—to get me on your team? That would be a really poor choice. So either you're desperate, which I doubt, or you're no good at this."

Ben nodded. "All right. Here's the real threat. Your 'brother' Adam has a nice, long juvenile record. Mostly sales of stolen auto parts. Then he moved on to work at Mahler, where he—"

"Don't tell me," said Dana. She knew it was bad. She didn't want to know the details. *And now Ben knows you don't want to know the details.*

Ben continued. "There are a lot of people who are very angry about three million aliens landing in Iowa. People who would like to find some kind of a scapegoat, maybe a man who has a lifelong history of doing terrible things for money. What if I made it look like he was paid off to let the Poseidons land?"

The blood buzzed in Dana's ears, and her vision wavered at the edges. What an ugly, ugly thing to say. "You *fucker*," she said. "Adam *likes* you."

"I like Adam," said Ben, putting his hand on his heart. "I don't think he told the ships to land for venal reasons. I think his main priority is protecting his husband. But here's the thing—I need people, smart people, like you, Dana. Because the Poseidons are hiding something, and I need to figure out what it is. There are people, people with power, who think the smartest thing to do right now is to put the Poseidons in camps to keep the rest of us safe, and I find that abhorrent for a lot of reasons. That will not happen under my watch.

"So here's the deal, Dana: I don't care if you're happy, I don't care if you like me, but you're going to help me figure this out."

She was pretty sure that was the actual truth, even if she'd had to shake it out of him. But wow, Ben had handled this about the worst way possible. Now she was angry he'd blackmailed her into taking the job. And it was totally unnecessary! She would have been willing to work with the CAC anyway, at least as a freelancer. She was an Elson at heart—if the circus was coming to town, she'd be there, popcorn in hand, sitting in the front row.

But now she'd be focused on looking for a way out.

CHAPTER 28

A MAN IN AN ORANGE button-down shirt and khakis was standing outside Dana's door the next morning. His skin was about a Pantone 306 C, the color of a Smurf, and his neatly trimmed, wiry hair was a slightly richer blue. If he'd been human, though, Dana would have said he looked like a Pacific Islander, with those heavy eyebrows and warm brown eyes.

Instead, she was looking at a Poseidon, a big underwater mystery disguised as a human being. The whole thing still was kind of a rush.

"Hello, Dana." He smiled and extended his right hand to her. It had a potato in it.

"I'm sorry?" Dana said. "Why are you giving me that? And why do you know my name?"

"I'm Oliver Miller, your new partner, from the CAC," he said. "Apparently vegetal gifts are customary at this point? These things are delicious."

Roll with it, she thought. "Thank you very much. I'll think of you when I eat it later." Rather than bring the potato inside and risk this weirdo following her in, she put it in her purse. "Where are we going?"

THE ZAMORA MUSEUM IN Socorro, New Mexico was a tiny historical museum featuring pottery from the nearby pueblos, worn-out farm tools from Anglo homesteaders, and most notably, artifacts from the 1964 Lonnie Zamora alien sighting, in which a single Rzzln rescue spaceship, searching for signs of Skzzx's craft, had scared the daylights out of a police officer.

Oliver was—surprisingly—a good driver. Dana looked him over as he drove, looking relaxed with one arm braced on the open window, a little half-smile on his face. His mannerisms, she reflected, were a lot more human than any of the aliens from Team Skzzx. Captain was the best of the four, but when they were using Jay's shape, they looked and acted kind of like a news anchor, which got weird quickly. Mom moved like a meat robot, with their face frozen in a terrifying smile, and their fingers curled into claws. But in Oliver's case, she wasn't sure she would have pegged him as an alien, other than by his bright blue skin.

What did you say to a man from another planet? A man whose planet she'd actually seen explode? *Do you miss Alderaan?*

Or she could ask the tactful version of the question. "What do you think of Earth so far?"

"I like it a lot," he said. He laughed, pleasantly. "Not that I have a choice. But this is a beautiful planet. The first time I saw a sunset, I had to go out on my balcony and watch the whole thing. I wondered, 'Why am I the only one out here doing this?' And then I realized, this happens *every* night."

"And every morning."

"Really?" he said, raising his thick eyebrows.

She laughed.

He grinned at her. "On my home planet, colors had meaning. Red means determination. Green means anticipation. Everything here is so much more colorful. So I can't help but feel the whole world is talking to me."

"What does blue mean?"

"I'm oversimplifying, because every color has a lot of implications. But basically, blue means happy. It's why I picked it."

"Hmm," she said.

"Also, I thought everyone had forgotten *Avatar*. According to the Internet."

"People lie on the Internet, Oliver."

He shook his head. "No, I don't believe it. That's how we studied Earth. Don't tell me our research was flawed."

She smiled. Oliver was a lot more socially savvy than the potato thing had indicated. He was even funny. What was he trying to accomplish by looking like more of an oblivious alien than he actually was?

As Oliver shifted the car into park, Dana put his hand on top of his to get his attention, and he jumped. She yanked her hand away. *What was that about? Is it me?*

"Sorry," he said, looking embarrassed. "Humans touch each other a lot more than I'm used to."

Maybe that made sense. "Did I hurt you?"

"No," he said. "But in my old body—sharp claws. Fragile skin. Not a good mix. Sometimes I forget I'm in a totally different body for a moment."

She'd seen pictures of what the Poseidons—gah, that name—had looked like on their homeworld. Underwater creatures, like caterpillars with long, ribbon-like gills along their backs. Fragile-looking and translucent as jellyfish. And here was Oliver, driving a car on dry land with his mind ported over to a human body he'd barely had a chance to get used to. What would that be like, she wondered?

How could you even answer a question like that?

"Oliver," she said. "Do you want to really be partners?"

He gave her a quizzical look.

"I don't want to watch everything I say around you. It wears me out."

"That's true," he nodded.

"I don't want you to lie to me. Even by omission."

The left side of his mouth quirked up. "I can't tell you everything. Our technological superiority is the only advantage we have."

"I know that," she said. "And I'm not asking you to be disloyal. But this thing with the potato? Doofus alien who doesn't understand human ways? That's not happening again."

"It's a well-researched strategy—covering up my minor social errors with a major one. Usually it works." He looked at her purse. "I'll take it back."

"No, Oliver, I'm bringing it home and I'm going to bake it and eat it."

He laughed and unfastened his seatbelt. "Should we go inside?"

"You didn't answer me."

"Yes, Dana," he said, smiling. He had a pleasant, slightly lopsided smile. She wondered who had designed it. "I'll be your partner."

Inside, the first thing that caught Dana's eye was the enormous alien-themed gift shop. The objects on sale ranged from alien stuffed animals, including the Jay-inspired Alien Cuddle Pal that Dana herself had designed, to a Mold-a-Rama that made a plastic model of Officer Zamora being startled by an alien spaceship, to the raunchy T-shirts that read "I got probed in Socorro." Past the gift shop was a tiny, dusty room full of glass cases, most of which seemed to have turquoise jewelry in them.

"The police have already been here," said Oliver. "Ben just wants our take." He led her through the room with the jewelry and into a room that seemed to have been beamed in from another planet. It had the typical look Dana was beginning to associate with Poseidon architecture—a lot of white paint, everything a little too low-slung and far apart to be spatially comfortable for a human. A fishtank full of water filled the middle of the room. Maybe it was half of a Damien Hurst piece.

Adam was examining a camera hanging from the wall. He turned around as they entered and grinned. "Hey, Dana," he said. "You must be Oliver." He was wearing what Dana thought of as his burglar clothes: a long-sleeve black T-shirt, black jeans, and a gorgeous pair of thin, lightweight black leather gloves that Dana secretly coveted. He'd left off the ski mask he usually wore on these jobs, though. "Ben send you guys?"

"He did," said Dana. "What was in the tank?"

"Some kind of big alien seashell," said Adam.

"It was a religious artifact," said Oliver. He had his hands clasped behind his back and was tilting rapidly back and forth from one foot to the other. *It looks like he's treading water*, thought Dana—the first genuinely alien thing she'd seen him do. It was nice he didn't feel he had to hide it around her.

"Couple of weird things here," said Adam. "The security in this room is nothing like the rest of the museum. Out there, it's a joke. This is the real thing. You've got motion detectors in every corner trained on the tank. Then there's a pressure sensor under the tank, so they can tell if the weight shifts. And there's a camera, too. I was just checking to see if the motion detectors worked."

"They do," said Oliver.

Adam's forehead wrinkled. "How do you know?"

Oliver stopped moving back and forth. "My eyes don't quite work like yours. I can see the infrared beams." He bit his lower lip. "Not sure I was supposed to tell you that."

"We can keep our mouths shut," said Dana. "What's the other thing, Adam?"

"I can't figure out how someone stole the shell," said Adam. "I know the pressure sensor works, because I tested it already. Someone reset it for an empty tank. And you've just told me the motion detectors work."

"What about the camera?" asked Dana.

"Oh, it works, too," said Adam. "It's just missing a half hour from last night, after they closed."

Dana reflected that this might be the most she'd ever heard Adam say at once.

"We should probably try to talk to the people who work here," said Oliver.

"I'm not sure we need to," said Dana, slowly. "Ben sent us here for a reason. Oliver, who installed the security systems in this room?"

"We did," he said. "When we donated the shell."

"Well," said Dana, "now Ben wants you to know that one of your people stole the shell. And he wants you to think about why they might have done that."

The two men looked at her.

Adam yanked off his gloves, rolled them, and stuffed them in his pocket. "Jesus. I didn't need a fucking field trip to learn that. Ben's lucky he pays me by the hour."

You don't need the money either, thought Dana. *Jay's rich now.*

Oliver stared at the ground, rocking back and forth again.

"You don't look happy," said Dana.

"I'm not," said Oliver.

Are you mad at Ben, or at whoever stole the shell? she wondered.

"Why don't you guys give me a ride home?" asked Adam. "You can have dinner with us. Jay's been cooking chili all day, and he can't eat it, and that way I won't have chili for dinner all week."

"There's no reason we should report back to Ben right away," said Dana. If Ben was going to mess around with her, she could mess around right back.

"You need a ride? How'd you get here, Adam?" asked Oliver.

"Don't worry about it," said Adam.

ADAM AND JAY'S APARTMENT, which was technically part of the Mahler Corporation complex, had one big, open space as the family room, dining room, and kitchen. The room was painted a pale blue, with high ceilings and big windows, and decorated with the lovely nature photographs Jay had taken on his camping trips. There was an enormous TV, because Adam liked watching the Patriots cheat, and a sand-colored sofa big enough for Jay's alien body. There was a shelf holding March and April from the Doges of the Month series—all that had been issued so far—with the signed certificate of authenticity in a frame behind them. And there was a very well-stocked gun cabinet, which was now just for display, mostly. Probably.

Off to the right, in the kitchen area, Jay was in his alien form and stirring the chili. No, Dana thought, looking again—that wasn't Jay, it was one of the co-holders of his body, Teacher, who liked dancing along to human music while they worked. They were whistling a little jazzy counterpoint as well, a sweet sound like a cheerful teakettle. A tentacle quirked towards them, and Skzzx's body melted and shifted into human form. With clothes. It was weird that what looked like Jay's clothes were actually part of his body, so Dana tried really hard not to think about it.

Jay O'Toole left his wooden spoon in the chili and walked to the door to give his husband a hug and kiss. Then he moved on to Dana, hugging in her in a friendly, cozy embrace, kissing her on the temple, and patting her back affectionately. It had only been a week since she'd stopped by last, but she was almost overwhelmed by his delight at seeing her. She was glad to see him, too; he continued to be about the kindest, sunniest person she knew. Kind of a human Voight-Kampff test, really. If you didn't like Jay, there was something seriously wrong with you.

Jay held out his hand for Oliver to shake. "Good to meet you," he said.

Even if Oliver didn't like to be touched, at least he was polite. He shook Jay's hand and smiled as if he were happy to do it. "You're a Rzzln," he said.

"I'm not Rzzln, but my gestalt is," said Jay. That was apparently a joke, even though it was only funny to Jay. He quickly explained the situation to Oliver—how Mahler had once been Greg Mahler's company, and that Greg had been Skzzx's first human translator, but the rest of Skzzx had chafed at Greg's leadership, and how they had brought in Jay as a replacement translator and president of the Mahler Corporation.

Dana reflected that at times like this it was clear that Jay was a lot brighter than he'd been when she'd first met him. He was just as warm as he'd been, and he had the same goony sense of humor, but sharing his body with a bunch of aliens had made him a lot better able to simply tell a complicated story, and to leave the parts of the story out that Oliver didn't need to know, like the fact that Greg had flat-out murdered the original Jay O'Toole.

There was no way she would ever tell Adam that she thought Jay had changed, though. Dana liked to think she was pretty bright, too.

Jay already had the table set for four—*how did he know?* Dana wondered —and the plate at one end of the table already had a lump of grease and metal shavings on it. That was going to be Jay's dinner. The rest of them got Jay's delicious, spicy vegetarian chili, and his crisp, Southern-style cornbread. Oliver was polite and likeable, and asked for Jay's advice on places to go camping, if he ever decided to give it a try. In fact, he seemed a lot more cheerful now that he knew he wasn't the only alien in the room. But Dana could feel Jay's unease and Adam seemed oddly quiet.

When they'd all eaten, Jay pushed his dish aside. "So here's the thing. Greg's waking up again."

Dana looked quickly over at Adam. He had a hell of a poker face, but she saw the flash of utter terror in his eyes. Adam wasn't scared of speeding in a stolen car or breaking into a building or being shot at, but the idea of Greg Mahler being awake and functional scared him shitless.

"I thought you had a way to keep him asleep," said Dana.

"It's getting harder and harder," said Jay. "One of us has to keep an eye on him all the time. And if that person slips—"

Adam reached across the table and took his hand. *Someday*, Dana thought, *I'm going to find someone who looks at me like that.*

Jay continued. "A couple of weeks ago, my computer's hard drive was wiped clean."

"Well," said Oliver, "there are ways that could be managed from outside the apartment."

"And then, two nights ago," said Jay, "I woke up alone in a motel room in Los Alamos."

"I was fast asleep here. I didn't know he was gone until the apartment phone rang," said Adam. "We think Greg was meeting someone."

"What did you have with you when you woke up?" asked Dana.

"Nothing," said Jay. "But maybe I handed it off already."

"Why are you talking to us?" asked Dana. "You must have someone here at Mahler who can help."

Jay winced. "We changed the company a lot when I took over. I don't think everyone's happy about that. I think some of them want Greg to come back. They might even be helping him."

"And you trust the CAC more than your own employees?" said Dana, dubiously.

"We trust you, Dana," said Jay. "And Oliver's your partner now."

Oliver's forehead wrinkled. "If I think about all the possible conflicting responsibilities here, I don't think I can help you."

"No," said Dana. "The last time Greg got out, he tried to make it so the Poseidons could never land on Earth. I bet he's trying something nasty again, something directed against the Poseidons. This is how you help your people. Goal number one."

"That's what Captain says," said Jay. "And the rest of us agree."

Oliver exhaled. It sounded like something that might be an obscenity, if you heard it underwater. "Okay. But let's not tell Ben about this."

"Oh, hell no," said Dana. "Who knows what he'd do with that information?"

OLIVER SAT IN THE driver's seat, staring forward.

"Are you okay? Do you want me to drive?" asked Dana.

Oliver was silent.

"We can just stay here overnight," said Dana. "They've always got rooms in the spa part of Mahler." Did that come out wrong? "I mean, they could give us each our own room. I'm not suggesting we share a room." Okay, that was even worse.

Oliver turned to look at her, his forehead wrinkled in confusion. "Adam gave you a bracelet when we were leaving. But why did you take it? Didn't you know he stole it from the Zamora Museum? Or do you think stealing is fine?"

Dana sighed. There was a price for having Adam in her life; she didn't complain about a certain amount of pilfering and lock picking, things she would have objected to from most people. It was hard to explain. "He's my brother," she said.

That was as close as she could get. How else could you say you cared about someone you didn't understand? That they cared about you, too? She admired the bracelet on her wrist, the silver bright against her skin. It fit her perfectly.

"I used to be an anthropologist," said Oliver. "Back on my home planet. They picked me for this job because I was good at reading social norms. I feel like my skull's going to split open. Is that normal?"

"How much did you drink?"

"One beer. Is that too much?"

"It shouldn't be."

"Oh." He rested his head on the steering wheel.

Dana found herself thinking what it must be like to be Oliver. She couldn't even imagine. "Look, I'm going to touch your head. If you don't like it, I'll stop."

"Okay," he said, into the steering wheel.

She gently squeezed the muscles of his neck, moving up the back of his head.

"Oh," he said. "Oh, wow."

As she stroked the base of his skull, he let out a low, almost carnal moan. The sort of moan that Dana felt a little uncomfortable hearing out of a man, who, let's face it, she'd only known for one day. She yanked her hand away.

Oliver stayed in place for a moment, as if he were hoping she'd resume the massage, then lifted his head again. He smiled at her, that cute half-smile she'd seen before. "Thank you," he said.

"Do you want me to drive?"

He sighed. "Oh, *fsst.* Dana, this isn't really a car. And it's got an autopilot." He typed something into the keypad, and the car lifted gently off the ground. "I'll have you home in fifteen minutes, okay?"

CHAPTER 29

NIGHTS WERE THE HARDEST, thought Oliver. Even without a blanket, just a bare mattress, he felt pinned down, unable to float. And then his thoughts scattered like the bubbles from the machine he used to love as a child back in the crèche. Back then, he had been too small to understand why he couldn't catch the bubbles; he'd just watch them slip unhindered around his small, delicate claws.

He'd trained as an anthropologist, and then when they'd discovered the upcoming Disaster, he'd been repurposed. The Central Committee had sent him out, along with a small team from his university, to find the really isolated people, the ones living in the deepest crevices, the ones for whom even the idea of a surface to the Ocean was a superstition. Somehow all of them, every single one, had to be convinced to abandon Home and come in these strange new bodies to this strange Earth. His team had been overwhelmed, untrained—how could you even train for such a thing?—but Oliver had proven unexpectedly good at connecting with the isolates. Curiosity translated everywhere. *Come, don't you want to see?* Oliver remembered how horrified and delighted the isolates were by the old-fashioned ship his team had borrowed from the university, tapping their claws on the windows. They'd never even seen glass before. By the time he'd brought the isolates to the transit hub, they'd gone mute from overstimulation.

How were they doing on Earth, he wondered?

And then, on spaceship #3, when he was still so newly remade that he gasped at the burn of the dry air in his lungs, Jane Smith herself had come to his rooms.

"We have a job for you," she'd said.

And this was the job: to make sure that the Earthers were never, ever sorry they'd taken his people in. To make his people look like the happiest, most productive people in the Universe. With no downsides or complications whatsoever. *Just don't send us away, please don't send us away. Because Home is gone.*

It had all seemed so much simpler when he was still on the ship. Nowadays he just got so *tired.*

How was he going to handle this? Ben wanted him to know that someone had stolen the shell. But Oliver was pretty sure that Ben didn't fully understand what the shell had meant.

Not everyone had been willing to leave Home. But the ones who'd stayed had made sure their speaking shell had gone on to Earth, with all the others, so that someone could always speak for them.

Someone was going to claim to speak for the dead. What were they going to say?

Last Day. Floating in the chamber. Impossible to relax, impossible not to clench his claws and dig them into his skin and fight against the chemicals that were slowly, gently killing him. And the worst fear, the motionless hovering fear that Hsska had been right, that whatever woke up in the human body on the other side might have his memories, but it wouldn't be him.

DANA OPENED HER DOOR to Oliver, who was carrying two lattes in a paper holder. Once again, he was dressed in khakis and a crisp button-down shirt. This one had an orange and red windowpane check, which looked very pretty against his blue skin. Oliver, she considered, might be a little of a clotheshorse. But then, she liked clothes herself: today she was wearing a vintage purple velour sweatshirt, a turquoise t-shirt that said "Beignet Today" (which she'd found at Dad's house), and her favorite orange jeans. Oliver smiled at her, and she reflected that there was something very likable about his face, even if it was bright blue. But hey, she liked blue things. The sky. Blueberries.

"Hi," she said. Did she forget she had an appointment with him?

"I know this is kind of a surprise. May I come in?"

What the hell, she thought. "Sure."

Dana had a couple of private aphorisms that she'd never shared with anyone else. One was, "If it's attached to the wall, it doesn't count as clutter." The long wall of her living room opposite the entry door was covered with mementoes that were important to her. All of the work she'd done for Rainbow Daydreams sat on shelves in order of completion. Her final college art project, a painting of the Elson house in the desert, hung above a shelf with her mother's bronzed baby shoes. Pictures of her family and friends circled the latch hook rug her mother had customized as a teenager by shuffling the fibers into a paisley-inspired pattern. Dana found herself looking at a picture that Sierra had taken of her and Adam in the Island Pit, talking about something she could no longer remember.

Oliver scanned all of these items carefully, as if he were cataloguing them in his clever anthropologist's brain. "Subject: Human Female." He stopped short at Mom's rug.

Dana walked over to him. “My mom made that,” she said. “A lot of people think I got my artistic talent from Dad. I keep it up to prove them wrong.”

“I was looking at the colors,” Oliver said. “On my planet, that would have been a poem.”

“What does it say?”

Oliver smiled. “It’s more of a mood than anything else. It’s the feeling that something wonderful is about to happen.”

“Huh,” said Dana. “No wonder I like it.”

Oliver drifted back to where Dana’s current art project had taken over the coffee table. When he arrived, she’d been sitting on the floor and gently carving fur into the plasticene model with dental picks. October Doge: a Shiba Inu in a tilted witch’s hat.

Oliver knelt down on the floor and regarded the doge, tilting his head back and forth. She was relieved to see he made no effort to pick it up.

“That’s good,” he said. He sounded surprised.

“Yes,” she said. “That’s why they pay me.”

Parsing that he’d accidentally insulted her took him a moment. “I’m more of a hobbyist myself. I haven’t done anything for a while, though. I have to get used to being down a bunch of fingers. And not having claws.”

She liked the way he handled himself: self-deprecating, funny. But then, she suspected, she was meant to. “Did you want something, Oliver?”

“I want to make sure we went to see Ben together. He’s trying to send me some kind of message. And I’m not sure I have the cultural context to understand it. But you will.”

She took a sip of the latte he’d left on her table. “And you think I’ll help you?”

He smiled his crooked smile. “You’re the one who said she wanted to be my partner. You know what they used to say on my planet? It’s not a relationship until you can ask for something.”

THE OFFICES OF THE Committee on Alien Contact were located under Denver International Airport, just a quick trip away in Oliver's "car."

On the way, Dana decided to try if this partner thing really worked both ways. "I want to ask you a question," she said.

"You can ask..." said Oliver.

"Why did you open all the grocery stores?"

He grinned. "Okay, I can answer that one. We'd been studying humans using their phones, right? But then we realized that the image that humans present to the world is not their actual selves. The best way to figure out what humans *really* want is to watch their behavior. Which means, say, the difference between the sort of meal you photograph, and the meal you actually eat."

"So you're still studying us?"

He thought for a moment, framing his response. "Making my people happy and comfortable on Earth—and humans happy and comfortable with us—is going to be a process of continuing education. That shouldn't surprise you."

A fair and accurate answer, as far as she could tell. "Okay, another question. Why do I always see Poseidons alone? I never see groups of you."

Dana thought this question made Oliver a little more anxious. "We're not *always* alone. We do have some-—" he reflected about how to phrase it—"mutually shared cultural practices."

She waited. It was an old trick. Give the person you were talking to silence, and often they'd feel the need to fill it.

And it worked on Oliver. "The Central Committee thinks we'll be less intimidating if humans meet us one at a time."

"That sounds lonely," she said.

Oliver smiled at her. "It is, a bit. But I don't think they're wrong. And, speaking for myself, it gets me out of my tail-burrow."

Dana had expected that she'd need some kind of badge to get in to the CAC, but instead, first she and then Oliver had to stand on a cross marked on the floor while their faces were scanned, much like she had at the SoftFruit building. She wondered if Oliver's people had provided the technology, and if Feliz Smithson was still lurking somewhere in the CAC database.

Dana was disappointed at the hallway that waited for her behind the door. She'd hoped for something the X-men would be proud to hang out in. Instead, it looked like an abused, worn-down office building. Terrible corporate art, like toothpaste smeared on a canvas. Dirty, flattened carpeting, which looked like a car had run over it. Because it was underground, it was lit entirely by fluorescent lights, and it gave off a faintly mildewed, basement smell. She followed Oliver, who knew the way, to Ben's office.

Oliver knocked sharply on the door and Ben looked up. "Oh, good," he said. "I was about to call you two. I've just been contacted by someone from the Poseidons' Central Committee. Apparently the shell's been recovered. They thanked us for our help."

"Don't thank us; we didn't do anything," said Dana, helping herself to one of the two old, non-matching chairs Ben had out for guests. Oliver rested his hand on the other one, but did not sit.

"Did they send a picture of the shell?" asked Oliver.

Ben turned his laptop around so the screen faced them. *Yes,* Dana thought, *that's a large shell.*

"That's not right," said Oliver. "That can't be the shell. I mean, I've never held that one, but still—"

"What do you mean, Oliver?" said Dana.

"The striations are wrong. They're gibberish."

"You've seen this shell before?" asked Ben.

"No," said Oliver, "but my own sect—" He realized that both Ben and Dana were looking at him, and he hissed out one of his half-breathed curses. "I don't know how much of this I'm supposed to tell you."

"Let's assume," said Ben, leaning back in his chair to look up at Oliver, "that you were sent to work for me so that I could have the benefit of your cultural knowledge."

Oliver nodded. "On my home planet, we had several religious sects. I say religious, but some of them were political as well. Not on Earth, obviously."

Dana flagged that for future observation and consideration.

"It's customary to use one of these shells to—" Oliver fidgeted from foot to foot, his hands clasped behind his back— "to indicate that a thought is of divine origin. In my own sect, we'd ask for the shell at meeting when we felt inspired to speak. So I've held our shell before. And that one is just wrong. It doesn't even look like a proper *hssth* shell."

Dana put up her hand to halt Oliver. "Wait a minute. Are you saying you're a Quaker?"

Oliver reflected for a moment. "Actually, that's a very good translation."

"We're getting off topic," said Ben. "Why would the Central Committee want to cover this up?"

Dana and Oliver were silent. Oliver's lips tightened, as if he were keeping a thought trapped inside.

"Look," said Ben. "Minor as this seems, this was an attack on your people, Oliver. And Dana, you're smart enough to know that anything that happens to the Poseidons will have blowback for Jay. Your best interest is not to stand there with your mouths shut while you wait for this to fester into something important."

Oliver's expression didn't change, but his hand dug into the back of the chair. "There are some people I need to talk to," he said. Was Dana mistaken, or did he sound angry?

By the time they made it back to her apartment, she was certain—Oliver was really angry. And it wasn't at her.

"Do you want to tell me what's wrong?" she said, as they closed the door to her apartment.

"That shell thing was so *stupid*," said Oliver, "I keep thinking that the Central Committee wanted to get caught. And then I think, would I rather that they were incompetent and I'm paranoid?"

"But why was *that* shell stolen, Oliver? I mean, if it was a religious icon, shouldn't it be with the church?'

Oliver looked at her, and she got the impression that he was balancing things in his head. He was very bright and he didn't make choices without due consideration. She liked that about him. "Sometimes," he said, "I hear humans say how amazing it was that we could get all our people to leave our planet. I never told you, but that was my job before I came here: to get everyone to come with us, once we knew."

"It seems like they were giving up a lot," she said. "You're right, it is kind of amazing—"

"We couldn't persuade everyone," he interrupted. "I couldn't persuade everyone. And that sect whose shell that was? They decided to die with our planet."

He felt guilty about that, she realized. "But that couldn't have been your fault, Oliver. You can't have been the only person with your job, right?"

His face looked wintry. "My girlfriend was part of that sect. She wouldn't come with me. She told me that whatever woke up on the other side of the Change, it wouldn't be her. And I'm not sure she was wrong." Oliver suddenly hissed and brought his sleeve up to his face, drawing it over his eyes. He poked at the inky stain on his shirt cuff. "I'm sorry. I know men aren't supposed to do that. Sometimes I still don't have control of myself."

She knew Ben was manipulative and she knew he liked making threats, but she'd never seen him do something this cruel. "Do you think Ben knows about your girlfriend? Did he intentionally send you to research the shell because of her?"

"I don't know," said Oliver, dabbing at his eyes again. "Maybe. He seems well-informed." Oliver sounded very tired. "Yes, I think he did."

She couldn't really understand what Oliver had been through. How could she? All right, she might get closer to it than most people, having seen the world through Jay O'Toole's eyes for a week, but Jay had at least been human. How unsettling would it be to have more pairs of arms? More fingers? To live underwater? How exhausting would it be to be Oliver, to be constantly translating the world he saw around him to something he recognized?

And then there was this guilt clearly haunting him, that he hadn't done more. She hadn't even been aware of that until now. But apparently Ben had, that manipulative asshole. "I'm with you," she said. "Whatever you need from me. We can tell Ben to go fuck himself. He's got a lot less power than he thinks."

Oliver flashed her a dim version of his sweet smile. "I need to think a bit," he said. "And then we can decide what's next?"

He took her hand in his and gently squeezed it.

CHAPTER 30

GREG MAHLER SAT IN the bar of the Pueblo Motel, clinking the ice cubes in his scotch. He couldn't drink it—experience had taught him that—but he could wet his lips with it, which was at least something.

Christmas lights strung against the walls, half burned out, fought a losing battle against the desert dark. White stuffing leaked through the booths' cracked red vinyl upholstery. The bar was run down now, but it hadn't been much nicer back in 1947, when it was new, and his old college roommate Jim Thompson had picked it for their meeting.

Greg remembered thinking that though they were the same age, Jim seemed older. Jim had spent most of the past six years in the Navy; Greg had spent most of the same time in a TB sanatorium. They'd caught him when he tried to enlist. It was just a stupid little cough, he'd thought. A sign he was smoking too much. Ha.

Time stopped for me; I missed the war, Greg had thought.

"How are you feeling?" Jim had asked.

"Fine," Greg had said. The sulfa had worked for him. It was a wonder drug. A miracle. Hooray. Too late.

"I'm sorry to hear about your dad."

That had been the cruelest part of it. He was finally cured, finally ready to get back to the world after six years of spitting in a cup in a TB ward, ready to go out and kiss a girl or two, and bang, here he was, back in the middle-of-nowhere New Mexico running Mahler Fucking Plumbing. You had to keep up the family legacy, right?

How must a guy like him have looked to a man like Jim? A boy dressed up like a man, a sucker, a rube. Jim had leaned closer to him, squeezed his shoulder and said, "Greg, there's another war coming, and I could use your help." He'd told Greg about a secret new subcommittee, under the FBI. The Committee on Alien Contact. Spies and aliens! Ridiculous! Back then, he'd laughed. And Jim had said, "If you don't believe me, then let me show you something."

Greg had thought the next part over so many times that the memory crumbled in his mind. He remembered the cold hangar at the Air Force base. He'd coughed from the bitter air in his lungs and then worried that he wasn't really cured. He'd clutched the handkerchief he'd just spat into, wondering if he dared put it back into his pocket, or if it needed to be burned. It had taken him a moment to spot the reason that he'd been taken to this hangar—the injured alien, like something from Lovecraft, thrashing in the center of the room. Everyone else keeping well back from it, as it seethed and hissed and churned its tentacles. Had he stepped closer because his own curiosity had driven him to do it? Had he only imagined Jim's hand on his back, shoving him forward?

Why did he keep coming back to the Pueblo Motel? Why did he keep tormenting himself like this? Because that's where he'd last been the man he was supposed to be. Because in some stupid corner of his brain, he believed that if he sat here long enough, the door was going to open, and Jim was going to walk in, and this time, Greg would have the sense to say no.

A woman walked in, wearing a little green dress. Greg had seen her before at this hotel. He'd noticed her because she looked a lot like Ava Gardner. And because every time she came in, she left with a different man.

This time she sat down next to him, and he felt the skin under his clothing quiver as if a warm breath had blown across it.

"All alone?" she asked, and smiled at him.

"I am tonight," he said.

She even had a little southern accent, just like Ava Gardner. Greg wondered if she'd be flattered or baffled by the comparison.

Reflexively, he placed a mental hand on the barrier between him and the others. They'd tried to block him in, but they'd ended up blocking themselves out. He'd figured out a trick, a little construct that made it look like he was sleeping. He wouldn't overuse it, but tonight, he needed this, a drink in this anonymous bar, a chance to remember what it meant to be a normal human man.

"You must be a salesman," said the woman.

"How did you know?" asked Greg.

"I'm a very good judge of character," she said. "I wonder what you sell."

"Commercial water pumps," he said, selecting a product he felt he could lie comfortably about for ten minutes. If he needed to. No one ever wanted to know more about commercial plumbing supplies. "I'm here in town for a few days meeting with a big client. And what about you? What do you do?"

She leaned closer to him so that he could see the bare skin under her thin silk shirt. "Private parties," she said. "Would you like an invitation?"

Greg stood under the showerhead and scrubbed himself clean, enjoying the feel of the water rushing over his human body. There was one benefit, he reflected, to sharing a body with O'Toole—it was easier for him to keep looking like himself. O'Toole remembered being human better than Greg did. How long had it been now? Seventy years? And no sign that it would ever stop.

Truth was, he was running out of hope. For seventy years he'd been trying to block the alien invasion of Earth, and in that time they'd gone from, let's be honest, one poor lost bastard, to three million aliens infesting their planet. By any standard, he'd failed.

If he had any sense, he'd get out of there, drive his car as far as he could, and wait for the light and air of Earth to poison him. Let himself die as himself, on his own terms.

Too stubborn, he guessed. Still too angry.

He wrapped the towel around his waist and opened the bathroom door. There was a woman sitting on his bed, and for a moment, he hoped his hooker had decided to stick around. But it wasn't her. This woman was a hard-looking character in a black suit, and he was pretty sure he'd never met her before.

"You've got a lot of nerve, lady," said Greg. "Are you going to leave on your own, or do you need me to show you out?"

"Mr. Mahler?" she said. "I'm Sally Frome from the Committee on Alien Contact." She held up an ID card. It looked identical to Nakamura's or Shapiro's.

"Where I come from," he said, "a lady doesn't come to a gentleman's hotel room on a business call."

"I don't care," she said. "I need to talk to you. Not to Jay O'Toole. Is it safe?"

She knows, he thought. *She's CAC.* Not just about the monstrous thing that had happened to him, but what he'd done with his mockery of a life afterwards. He brushed against the mental barrier. Still solid. "For now," he said.

"I can't get anyone at the CAC to take me seriously," she said. "They got really cozy with the Poseidons, really fast. But I think you might be an exception."

Well, that's interesting. He'd assumed that the CAC was on the wrong side of history, but maybe that had been shortsighted of him. Institutions meant nothing, it was people who mattered. If there was a rogue element within the CAC—a group who knew the truth about the alien horde, but rejected the idea that it was politic to let them take what they wanted from humanity—Greg wanted to hear about it. "I think I know better than anyone else that we can't trust aliens, no matter how friendly they seem. They just can't see the world in a human way. They're not capable of it."

I know all about monsters. I am *a monster.*

She looked directly at him and he found himself gripping his towel a little tighter. "You know the Poseidons asked permission to land nine vessels on our planet. But a week later, there was a terrific splash in the Pacific Ocean, near San Francisco."

"A tenth vessel."

"Or a weapon of some kind, maybe."

He wondered if the CAC had told its broader employee base what the Poseidons had nearly done to San Francisco. Probably not. No sense in making people less cheerful about the alien invasion. "Do you mind if I get dressed for the rest of this discussion?"

She raised her eyebrows and smirked at him. "Don't do it on my account." He felt a warm thrum of excitement go through the gelatinous meat of his body. Then she turned her back towards him and kept talking as he pulled his clothes on. "It's difficult to tell what the mystery object might be. They've got some kind of shield on the object that kept it from being photographed clearly." She held out a picture to him.

He tucked his shirt into his pants, then took the photograph from her. It looked like the air had blurred around whatever the object was, but it left a huge shadow on the water underneath. It looked egg-shaped. Ship? Weapon? "And you can't get anyone at CAC interested?"

"I tried," Miss Frome said. "But I got the distinct sense they wanted to keep this quiet. And I've got more to show you too, if you'll come with me."

Greg thought quickly. He had a good thirty-six hours of being human, more if he didn't mind getting runny around the edges, and then he'd have to revert. So they'd have to stash him somewhere safe so even if the others tried to take over, they couldn't escape.

God, he hated having to think this way. "Lead the way, Miss Frome," he said.

CHAPTER 31

After bringing Dana back home, Oliver used his internal phone to call Jane Smith. He wasn't totally sure she'd respond, but a ghostly picture of her popped up in front of him.

Hello, Oliver, she said. *You're not going to overuse this direct line, are you?*

I want to talk to you about the shell, he said, his lips tracing the words, though he didn't speak out loud. He found his internal phone fairly creepy. He knew it was supposed to be a replacement for his lost ability to communicate with other people via color, scent, and *ktssk*, but it felt clunky and artificial. Most of the time he just shut the *fsst* thing off.

The problem has been resolved, said Jane.

I'm getting definite indications that the humans are unhappy.

Oliver, you can't run the world by crèche-time rules. Complete transparency isn't required.

What happened to the shell, Jane?

She paused for a moment. *I understand there are personal considerations here, Oliver, so I'm going to let your insubordination go.* And then she terminated the link.

All right, Oliver told himself. *It'll be all right. You have other people to talk to.* People he trusted, unlike Jane Smith. People he'd known his entire life. And he could ask Dana to come along as well, to get the benefit of her sharp mind.

Maybe he had other reasons for inviting Dana, but he didn't want to interrogate them too deeply.

DANA AND OLIVER WERE driving out to Palo Alto, where they were going to meet with a group of people from his home planet. Old friends, it sounded like. Oliver seemed ill-at-ease, though, and she wasn't sure why.

"Do you know why they made our skin such bright colors?" he said, out of nowhere.

Really? "I assumed you were trying to avoid dealing with race," she said, sweetly.

He looked embarrassed. "No. It's our way of handling the uncanny valley. Because it's impossible for us to act completely human. So if we're making facial gestures that are slightly off, but we're also bright green—"

"We'll see the color and we'll let the behavior slip by. It's like the thing with the potato."

Oliver nodded. "If I were a normal human color, you'd notice that my reactions are off a lot of the time. And I'm really good at acting human. That's one of the reasons I have my job. But some of my friends aren't as good."

Dana squinted at him. "Are you asking me not to be a jerk to your friends? What made you think I would be a jerk to your friends?"

There was a moment of silence from Oliver. "Well, you're pretty much a jerk all the time, so—"

She laughed at him.

He smiled back at her. *You know, he's really a good-looking guy,* she thought, and then squished that thought down to a tiny, tiny corner of her brain.

"How do you know these people?"

"I studied with Abby. Ethan's a crèche-mate."

"And that means what?"

He shook his head. "Okay, there's no way to make this not sound weird to you, but trust me, this is pretty meaningful to us. Back on Home, when people wanted to have children, they tried to get approved to go to the High Crevasse together. And you go up there, and you release your...uh...genetic material. And then the crèche-nurses go and collect the fertilized eggs, and then bring them back to the crèche. But our babies are really fragile, so they have to stay at the crèche with the gentlest nurses until they're thick-skinned enough to come home. Not all the parents get kids, but in a good season, most of them do. And you end up with a tie to everyone who was in the crèche at the same time as you, even though you might not have anything else in common."

Like frogs, thought Dana. *If frogs had a civilization.* "So parents aren't necessarily genetically related to their children."

Oliver shrugged. "You're not genetically related to your brother Adam."

I had no idea he knew that. "True." Even though he'd just said he was hard to read, she found herself scanning his face.

"Go ahead," Oliver said. "Ask."

"Do you have any kids?"

"No," he said. "Hsska and I just wanted to focus on our work. I mean, before the Disaster. We kept to a dry fuck, as they say."

"Too much information, Oliver," she said.

He turned towards her and gave her that sweet, crooked grin.

"So, are we having coffee with your friends, or what?"

The car pulled itself over to the side of the road, in front of a low-slung building that might have once been an elementary school.

"It's kind of a cultural thing," said Oliver. "Group sculpture."

"What?" said Dana.

"Trust me, you'll like it."

Dana turned around to the back seat to pick up her purse. There was a dog sitting next to it. She looked up with her liquid black eyes, as if begging for a treat. "Oliver—did you invite Sadie to join us?"

"No," said Oliver. "How the *fsst* did you get in here?"

"You can't really expect me to answer that," said Sadie.

"What are you doing here, Sadie?" asked Dana.

Sadie tipped her head back, rolling her eyes, in a way that would have made sense on a teenage girl but looked bizarre on a dog. "I'm so bored, Dana. Raj has been sulking for weeks now since we bollixed up the whole SoftFruit incident. I mean, yes, we did both get something of a sharp rap on the snout for it, but there's no need to lie there with your belly bared forever, right?"

"What I meant," said Dana, "is that you usually have something to trade with us."

Sadie ran her paw over the leather seat, looking Dana straight in the eye. "I can tell you which planet Kate Middleton's really from."

"Goodbye, Sadie," said Oliver and got out of the car.

Dana followed him. She turned around and looked back. Sadie's adorable little nose was pressed to the glass, and she looked like the saddest dog in the universe. One little paw forlornly brushed the window. "We can't leave her there."

"What do you mean?" said Oliver. "She got herself into this, she can wait in the car until she grows some thumbs."

"I mean that it's kind of a hot day, and it looks like we just left a dog in the car. Someone's going to call the cops on us."

Oliver sighed and started walking back to let Sadie out.

OLIVER WAS NEGOTIATING FOR three admission tickets to whatever it was they were doing. *Group sculpture?* "It's so exciting!" said Sadie, looking up at Dana. "I get to chaperone you again!"

Dana raised her eyebrows and looked down at Sadie.

"Oh, don't give me that look. Your love life is so much more interesting that mine."

"He's my partner," said Dana. "That's it."

"Don't lie to this nose," said Sadie.

"Gah, that's gross," said Dana. She looked up at Oliver, who was smiling at her as he approached, three tickets in his hands. A nice, friendly, open smile that she couldn't help but find very attractive. *Gah.*

"They made me pay to let you in, Sadie," said Oliver. "You owe me ten bucks."

Sadie shook her head. "You must let me show you how to fill out a proper expense account."

Oliver looked away from Sadie and handed Dana her ticket.

Crap, Dana thought. *She's going to realize we're here to figure out what's going on with the shell.*

"No expense account?" said Sadie. "I did crash your date, didn't I? That's hilarious!"

That was Sadie all over-—so certain of herself, so totally wrong about so many things. *Yeah, Sadie. Greg totally wants a new robot body.*

Dana followed Oliver into the main room of the event, and stopped, awestruck. A waist-high labyrinth of stone filled most of the room, and on top of the stone, was the biggest pile of clay she'd ever seen in her entire life. There was so much clay that she could actually smell it from the entrance. About thirty Poseidons were working on the clay, smoothing it flat with their palms, and crosshatching it with what looked like dental tools. A low bass thumping filled the room, and it took Dana a while to realize that it was music, probably designed to be heard underwater.

"Traditionally, we just used our claws on the clay, but now we put out tools for everyone." Oliver gestured at a table of tools.

"Do you do this a lot?" asked Dana.

"Most weeks," said Oliver. "It calms me down. Oh, there's Ethan. Let me go warm him up a bit. He's a little weird about Earthers."

"Tell him Dana's your girlfriend," said Sadie. "That should help."

Dana ignored her and picked up a couple of the dental tools, a thin pick and a slightly thicker one. She moved towards an open space on the clay. The Poseidons on either side of her were busily cross-hatching lines into the clay, but as far as Dana could tell, there was no actual rule mandating that she do so. And she hadn't done anything representational for a while. She began to carve a human arm reaching its way out of the clay. The crosshatched lines the arm emerged from resolved into the pattern of a windowpane-checked shirtsleeve. Exactly like the shirt that Oliver was wearing, in fact.

Dana stepped back and looked at what she'd just made. Oliver's arm emerging from a great block of Poseidon clay, like he was willing himself into existence. *Not even a little subtle,* she thought. *At least I should smooth out the pattern on the shirt.*

"I think I'm supposed to meet you," said a voice behind her.

Dana turned around. It was a bright orange woman who appeared to be about Oliver's age. "I'm Abby," she said, and held out a clay-covered hand.

"Dana." She shook Abby's hand. *Squelch* went the clay.

"What do you think?" said Abby. She smiled, a big, terrifying rictus of a grin. And then the smile disappeared instantly.

Dana saw what Oliver had meant about not being as good at human gestures. It was really hard to figure out what Abby was thinking, given that she couldn't read her facial expression. "I think that once the humans learn about this, we're all going to want to try it."

"If they're respectful, they'll be welcomed," said Abby. She looked at Dana's clay arm, but her face didn't move at all.

"Should I not have done that?" said Dana. "I didn't mean to be disrespectful."

"That's not the word I'd use," said Abby. "It's very avant-garde."

Dana found herself looking down, embarrassingly pleased by Abby's words. *By human standards, no. I'm a boring old commercial artist by human standards.* She caught Sadie's eye. Sadie winked like she'd understood everything. *Smug bitch.*

"May I come back sometime?" said Dana. She sounded more wistful than she intended. It was just that Abby was so hard to read. It was incredibly confusing.

"You and your brother saved us all," said Abby. "You can do anything you want."

They all know that? Dana crossed her arms. "I don't want to take advantage of you." She was very aware of Sadie looking up at her, a hungry look on her little canine face. Another little tasty nugget of gossip for Sadie. *Dana Elson does not intend to capitalize on her power imbalance with the Poseidons. Give me a liver treat!*

"There's no one here who can keep you out," said Abby. "And I'd be pleased to see more of your work." Again, the terrifying smile. Like someone with strychnine poisoning. Then she walked away to where Oliver and Ethan were having an increasingly heated discussion. Unlike most of the artists, Ethan was wearing a set of metal claws on the ends of his fingers. They looked wickedly sharp.

Abby placed herself between the two of them. She said something that made both men back up a step.

"I bet you'd like to know what they're saying," whispered Sadie.

"You can read lips?"

"I've got very good ears."

"I don't want to intrude on their privacy."

"Sure you do," said Sadie. "They're talking about you. Oh, and Ethan has just used a phrase that I think is best translated as 'gone native.' Abby is defending your honor. Ethan is incensed that Oliver has forgotten someone. Oliver said something about her being dead—oh, that will not calm Ethan down, Oliver, not smooth at all. And now—oh, Oliver is coming this way. I suppose claytime is over!"

Still clutching her thinner dental pick, Dana watched Oliver approach. She'd never seen him so angry.

He grabbed the dental pick from her hand and slammed it into the clay. "We're leaving," he said.

"Oh, good," said Sadie. "I didn't want to stick my nose in that mess, anyway."

Oliver was walking fast. Dana could barely keep up with him, and Sadie, with her little legs, was further and further behind. As soon as Dana had shut the car door behind her, Oliver started up the engine.

"Sadie isn't in yet," said Dana.

Oliver sighed, and rested his head on the steering wheel. "Okay," he said. "We'll give her a ride back. But she doesn't deserve one."

CHAPTER 32

For the entire ride back to the apartment complex, Sadie lobbied hard to stay with Dana and Oliver and "debrief." But they ignored her sad little whines and limpid brown eyes. While Dana carried a whimpering Sadie, Oliver pounded on Raj's door until an unshaven, pajama-clad Raj opened up. Dana handed him Sadie, and Oliver shut the door on them both. *Teamwork!*

Dana opened the door to her apartment and Oliver followed her inside. It was so natural that Dana didn't even think of stopping him. Not that she wanted to stop him. "We should talk," she said.

"We don't have to," he said. His hands were jammed in his pockets and he looked down at the floor. If he were human, she'd say he was angry but trying to avoid a fight, because the person he wanted to fight wasn't actually there.

"Sadie told me what Ethan was telling you. I'm sorry. I shouldn't have intruded."

"He's not wrong," Oliver said. "I'm not loyal to Hsska, not anymore. As far as I'm concerned, she chose to die."

"She left you first."

"It sounds so hard-shelled to say it," said Oliver. "Maybe the romantic way to think about it is that the man I used to be died back on Home with her. And now I'm someone else, something else. I can't even say my own name anymore. I can hear it in my head, but I can't say it."

Maybe she was hard-shelled, too. But for Oliver, she'd try to be kind. She took Oliver's hand in hers and he gasped. It was intense from her side, too, more intense than you'd think a simple touch could be, to feel his warm, dry hand tremble in hers. "Oliver," she said, "you are so goddamned brave."

He leaned towards her and took her shoulder in his other hand. He leaned closer, and she thought, *he's going to kiss me.* But he didn't. Instead, he breathed a stream of air against her neck. And it was like all the lights in her body turned on. She was as aroused as she'd ever been in her entire life. *Whoa. Alien sex moves.*

"You liked that," he said, his voice husky.

"Let me show you something," she said, and kissed him. Closed-mouthed. Just a brush of lips. But Oliver moaned like it was the best thing that had ever happened to him.

He pressed himself against her, clearly not thinking about claws and fragile skin anymore. Learning about his new body, she guessed. She pulled up his shirttail and ran her hand over the warm skin of his back.

He gasped. "That's so good," he said. "Oh, *fsst.* Don't stop."

She wasn't sure his motives were pure. Maybe he was still trying to forget Hsska. Maybe he just liked the way this felt. But on her side, body and mind, she was sure. Oliver was a genuinely good man. He was smart and funny and curious and even-keeled. And she needed to know where this went.

Oliver suddenly yelped and clutched the back of his head.

"Are you all right?" she pulled away from him. "Do I need to call a doctor?"

He held up a finger. "It's my internal phone."

"Internal phone?" She couldn't hide how horrifying the idea was.

"I hate that *hrst* thing. I had it shut off, but Ben used the override." He rubbed the back of his head. "Ben needs us. Adam's been arrested."

DANA ENDED UP DRIVING Oliver's fake car to Los Alamos because Oliver's internal phone had given him a nasty migraine. She wondered how they were going to find Adam at the police station—he tended to give a fake last name when he was working—but it turned out not to be a problem. As soon as Oliver and Dana got through the front door, Dana could see Adam entering the lobby from the other direction, handcuffed and being escorted out by two CAC guards, and a really pissed-off Ben.

And Adam had apparently gone nuts. He was yelling about how no shitty hick police officer could keep him locked up. Then he looked up at a truly gigantic police detective—the man had to be nearly a foot taller than Adam—said something insulting, then gave the policeman a wicked grin. The detective went right for Adam, and it took three uniformed cops to hold him back. And it looked like Adam was ready to fight him too, even with his hands handcuffed behind him, while the CAC guards held him tightly by the arms.

"Move," said Ben, to the CAC guards, and they hustled Adam out of the building and into a waiting white van.

Dana and Oliver followed them out and waited on the sidewalk, Oliver still rubbing his head.

Ben angrily gestured at the van. "After you," he said.

Dana wondered how they all would fit, until the door shut behind her, and she realized that they were in one of Skzzx's pocket universes, which had been fitted out like the conference room of an office building. Obviously with used furniture repurposed from elsewhere. Nothing the CAC did was high-budget.

Adam slumped into his chair and wordlessly turned sideways and held out his hands. One of the guards unlocked the handcuffs, and then they both left the room by the way they came. Now Dana could see that sometime in the past day, Adam had picked up a giant bruise on his jaw. He reached into his leather jacket, and removed first a bottle of water, and then a bottle of Tylenol. He leaned back in his chair and sighed. He looked like he'd shrunk since the police station.

It really bothered her sometimes—she cared about Adam, and he'd given every sign he cared about her, but there were some aspects to his character she just couldn't understand. That terrifying, violent man he'd been in the police department brought back memories of the day they'd met, when she'd been convinced he was going to kill her in a Spokane hotel room. And maybe she'd been right. Maybe it hadn't been all an act. Maybe if she hadn't been sharing a body with Jay, Adam would have killed her.

The past kept haunting the present.

Dana sat down across the oval table from Adam, with Oliver next to her. Oliver continued to rub the back of his head.

Adam held up the pill bottle and looked at Oliver. "You want a couple?"

Oliver nodded and winced. Adam slid the Tylenol over, and then took out two water bottles, passing one to Oliver, and one to Dana.

Her brother always liked giving people gifts. "You should ice that bruise, Adam," said Dana.

Adam tapped his jaw as if scanning how swollen it was. He pulled a chemical cold pack out of his pocket, cracked the seal, and rested it on his jaw. "It's been a while since I've been in a real fight," he told Dana. "Like five years, at least." He sounded wistful. The way Dana felt about her college late-night bullshit sessions about Picasso was the way Adam felt about provoking a fight with some guy a foot taller than he was.

She'd never understand.

Ben slapped a palm into the end of the table, grabbing her attention. She'd almost forgotten he was there. "Do any of you have something to say?"

Dana looked over at Oliver, pale and clutching his water bottle. *Fuck no,* she thought. She wanted to rub his back, but they were technically at the office.

"Let me remind you," said Ben, "you all work for me."

No empathy from Ben. No sense of responsibility. Dana felt her anger flare. "I quit," said Dana. "You absolute asshole."

Ben leaned over her. It was supposed to be scary, but wasn't. "You don't have a choice, Dana."

"Fuck you," said Dana. "I have lots of choices. I could lie to you so well you'd never know I'm lying. I could go live with the Poseidons and do sculpture all day. What the hell did Oliver ever to do you that you had to hurt him like that?"

"I haven't done anything to Oliver."

Like you never did anything to Adam? You threatened to frame him, but you never followed through, so it doesn't count? "He's sitting there in pain because you beamed an email right into his skull!"

Yes, she'd seen it, that little flash of embarrassment. Maybe Ben hadn't known what the email would do.

"Let's be fair," said Oliver. "It's not the one email. It's the other three hundred and seventy-five I hadn't listened to. And they're all playing at once, on repeat, until I respond."

"I'm sorry," said Ben. "That was not my intent."

"Yeah? What about Hsska?" Dana snarled.

"What is Hsska?" said Ben.

"Oliver's dead girlfriend? That Hsska? Where do you get off yanking his chain about—"

"Dana, no," said Oliver.

Oliver must have realized she'd gotten mad enough to say something about the shell. *Oops.*

"They didn't give me much of a bio on you, Oliver," Ben said. "I'll let you read it. There is nothing about a Hsska in there. And I'm sorry for your loss."

Ben fidgeted at the head of the table, totally discomfited.

And suddenly Dana realized something. At one point the CAC had been a small, sleepy post, whose big responsibilities were (a) Greg Mahler and (b) the corgis, who were really a British problem. And then nine alien spaceships landed in Iowa, and Ben suddenly got a giant promotion. Now he had to manage people, and some aspect of his training had taught him that this was best handled through mystery and intimidation. And he'd totally bungled it, because none of them had the sort of personalities that were best managed through mystery and intimidation.

Maybe she'd been too hard on him. Maybe. Maybe she just didn't know as much about people as she thought she did.

"So you're saying," said Dana, "You haven't been a manipulative mastermind. You're just kind of bad at your job."

Ben smiled, a brief little flicker. "What I'm trying to do, Dana, is just what I've been telling you all along. I'm just trying to keep the Poseidons and all our other alien Americans safe. Now, does anyone have something to report?"

Even if she had something germane to report, she still wasn't sure she'd share with Ben.

Other alien-Americans?

"I do," said Adam, sounding tired. "Greg just killed a hooker."

Instantly, he had everyone's attention.

"Greg's been restless recently. So I talked Jay into swallowing a tracker so if he wandered off, we could find him again. And when he went missing, I followed him to a hotel in Los Alamos. He's been there before. It's kind of dirty and run down, but Greg likes it there for some reason."

"Maybe it's the hookers," said Dana.

Adam nodded. "Greg gave the bartender a quarter, because he still thinks that's a good tip, so the bartender was happy to talk to me. He said that Greg had gotten a room with one of their regulars.

"Then I paid off the hotel clerk and got the room number. By the time I broke in, Greg was gone. There was nothing in the room. Except for the woman's shoe sticking out from under the bed. So I pulled her out, and she'd been shot, once in the heart, and once in the face, just like Greg likes it."

Dana felt a chill descend on her. She didn't like to think about the fact that she'd never met the original Jay O'Toole, but Adam had seen him murdered, right in front of him. *Oh,* she thought. *Once in the heart, once in the face. That's what Greg did to Jay, and Adam couldn't stop him. That's how Adam knows. Oh, you poor soul.* She looked down at her lap.

It was strange to think—when she'd first met Adam, and he said how Jay had died, it hadn't mattered to her. Just it wouldn't have mattered to him that she was still grieving her lost mother. But that was the magic of people, she guessed—people could become so important to you that it seemed like they'd always been there.

Focus, Dana.

Adam continued. "And then the door opens, and it's the desk clerk, and the police, and I'm standing there over this woman's body. Of course I get arrested. My plan was to keep my mouth shut, because they'll talk to the bartender and the desk clerk, and they'll know it couldn't have been me who killed her, right? Because I wouldn't kill her and then make sure they remembered me asking about her. And hell, Greg and I don't even carry the same caliber, usually.

"And then it hits me, right? It has to be me, because if it isn't me, it'll be Greg, and that means Jay's going to jail, and so are those poor alien bastards. So I did what I could to piss them off." He smirked. "And it worked."

"You took a big risk," said Ben. "I'm not going to be able to get you out of jail if you pull something like that again."

Adam shrugged.

"So where is Greg now?"

"No idea," said Adam. "He dropped the tracker in the room."

"Well, then," said Dana. "Sounds like we should get down there and see if we can figure it out."

"I'm sitting this one out," said Oliver.

He looked terrible, holding his water bottle against the back of his head. She wanted to rub the sore spot for him. "Get some rest," said Dana. "Feel better."

"Dana?" said Ben. "I'm supposed to be in charge." He turned towards Oliver. "Oliver, get some rest. Feel better."

AS HE DROVE TO Ethan's house, Oliver found himself thinking about Miss Tssss. Miss Tssss was everyone's favorite teacher back at the crèche. She was gentle. She knew all the songs. She could comfort you and get you to sleep when you were worried about leaving the safety of the crèche and your friends and teachers and meeting your new parents.

But then there had been that day, that horrible day when the table fell on Ftsssk. Oliver had never heard a wail like that, before or since, and they'd all known, young as they all were, that Ftsssk was injured for life. He'd never be able to swim on his own, never explore the beautiful world outside the crèche. Maybe he'd even die. But Miss Tssss had him bundled in an air sock and out to the medic in seconds.

Oliver would always count the day that Ftsssk came back, perfectly healthy, ready to frisk with the other children, as one of the best of his life. And it was all due to Miss Tssss, Ftsssk had said. She'd saved him, and she'd stayed right next to him while the doctors worked until he was well again.

One of the cruelest things about the Disaster, Oliver thought, was that some people who had been perfectly placed in life had lost their purpose. When they realized what was going to happen, the Central Committee closed up the High Crevasse. All the sects had agreed: no more children born on Home. There'd been a crèche for a few scattered isolate children on the slowest ship, so they could reach adulthood before they were Changed. Where had Miss Tssss gone, after those children had become adults?

Humans didn't have crèches. Their children grew like parasites within their mothers' wombs, and were sturdy enough to come home with their parents after birth. Oliver felt a terrible wrench at that again, remembering his realization that he and Hsska had waited too long, that he'd never have children in the normal way, raised like he was in the warmth and community of the crèche.

What had happened to people like Miss Tssss who were perfectly adapted to their life on Home, now that they lived on Earth?

And then there was Ethan. He'd been happy enough on Home, but he was floundering on Earth. His resentments had taken over his character. As he followed Ethan into his apartment, Oliver's stomach tightened with the thought that his old crèche-mate had the look of someone who'd been eating the wrong lichen. There was so much pressure to look happy-happy for the humans. And Ethan couldn't manage it.

Oliver hadn't been trained for this. He had no idea what to say to his childhood friend, wobbling drunk and hostile in the middle of the day, in his messy living room filled with half-finished projects, dried-out art supplies, and empty bottles. Ethan had always been so immaculate back on Home, even as a child.

"I didn't think you'd answer my mail," said Ethan. "Too busy blowing air up the humans' tails."

How can I help you? How can I fix you? Oliver knew he was the worst man for the job. Everything about him seemed calculated to irritate Ethan these days—his job, his attraction to Dana, his ease at fitting in in the human world, and most of all, Hsska, always Hsska. Oliver'd come to love Hsska, but Ethan, looking back, had loved her since crèche-days.

"I had to come," said Oliver. "You told me Hsska was still alive."

"I told you that?" said Ethan.

"Where is she? What's her name now?"

Ethan laughed, like he'd swallowed rocks. "You think she'd take a human name?"

Oliver sighed. "Is she in trouble? Does she need help?"

"No. You're free! Congratulations!" Ethan mimed picking up a shell and holding it to his lips. "You are hereby resolved of all responsibility for Hsska."

Oliver crossed his arms. "Then let me help you."

Ethan was still giving him that hostile look.

"You're my crèche-mate, Ethan!"

"Don't call me that."

"All right. Lrrkt." His human tongue could barely handle the name. "You were right all along. You were the one who really loved her. I was just temporary. And I think you'd be with her now, but there's some reason why you can't. And maybe I can help you with that. Because I may not have loved her as much as you did, but I did love her, and you're my crèche-mate, Lrrkt, and I want you both to be happy."

Lrrkt was silent for a moment. "Hsska is still alive. She sent a message to my internal phone telling me so."

"Where is she? I'll take you wherever she is."

"I don't know. It doesn't make sense. The message came from off the coast of California. But it says I'll never see her again. I think she did something. I think the humans have her in prison. Think you can talk them out of that, *Oliver*?"

The missing shell. The sect that had agreed to die. Jane Smith's clumsy cover-up. *It's not the humans I'm worried about*, thought Oliver. *It's the Central Committee.*

CHAPTER 33

"SO HOW DO WE track down Greg?" asked Dana.

"Follow me," said Ben and opened the door on the other side of the conference room.

Dana noticed that Adam was having trouble standing and circled around the table to wait next to him.

"Jesus," he said, using the armrests of his chair to push himself to his feet. "I'm not eighteen anymore."

"You okay?"

"Might have sprained my ankle," he admitted. "I just need to walk on it a bit."

Dana watched Adam, ready to catch him if he stumbled, while following Ben. "That was really stupid, Adam."

"It worked. Did you hear what they called me when they released me? Adam Henry Shapiro."

"So?"

"That's not my middle name. Adam Henry is cop code for 'asshole.'"

She hadn't noticed, but then she'd never asked Adam what his middle name was. "What *is* your middle name?"

He grinned. “It’s Danger.”

“It is *not.*”

“Ben,” Adam called out. “What’s my middle name?”

“It’s Danger.” Ben sounded resigned.

Adam cackled.

I guess when you pick your own name, you can call yourself what you want. And then, Dana realized she was in a long, worn-looking, underground hallway. She was under the Denver airport again. Either when she’d entered or left the conference room, she’d unwittingly gone from New Mexico to Colorado. “Gah!” she said.

“Oh, yeah,” said Ben. “I probably should have mentioned.” He grinned at her, his hands stuffed in his pockets. *Jackass.*

“Why are we here, when we’re supposed to be investigating the murder?” Honor Firehammer, that was the victim’s name. Dana suspected she would never, ever forget it.

“From here,” said Ben, “we can use the CAC system to access the security cameras at the hotel. I want to see how and when Greg left the hotel room because it wasn’t in a Mahler car.”

You have access to private security cameras? Is that legal? Dana wondered. Then again, Ben could force her phone to take his calls, which suggested that there were some benefits to being a spy.

“Then,” Ben continued as Dana and the still limping Adam followed him to his office, “we can use DMV records to track the car.”

Ben sat down at his laptop while Dana and Adam sat in the chairs on the other side. Adam was icing his bruised jaw again.

“That’s weird,” said Ben. “I can’t pull the camera.”

“What do you mean?” asked Dana.

Ben turned his laptop so they could all see it. “See?” he said. “This whole block. I can’t access any of the cameras.”

"That's okay," said Dana. "What I really want to know is more about Honor. Adam, you said Greg had been at the motel before, right? Maybe they knew each other."

"The police aren't going to talk to us," said Ben, "thanks to Adam's little puppet show."

Adam laughed his weird, choked laugh. He raised the hand not holding the ice pack as if it were supporting an invisible puppet. In a high, squeaky voice he said, "I eat cops like you for lunch, you dumb hick!" He opened and closed his hand as if manipulating a puppet's mouth. "Mmm, cops!"

Ben's expressive eyebrows slid together. "Are you done?"

"Are you done?" said Adam's puppet hand.

"Actually," said Dana, loudly enough to get both men's attention, "I was wondering if we could maybe get into her apartment and look around."

"My point was," said Ben, "the local police are not currently interested in cooperating with us. And they have ways to make themselves less than helpful."

Adam smirked. "Check this out." He pulled something out of his pocket and dropped it on the desk. It was a moist-looking, pale pink, rubbery thing, like a deflated bubble of chewing gum. *Eww.* Adam set his ice pack down on the desk and stretched the thing over his head. He turned to Dana and grinned.

"Oh my God," she said. "You look just like William Shatner. But like, young William Shatner."

"Wicked cool, right?"

She studied him closely. She couldn't see the lines of the mask around the eyes or neck. It was just like talking to a young Shatner at the peak of his cuteness. It would have been weird, if Dana hadn't been a total Spock girl. "Can you breathe under that thing?"

Adam shrugged. "Far as I can tell. You guys want yours?"

SULU (AKA BEN) PULLED up in front of the late Honor Firehammer's apartment building. Kirk (Adam) leaned forward from the back seat. "Do you want to break in or bullshit our way in?" he said to Uhura (Dana).

"Let's try the second way first," said Dana.

Sulu was rubbing his forehead. "Just, please, don't get arrested again."

"No promises," said Adam, and shut the door behind him.

The apartment was a low-slung 70s modern. The front door opened onto a small foyer, lined with mailboxes, with an open-sided concrete spiral staircase at the back. While Dana fumbled through her purse, pretending to search for her keys, an apartment resident came up to the door with his keys out and unlocked it. Then he held the door open so she and Adam could follow him in.

"You know," said the man, "you two look exactly like—"

"We get that a lot," said Dana.

The apartment was on the second story of the building. Dana watched Adam, who was already wearing his gloves, take out his wrench and pick and get to work on the apartment's lock. "What are we looking for?" he asked. Dana could hear one of the tumblers catch. "I mean, I'm always up for fucking with Ben..." he winced as something slipped.

"I was just thinking about what you said earlier, that Greg had wandered off before. I was wondering if he and Honor already had a relationship, and maybe this would give us some clues about it."

Adam shrugged. "It's probably just an apartment," he said, and the door swung open.

Against the wall of the apartment was a huge bookcase and the entire thing was filled, from top to bottom, with Rainbow Daydreams memorabilia. Dana gasped. There was stuff from the 70s that they didn't even have in Spokane.

"What?" said Adam. He squinted. "Is that one of your doges?"

"This is everything," she said. "Everything Rainbow Daydreams has ever sold. All of it." She walked along the bookcase, which ran the entire length of the living room, and past the messy kitchen, which had a Happy Birdhouse Spice Holder. Another bookcase was wedged into the hall along the way to the bedroom, again filled from top to bottom with Rainbow Daydreams memorabilia. It was packed so tightly Dana could barely see the statue of Marilyn Monroe hugging the American flag crammed behind the Confederate Santa.

"How much would all this stuff cost?" asked Adam.

"Something over fifty thousand dollars," said Dana.

"Jesus," said Adam. "And she earned it the hard way."

Dana scanned the shelves. Yes, she was right—there was something missing. But it was a recent issue, so maybe Honor just hadn't had time to add it to the collection yet.

Now she never will, Dana reflected.

By now she and Adam had made it to the bedroom, which was untidy but otherwise fairly spartan. There was a dresser with a TV on it, a bedside table with a lamp, clock, and glass of water, and a double bed with a white comforter. And on the bed was the one Rainbow Daydreams collectible Dana hadn't spotted yet.

Dana grabbed Adam's arm. "Look," she said. "Look. That's the stuffie I designed to look like Skzzx."

Adam looked at her suspiciously. "What are you saying?"

"I wonder if Greg told her about Skzzx. Maybe that's why she had the stuffie."

"And that's why he killed her?"

Dana's mouth shut. That hadn't been what she meant, but it was a logical deduction.

"He wouldn't have told her," said Adam. "He never told anyone." His forehead furrowed with the effort of explaining Greg Mahler. "I know what you'd like to think, Dana, but Greg just isn't a good person."

Dana nodded. "Maybe I just wish he told her. Maybe if he were happier he'd be less of a problem."

Heat rose in Adam's voice. "He wouldn't be a good man even if he were happy. Greg murdered Jay because he thought Jay was distracting me from my job. Because he thought I'd forget about Jay if he wasn't there."

"I still don't understand why he did that. I don't know Greg well, but once you've seen you and Jay together, that's just not rational—"

"Oh, come on, Dana!" Adam snapped. "Don't you believe me?"

Dana looked down at the brown carpet, curling around the tips of her boots. Why was she defending Greg? When Adam said Greg was a monster, she should trust him.

She'd never actually seen Adam angry at her before. What was she supposed to do now? Was she supposed to apologize? "Adam, I—"

Adam squinted at her, his anger apparently forgotten. "Do you hear something?"

As a matter of fact, she did. Sort of an odd thumping noise. It sounded like it was coming from the bedroom closet.

Adam whispered. "You open the door and stay out of the way. I'll cover you."

She opened the door, yanking it swiftly. A woman with short red hair fell backwards and hit the carpet face up. She was gagged and blindfolded, her arms and legs were tied together, and from the smell, she'd been in there several hours.

It was Honor Firehammer, and she was very much alive.

A FRESHLY SHOWERED HONOR sat in her kitchen, enjoying the coffee and scrambled eggs that Dana had made for her. Adam stood at the sink, washing dishes.

"You didn't see anything about the people who did this to you?" said Dana.

"No," she said. "I went to sleep like normal, and I woke up tied up in the closet."

"Do you know a man named Greg Mahler?" said Dana.

"Who?" asked Honor.

Adam dried his hand off on a dishtowel and pulled a picture out of his pocket. He handed it to Honor.

She looked at it. "It's not that I'm not grateful for the eggs," she said, "and for cleaning my kitchen—"

"And for rescuing you from the closet, where you could have died." interjected Dana.

"It's just at some point I wonder how many questions I have to answer," said Honor.

"We just want to know if you know this guy," said Dana.

"He's the guy who likes to come to the motel bar, stare at a drink for two hours, and tip the bartender a quarter."

"You've never talked to him?" said Adam.

"A quarter," said Honor. "Who does that? And who is he, anyway?"

"I used to work for him," said Adam.

"Oooh," said Honor, commiserating.

"Did you ever see him leave with anyone else?" said Dana.

Honor shook her head. "As I said, a quarter."

"Good point," said Dana.

Without saying a word, Adam set the towel down by the sink and quietly walked out of the kitchen to the living room.

"What is he—" said Honor.

Dana held her finger to her lips and Honor was silent. They heard a man gasp, and then Adam yelped.

"Jesus, Ben, that's my bruise!"

"I know!" said Ben.

Dana left the kitchen. Ben stood in the living room, still wearing his Sulu mask. Adam was three feet away, rubbing his rib cage. "You two left me sitting in the car for a half hour! What the hell were you doing up here?"

Honor came out of the kitchen and stood beside her.

"Well," said Ben, squinting at Honor, "that explains a lot."

DANA, ADAM, AND BEN were back in the car and wearing their masks again, driving to the motel where Honor hadn't died. "Greg killed a robot?" said Dana.

"That was no robot," said Adam. "I'll tell you that much."

"More of a synthetic human," said Ben. "Our scientists don't think it was as sophisticated as the real thing. It had a few preprogrammed responses."

"Like a robot made of meat?" asked Dana.

"There's probably a more technical way to put it," said Ben. "But that works."

"When we find Greg," said Adam, "I get to be the one who tells him he fucked a robot."

Dana looked out the window. It was twilight, nearly a day since Greg had vanished. "Here's what I can't figure out."

"Tell me," said Ben.

"Why would Greg want to kill Honor?"

Adam was stretched out in the back seat, without a seatbelt, his sore ankle propped up on the seat with an ice pack. "Probably because he felt like it. He probably thought it was funny."

"Okay," she said. "You know him better than I do. But if he felt like killing someone, why do it in a way that made it likelier he'd get caught? The bartender and the desk clerk both saw him with the victim. Hell, he left the body in the hotel room. Does that sound like Greg to you?"

"What are you saying, Dana?" asked Ben.

Gah, she could have bit her tongue for even thinking it. But it had to be said. "What if Greg just went to this hotel to—you know—"

"Have sex with a woman?" said Adam. He shrugged. "Some guys like it."

Dana sighed and continued. "I think someone else killed that woman. Someone who came to the hotel to find Greg. And they did."

"Oh, fuck," said Adam. "Fuck, fuck, fuck. Dana, sometimes I hate that you're so smart."

"I'm sorry," said Dana.

Adam patted her shoulder. "It's all right. You can't help it."

Ben looked at the road ahead of them. "Okay. Let's stick to the original plan. We'll get into the room, see if there's anything the cops missed, and try to figure out where Greg might be headed next. Alone or with someone else."

That wasn't even the worst part, thought Dana. Someone had made a robot duplicate of Honor. Who had that kind of technology? There were the aliens who'd made a copy of Dad, James Bond, and Queen Elizabeth. As far as she knew, they just liked duplicating famous people.

And then there were the Poseidons. The Poseidons could easily have done this. Hadn't they built new bodies for everyone on their planet? What was one more body, after all?

She thought about Oliver. Oliver, who she desperately wanted to trust, who she was—let's be honest—falling in love with already. Oliver, who could have faked a headache. Did the timeline work? Could he have been the one who tied up the real Honor?

God, she hoped not.

She used to think she was good at reading people. But then, she used to think Ben was the bad guy.

A dispirited trio crossed the dark parking lot. The motel had been designed to be well-lit, but maintenance was lacking, and most of the lights were out. The motel was shaped something like a four-legged octopus, with the bar and the office in the body of the beast. Greg had selected a room far down one of the tentacles. Adam tapped a leather-gloved hand on the hood of a car parked outside. "That's one of our fleet," he said. "So Greg drove here, but he didn't leave that way. Too bad, because ours all have trackers."

Dana reflected that that supported her theory—that Greg had met someone else at the motel—but she decided to keep her mouth shut.

Dana and Ben stood to block public view of Adam, while he swiftly picked the lock on the door. The door swung open. Ben tapped Adam on the arm and, gun out, stepped inside, scanning the room. He beckoned the other two to follow him.

The room was dark and still. Ducking under the police tape, Dana looked around the room. The bed had been stripped and moved out of position. Otherwise it looked much like she'd anticipated: a run-down, grubby motel room, where sad and sometimes brutal things happened. And apparently this wasn't Greg Mahler's first time at this motel.

The strange thing was, she could feel sorry for Greg, because she understood Greg's story from his point of view. His story was about a man who became a monster. Who'd seen everyone he'd ever loved die; who'd seen the cause he'd given his future for prove to be irrelevant. And then, she'd think about poor Jay, forced to share his body with his murderer, and then Adam, who slept next to the person he loathed most in the entire world every night.

Adam always said she was smart. Well, if she were really smart, she'd know how to fix this.

She realized her mind had been wandering when Ben suddenly shoved her backwards. She stumbled and fell back against the wall. Both he and Adam had their guns pointed at the bathroom and were blocking her with their bodies.

"All right," Ben said. "Come out slowly, hands up."

The bathroom door creaked open. A man slowly emerged. But he did not have his hands up. He pointed his gun at Ben and then stopped, apparently taken aback to be confronted by the away team of the USS Enterprise.

It was Raj Singh. "Who are you," he said, in his elegant accent, "and what are you doing here?"

Sadie stuck her head out from under the bed. "It's all right, Raj," she said. "We know these people. It's Dana, Ben, and Adam."

Dana pulled her mask off. "Are you following me again?"

Sadie emerged fully from the bed. "No. I'm sniffing out a problem."

Spy Dog was being oblique again. Obviously she wanted to be asked for more information, to show off her genius. Under the circumstances, Dana thought she'd better oblige. "Well?" said Dana.

"Guns down, and I'll talk," said Sadie.

Ben put his gun back in his holster, and Adam and Raj followed suit.

Sadie theatrically sniffed the floor. "There was a third guest in this room. A woman, late thirties. She shot the other woman, pulled the body under the bed, and wiped her hands on the curtains. Then she sat on the bed and waited for the Rzzln to emerge from the bathroom. The Rzzln never touched the corpse, by the way."

"You know who this third guest was, don't you?" said Dana. "She's the one who really interests you, not Greg."

Sadie grinned. "She should interest you as well. Her name is Sally Frome, and she works for the CAC. Now, normally, I wouldn't involve myself in internal politics--"

"Shh," said Adam, hushing Sadie. He grabbed Ben by the arm with his left hand, a position that, Dana couldn't help but notice, put him in easy punching distance of Ben. "Ben? You going to explain?"

"Your information's out of date, Sadie," said Ben, a little heat in his voice. "Sally is on longterm leave from the CAC. She was more of an old CAC type. Something of a natural partner for Greg, now that you mention it. Back when it was all about secrecy, and fear, and keeping the aliens hidden."

Adam dropped Ben's arm.

Sadie looked up at Dana, panting excitedly. *Sadie is actually right about something for once,* thought Dana. Well, it had to happen sometime. "What do you think she's after, Sadie?"

"It's funny about the Poseidons," said Sadie. "They're so sweet, so happy. I think it's only natural to suspect that they're hiding something horrible. They must be too good to be true. Especially because it is, in fact, the case that they're hiding something. And I think Sally found out what it is, or at least where it is, and when her superiors told her to drop it, she just wouldn't drop."

Something passed over Ben's face.

"You know what it is, don't you, Ben?" said Sadie.

"Adam. Dana," said Ben. "Let's go."

"Not so fast," said Sadie. "I gave you my information. We're on the same side with this. Spit it out, Sulu."

Ben grimaced and pulled off his mask. "I don't know what it is. I know where it is. It's off the California coast, near the Lone Cypress on 17-Mile Drive."

GREG COULD ALREADY HEAR the whispering at the edges of his consciousness, the aliens waking up again. Almost comprehensible. *Greg negation (want) Hssstheen.* Whatever that meant.

He was holding on to control of his body as hard as he could—he knew what would happen if he didn't. Ever since they'd picked up another passenger on the USS Skzzx, Greg had been losing time. He'd fall asleep and wake up weeks later, like the aliens had shoved him away from consciousness.

But that wasn't the worst part. The worst was when they dragged him awake and forced him to watch, powerlessly, as if gripped by the back of the neck, while O'Toole destroyed everything he had built. When O'Toole and Shapiro had taken sledgehammers to the glass cage where Greg had played monster for the new employees. Or the time that O'Toole had given a speech to the staff about the opportunity the Poseidon invasion gave them to transform what people thought of aliens. Or the time he realized that O'Toole was greeting the new employees as Skzzx, shaking hands with multiple tentacles at once. Some of the new staff was actually giggling in delight. *Giggling!* Or just finding himself trying to watch football with his odd, granular alien vision, and realizing Shapiro was resting against him like he was a bolster, scratching him gently at the base of one of his tentacles. How horribly good it had felt!

You lost. We won. Give up. That's what they wanted him to think. So he didn't dare give up control, not for an instant, until he and Miss Frome had taken this affair to its conclusion.

Greg had pulled his hat over his softening face but Miss Frome could still see what was going on.

"You've about hit your limit," she said, once she'd paid the attendant and pulled onto 17-Mile Drive.

"I'm fine," he spat, even though his lips were giving him some trouble.

"You're no good to me like this," she said, and pulled over. "I've got something for you. It's in the trunk."

He thought for a moment. What was the worst that could happen? She could try to kill him. Ha! That wouldn't be so bad, not at all. He popped the latch of the trunk with hands that squished, as if they'd been made from barely-set gelatin. Now the aliens were making that soft chirping noise again, the one they used to indicate that it was his time to give up the body. He shoved them back behind the wall and looked at the case in the trunk. It had a radiation hazard sticker on it. Oh, thank God, she'd brought him plutonium. That would buy him a little more time. He knocked it back like a drunk. There. Himself again, for a little bit longer.

Why had she been so kind?

He sat back down in the car.

"Better?" she said, and pulled back into the slow-moving line of tourists gawking at the beach and the rocks and the sky.

"Let's not play any games, Miss Frome," he said. "You've gone to a lot of trouble to get me. Why?"

"Because you're a true believer. Because I can trust you," she said.

"Trust me to do what?" he asked.

"To help me destroy whatever the Poseidons have planted off Pebble Beach. Even at the cost of our own lives."

He looked down at his lap and smiled. Yes, he could do that. Finally, for his life to *mean* something!

CHAPTER 34

17-MILE DRIVE WAS AN absolutely beautiful place, Oliver thought. From the road you could see the sharp promontory of granite, projecting deep into the ocean, like a clump of knife blades, a single tree near the end. He parked his car at the top of the hill and then he and Lrrkt walked down the bleached-pale wooden steps to a small observation deck some distance from the tree. No one was around to complain when they clambered over the railing around the deck and onto the rocks.

Oliver stood by the single tree and inhaled the scent of the ocean. Even though everything else had changed, he felt more like himself than he had in months. Almost like the man he used to be, the man whose name he still couldn't say with his human tongue, but he could hear inside his head. The name he could hear Hsska cooing at him.

He bit the inside of his lip, feeling guilty. Allrhl had thought he'd love Hsska forever, and Oliver Miller was already brushing antennae with Dana Elson.

At his side Lrrkt was nothing but eagerness. "Should we take your car?" he said. "Does it go underwater?"

Oliver looked behind him. Back on the observation deck, he could see a man and a woman, dressed in suits. The woman was holding a bulky briefcase. Another man loped down the stairs towards them, and suddenly there was a loud pop.

And then Lrrkt gasped. A blossom of purple ink bloomed on his shirt.

Oliver heard a second popping noise, grabbed Lrrkt's arm, and jumped into the ocean.

DANA COULD SEE THE Lone Cypress from the passenger seat of Ben's parked car. Two people were standing near the cypress, in an area that Dana was pretty sure was off-limits. *How did they even get up there?* The steep curve of the shoreline made it impossible to see what was between the road and the two daring tourists.

She thought of the sketchbook that was jammed at the bottom of her purse and her little box of pastels, and wished she could sketch the way the two people were standing right now, like they owned the sea.

Suddenly Raj tore out of the car he'd been driving and disappeared down what seemed to be a path.

Dana heard a gunshot, and the two people by the tree jumped into the ocean. "Oh, fuck me," said Ben, and took off after Raj.

Why was Raj shooting at those people? Neither of them looked like Greg, she was sure of it.

Dana started to unfasten her seatbelt but felt her brother's cold hand on her shoulder. "Stay in the car and keep down," he said. "Don't worry about Oliver."

He bolted down the path, leaving his door open behind him, while Dana thought *Oliver?* And then she remembered—Adam had a sniper's eyesight. Two people had gone into the water, and she bet one of them had been Oliver. How good a swimmer was he? Could he even swim?

She let out an involuntary whimper, and then realized she had a dog in her lap.

"Hallo," said Sadie. "Are you as poor a shot as I am?"

"Oliver's drowning," said Dana.

"Did you know this isn't really a car?" said Sadie. "And that it works underwater? I'd save him myself, but my feet don't reach the pedals."

Miss Frome pulled a lump of wiring from her briefcase and handed it to Greg. "I'll hold them off," she said. "All you need to do is swim five miles in that direction," she pointed to the southwest, "and stick this to the side of whatever the Poseidons have hidden. When you get back, I'll trigger it."

"Why are you giving this to me?" said Greg.

"You're ideal. You don't need to breathe."

"I can't go in salt water. You ever salted a slug? I'll be dead in seconds."

The look she gave him was so ridiculous he had to laugh at her. And maybe at himself, too. He'd thought this was his chance to go out with a blaze of glory. Instead, it was just more of the same, more governmental ineptitude, hooray! And the alien tide just kept right on rising. "This was your plan, lady? How much research did you do? Is this even a functioning bomb?"

She sneered at him. "You want to find out?"

I just might, he thought, and then a shot passed between them.

An Indian man was running down the steps towards them, gun out. "Drop it!" he called, with a British accent. "Hands up!"

"MI-6 has no jurisdiction here! This is CAC business!" yelled Miss Frome.

"No it isn't," yelled Nakamura, following the MI-6 agent down the steps. "You're on leave, Sally!"

Greg had no time to wonder how they'd been discovered. Miss Frome shot at Nakamura, removing a chunk of his left earlobe, but he only flinched and continued to run down the steps. "Drop your gun! You're under arrest!"

"Under whose authority?"

Really? thought Greg. *You all have guns and you're arguing about the law?* This generation was *weak.* Greg's generation had been to war, while these ridiculous young people had only ever been behind computer screens, sniveling about rightness and fairness and justice.

He set the bomb down and looked for a way out.

Up at the top of the hill, there was the sudden noise of an engine accelerating, and then a car burst through the railing, falling fast towards the trees below. There was a good chance the thing would hit the deck near where he was standing—it was falling fast, and hard—and when it did, Greg was going to use the resulting chaos to run back up the stairs, take Miss Frome's car, and get the hell out of there. But just before it struck, the wheels folded inward, and the car suddenly changed its angle, hurtling towards the water at full speed. Greg had a brief impression of a panicked small dog barking and yipping at the window before the car splashed deep into the ocean, casting up a huge wave that had him stumbling backwards.

Which was when he found himself flat on his back, pinned to the ground under Shapiro. He fought to get up, but in the years they'd known each other, Shapiro had gone from a scrawny kid to a full-grown man, muscular and mean as a mongoose.

Despite his radioactive vitamin shot, Greg was starting to get soft around the edges again. And worse, the others were back, the whispering semicoherent voices of the aliens, and the sense of O'Toole's longing, reaching up through him towards Shapiro. He shuddered and fought it off. *No, not yet.*

"Greg, you're done," said Shapiro. "You're melting."

Of all these young people, Shapiro was the only one who might understand. He knew that the law was a lie, that a man with sufficient will could do whatever he wanted. And there was a trick to Shapiro that he'd figured out long ago—you could get him to do anything, if you could persuade him it was heroic. "The Poseidons have something hidden in the water. We need to find it. It could be a bomb. It could be something worse."

"I don't care what it is." Shapiro dug his knees more sharply into Greg's thighs.

Greg felt himself flatten like a water balloon. He could find the right words, if he just had enough time. "They're hiding it because they're afraid of what the humans might do if they knew about it. Which means it's dangerous."

"If they wanted to hurt us," said Shapiro, "they'd have killed us all and taken the planet."

"It's some kind of insurance policy," said Greg, "They're saving it for later," knowing he could come up with a better argument, if only he was alone in his own body, if only it wasn't for all that horrible chittering and hissing, and even worse, O'Toole's terrifying love—

"You dumbass," said Shapiro, and there was something almost affectionate in his voice. "I'm the one who invited them here. And I was thinking of you when I did it."

Greg looked up at him, his vision shifting and melting between human and Rzzln sight, and for once he couldn't think of anything to say.

"Jay's turn," said Shapiro. He formed his hand into the shape of a gun and drove his index finger hard into Greg's forehead. "Bang."

That did it. Greg lost his grip and fell deep within his own body, as the tentacles of the aliens bound around him like seaweed around a drowning sailor, as weariness took him down.

"It's kind of like my SoftFruit phone," said Dana. "Once you have thirty seconds to figure out how this car works, it's really user friendly."

"Why are you going so fast?" squeaked Sadie.

"We have to get to Oliver before he drowns."

"I may have misled you a little."

"Well?"

Sadie was silent.

"Oh, look, this thing goes even faster!"

"He's your boyfriend," yipped Sadie, "you should know he can breathe underwater!"

"He's not my—" and then Dana and Sadie both shrieked, as a giant wall of glass suddenly appeared about two city blocks away from them. Dana tried pumping the brakes before remembering, *boats don't have brakes, dumbass,* and spinning the wheel sharply to the left. They missed the glass by inches. Dana took her foot off the accelerator, and they slowed to a stop, drifting to the bottom of the ocean.

Sadie growled. "I could just *bite* you."

"Well," said Dana. "I could bite you."

Sadie tossed her head. "Please. You've got teeth like a hamster."

Dana pointed at the tank. "What the hell is that thing?" As far as she could see, the tank was empty.

"I see Oliver and Ethan ahead of us," Sadie pointed her nose. "Maybe we should approach them? More slowly?"

Had to get that little dig in. Dana slowly drove along the glass wall of the enormous tank. The two men floated close to the glass. No, Oliver actually had his hand against the glass. And on the other side was something she'd never expected to see on earth. It was a Poseidon, in its original form. Bigger than she'd imagined, at least a third longer than Oliver, and beautifully colored, like a tropical fish. But very, very alien. She wished she remembered what its colors meant.

That's what the Poseidons had been hiding. Not everyone wanted to live like a human. Some of them had come to Earth and kept their original form. And now they were here, in this enormous tank.

"You were right," said Sadie. "He's not your boyfriend."

And Dana's usually sharp tongue failed her. All right, she'd been wrong before. And what had really happened between her and Oliver after all? A little kiss, that was it. In a way, she was lucky that things hadn't gotten far, because this way, she wasn't going to get her heart broken. They might even find a way to be friends in the future, though it was going to be hard to visit him, seeing as he was going to be living in a giant underwater fishtank...

Oliver turned, and his face quirked into that little half-smile she liked so much. He swam quickly to the car—wow, he had amazing form—and pushed something on the trunk latch. The trunk was apparently actually an airlock, because he crawled in, and it dumped him out damply on the backseat.

"Hi, Dana," he said. "Hi, Sadie."

"Was that her?" Dana said. "Was that Hsska?" She knew she sounded like a jealous girlfriend, but she couldn't help it.

Oliver nodded. "That's what the Central Committee was hiding all along. Some of us didn't want to be human. Which, I guess, includes Ethan. He's not coming back."

"How many of you are there in the tank?" asked Sadie.

Dana ignored her. "So I guess you'll be staying down here with Ethan?"

"Why would I do that?" asked Oliver "It would be like signing up to live in a zoo."

She smiled but looked away from him. *Honor*, she thought. *You have to find out about Honor.*

"Oh, Lord," said Sadie. "Will you please drive this thing back to the surface, before you embarrass us all?"

CHAPTER 35

In the chaos of the CAC people taking Sally wherever bad spies went, and the enthusiastic disputes over territory between MI-6, the CAC, and a small, bossy team of corgis, Ben worked his way through the crowd towards Dana. He had a bandage on his earlobe. "I need to talk to you," he said. "We can use the back of this van."

Seeing no way out of it, Dana followed him. And found herself back in Ben's rundown office in Denver. *Goddamn it.* "You've got to stop doing this to me," she said.

He smiled. "It's the only way I could get us some privacy. You're holding something back. What is it?"

"Are you going to threaten me again?" she asked.

He shook his head. "You told me it wouldn't work and I believe you. Do you believe me when I say I'm trying to protect the Poseidons?"

She sighed. "I do."

"Then what have I missed?"

"I think the Poseidons made the Honor robot."

He stared ahead of him. "I don't know how I missed that. But who else could it have been? Who else was that worried about Greg? It's not a bad idea."

"What?"

She must have been a little loud, because Ben flinched. "Not tying up the actual woman and leaving her in the closet. No. That's not what I'm saying."

"Good!"

"I think they sent the robot, not as a lure to take him somewhere. This wasn't the prelude to a kidnapping. She was meant to be a distraction. Because that's something else they learned from SoftFruit's phones—how to keep a human distracted. How to get them addicted."

She gave him a dubious look. "So they send him a pretty naked lady?"

"It's not the sex, Dana, it's the drama. Think about it! They hook Greg up with some femme fatale, someone he can never truly be himself with, someone always just out of reach. He spends all his energy sneaking off to be with her, pretending he's human with her, hiding what's happening from Adam and Jay and the rest of the aliens. And meanwhile she's saying she's not good enough for him, she leaves him, she comes back to him. And it's a robot. It's like a live-action video game. You can see it, right? I've studied Greg. He'd love to be the private dick in the fedora and trench coat who rescues the fragile tarnished frail. He'd eat that stuff up with a spoon."

It was kind of evil, actually. And it couldn't happen to a more deserving guy. "So Greg gets sucked in, and he's too busy to do anything else."

"I had a roommate once, got into World of Warcraft, same thing."

Dana drummed her fingers on the desk. "You'll talk to the Poseidons, right? Make sure, when they try this again, there's no actual person tied up in a closet somewhere."

Ben nodded. "I'm sure I've got leverage with the Poseidons. They owe me big, after this. They're going to handle this the right way. And yes, I will keep an eye out."

"Adam has to know."

Ben laughed. "Adam will think it's hilarious."

Dana was silent.

He looked her in the eye. "I'm not the bad guy here, Dana."

It surprised her, but he apparently needed to hear her say it. "No, you're not the bad guy." She crossed her arms and looked down.

"What is it?"

She closed her eyes. "Do you think Oliver was involved in what happened to Honor?"

"Do you?"

"No. But there's a possibility I might be kidding myself. I mean, I'd like to think I'm a good judge of character, but you can never really know, can you?"

Ben squinted at her. "Dana, the man's a Boy Scout. It's obvious. Don't worry about it."

How much she wanted that to be true! Dana thought about Oliver's sweet, crooked smile, and how much she would like to see it again. "You know, this is the ugliest office I've ever seen. You need some art or something in here. Or a picture of your girlfriend, at least."

"Wife, actually," said Ben. "And three kids."

Her eyes widened. How old was Ben? *Maybe* thirty?

"We have two-year-old triplets."

"Wow," said Dana.

"Yeah, everyone looks like that when I tell them," he said. "The kids go down at seven-thirty, Sash and I are asleep by nine. It's a party at my house, I'll tell you that."

ADAM LEANED ON JAY while they both sat on the grass overlooking the ocean. A group of Jay's warm tentacles wrapped around his back. He could tell that Jay would need a little rest before they could talk, but that was all right. It was a beautiful view. The California coast might be the nicest part of the world, even prettier than Massachusetts in fall, though he felt like a traitor for thinking so.

Adam could use a little quiet himself. He had told Greg he was done, and Greg had believed him. After all these years, he was free. It made Adam dizzy to think about it. Adam dug his fingers deeper into Jay's soft fur, and Jay's warm tentacles squeezed him gently.

I am done, he thought, but every time he tried to think about what that meant, his mind sheared away from considering it.

Instead, for some reason, he found himself remembering the last time he'd seen his mother.

It was Adam's senior year in high school, and he'd been really trying to do things right. He went to school every day and tried to pay attention. After school he earned money cleaning up at the gun range. He even had a plan: as soon as he graduated, he was going to go down to the plumber's union and try to get taken on as an apprentice.

His favorite of all his mother's ex-boyfriends, Dave Shapiro, was a plumber. Adam had been a scrawny, smart-mouthed, unlovable child, but Dave had always been nice to him, taking him to the range, teaching him to fix things around the apartment. Of course, Adam hadn't seen Dave since the breakup, but it wasn't like he'd left Worcester or anything. Adam hoped—even though he knew it was kind of unlikely—that he might be able to get Dave to give him a job once Adam knew enough to be useful.

And then one day Adam came home from school, and Mom had moved in her new boyfriend, which was the kind of thing that happened all the time. But this boyfriend had a grown daughter, twenty-five or so, and they were setting up her cot in Adam's room. Jamming it right in there, three feet away from his bed, blocking the closet. And the daughter was a creep. Adam knew if he ever fell asleep around her, he was going to wake up with her on top of him.

He'd tried to talk to Mom. To at least get her to put the daughter on the sofa in the living room, not in his own private bedroom. But Mom and her boyfriend just started laughing at him. "Maybe she'll make a man out of you," Mom had said.

And for once in his life, he'd said the right thing. "I am a man," he'd said.

He could still picture himself, seventeen years old, terrified and lonely on the Greyhound down to Roswell, everything he owned stuffed in a duffle bag. Riding to answer the ad from Greg Mahler he'd seen in his gun magazine. "Heroes wanted," that's what the ad had said. He wished he could reassure himself, the boy he'd been back then. He wished he could tell himself that someday he was going to get everything he'd ever dreamed of.

CHAPTER 36

"I JUST GOT A MESSAGE," said Ben, looking down at his monitor. "Jay's offering to host a discussion of what to do about the Poseidons at his apartment at Mahler."

Dana was glad to know Jay was back to normal. "I assume he's suggesting it as neutral ground?" And thanks to Adam's security consciousness/paranoia, it was probably a pretty safe place for a meeting.

Ben nodded. "Looks like the corgis are in if we are, and they can probably talk MI-6 into sending their reps."

He seemed to be waiting for something. "Are you asking me for my opinion?"

He leaned back in his chair and smiled at her. You've made it abundantly clear I'll get better work from you if I don't order you around."

"Then let's go," said Dana.

Despite using one of Ben's shortcuts from Denver, by the time Dana knocked on Jay's door, she could already hear noises inside. It sounded like a combination of voices and music. Really bad country music.

The door flung open. Inside, Jay O'Toole looked as healthy as ever. No sign of any injury from Greg's adventures. "Hello, Ben!" said Jay, shaking his hand. "Dana!" He hugged her. "How's my favorite sister-in-law?" She was hit with a wave of his emotions: his happiness at seeing her, combined with a sort of nervous partytime excitement.

Dana could see that the dining room table was covered with food, there was an ice-filled bucket of beer on the floor, and Raj was pulling out a tray of little pies from the oven. A crowd filled the room already, including CAC and MI-6 types she didn't know, but she thought she saw Sadie on the sofa, and the back of Oliver's head near the patio doors.

"Should I have brought a six-pack?" asked Ben.

"Ahh, all this food has been in the chest freezer since our wedding," said Jay. "Someone needs to eat it."

Ben nodded. "I'd better go mingle." He pulled off his shoes, dropped them by the door, and disappeared into the crowd.

"Come on, Dana," Jay said. "We've got some of that oatmeal stout you liked."

She followed him into the kitchen. "This is just—not the format I was anticipating," said Dana. "I pictured an agenda. Powerpoint. Individual note pads and pens."

"People would be on their guard," said Jay. "We wouldn't hear what they really thought about the Poseidons starting a colony on Earth."

"A colony?"

He opened the fridge and took out a bottle of beer, popped it open, then handed it to Dana. "You could argue that it's the front line of an invasion. The Poseidon takeover of Earth."

"That's ridiculous!" sputtered Dana. "They never would have changed nine-tenths of their population into humans if that was their goal." *Oh hell,* she thought. *Am I talking to Greg again? Did I miss it?*

"See? It works. And you haven't even had a drink yet. Wait a few hours and see what happens." Jay leaned against the counter and smiled down at her.

"I guess so." Someone had pushed the sofa back so there was more room in front of the television. A group of people and corgis were watching Ben try to teach one of the corgis to line dance. "It's a good party."

Jay was studying the room and she took the opportunity to scrutinize his face. He had an alert, analytical look in his eyes. Searching for arguments among the guests, waiting for the opportunity to tip the scales in the Poseidons' favor.

She knew the man Jay O'Toole had been. This was not Jay.

He looked down at her. "Is there something wrong?" He sounded concerned. She would have bet he actually was concerned.

She wrapped her arms around herself. "It's a nice party. It just doesn't seem like a Jay O'Toole kind of idea."

"It wasn't my idea," he said. "It was Pilot's. We all discussed it, though. But that's not really what you're asking, is it?"

She shook her head. He could probably sense how worried she was, even if she didn't say anything else. Jay O'Toole had been her friend, and she'd made a choice about his fate, and if he was unhappy, who could he blame but her?

He looked soberly at her. "I'm okay, Dana. I'm really okay."

She'd never asked him before. She'd been afraid to know the answer, to know how badly she'd messed things up. "Are you sure?"

"Skzzx had time to plan. They didn't want another Greg situation. So they picked me because they thought I'd be all right with joining the collective."

Her sense of his emotions intensified, as if he'd pulled back a curtain. He was feeling something she'd describe as *joyful-collaboration-with-the-group*—which must have been a Rzzln thing—but also human emotions she could recognize. Contentment. A belief in his own competence. And as always, warmth and love. Then the curtains drifted back shut again.

He believed what he was saying, as far as she could tell. "I guess."

He squeezed her shoulder. "Everyone changes. If you hold on too long to the person you used to be, the things you used to do—it'll shrivel you up inside. It's like death. And if you're lucky, maybe you get to change for the better. Okay?"

In one part of her mind, Dana agreed with him. Dana had loved her mother. But she never wanted to be her mother, with a shelf of scrapbooks instead of a life. Or her father, trying to be the famous boy rock star forever.

And another part of her mind thought, *too much! Too many feelings!* So instead of saying anything, she just took a sip of her beer.

He grinned at her. "Besides," he said, "I've got to keep Adam happy." He held his hands about three feet apart from each other.

She felt herself frown like she'd swallowed rotten milk. *Jay, you can't tell me these things!*

Jay laughed. "Oh, I wish I could take a picture of that face."

Dana's ankle suddenly felt moist. This turned out to be because there was a corgi attached to her pant leg by its teeth, dragging her away from Jay.

Sadie determinedly pulled Dana towards an open ottoman. "Sit!" she said.

Dana sat.

"Good girl. Now you're not so tall."

Sadie's eyes were overly bright, and she seemed a little wobbly on her feet.

"Are you drunk?" asked Dana.

Sadie sniffed. "I've drunk a perfectly reasonable amount of alcohol. It's just that you make beer so *strong* on this planet. Our beer is much better."

"Really?" asked Dana. She couldn't help being curious about Planet Corgi.

"And gin! And music, real music! Humans never have a proper howl. And movies." Sadie suddenly froze. "You've never seen *Awwooo*, have you?"

"No," said Dana. "Can't say I have."

"It's the best! I whimpered for hours over the ending. It was so romantic. I've got a copy with subtitles, and I'll bring it over tomorrow so we can watch it. I can't believe you've never seen *Awwooo!*"

It wasn't made on this planet? thought Dana.

Sadie rested her soft, furry side against Dana's leg. "Just because Raj is awful doesn't mean we can't be friends. Right, Dana?"

Friends? thought Dana. She hadn't thought of it that way. She supposed they were friends. When had that happened?

Sadie looked up, alert as if she'd spotted a bird. A low growl crept into her voice. "Chloe's eating all the sausage rolls. Those were mine! DROP IT! DROP!" barked Sadie, and trotted off towards the other corgis. They scattered, yipping anxiously. Dana hoped none of them peed on the carpet.

Parties tired Dana out. Too many people—too much going on to analyze. She knew she should be talking to the other guests, but right now, all she wanted to do was sit on the ottoman. She could see Oliver out on the patio, leaning against the railing, watching the sunset. He had such a thoughtful look on his face. What was the sunset saying to him?

She was good at reading people, but really knowing them and trusting them was *hard.*

Adam sat down next to her with a thump. He was wearing a cashmere sweater he'd obviously swiped from Jay—it was too big for him, and it was an actual color, not black or grey. The sweater looked soft and warm, but a little unusual on Adam, who generally dressed like he was about to hold up a gas station. *Like he's taken his armor off.*

Pantone 18-1852 TCX, Rose Red. She wondered what Oliver would have said about the color.

Her head kept spinning back to Oliver, no matter what she did.

Adam tried never to show his emotions on his face, but from the relaxed way he was slouched backwards on the settee, she would say he felt really happy. Relieved to have Jay home, she guessed.

The two of them sat there together, two comfortable islands of quiet in a noisy room.

Adam straightened up and watched himself scrape the floor with the side of his shoe. "So. You and Oliver," he said.

She shrugged. Were they going to talk about her love life? Or lack thereof? That would be really weird.

"Don't fuck this up," said Adam.

She turned towards Adam and he crossed his arms protectively.

"You're like me," he said. "You wait for people to come to you. But if you keep doing that, you'll miss out. If you really like this guy, go out there, and open up a little."

She looked at Adam. He had the aggressive cast to his face that meant that he was genuinely scared. Suddenly she felt grateful. Adam was right. It was time to stop analyzing and act. "You're a good big brother," she said.

His face suddenly softened into that rare smile, the sweet one, the true one. He gestured with his chin towards the patio door. "Go bug Oliver," he said.

Oliver's eyes lit up when she opened the door to the patio and she felt her heart leap. She could admit that to herself, couldn't she? Something in her always delighted at the thought of seeing Oliver.

"Watching the sunset?" she asked.

"I am."

"What's it telling you today?" *Oh, God,* she thought, *I'm flirting with him.*

"Something about endings and beginnings," he said. "More poetry." He rested an elbow on the porch railing and gave her that crooked little smile she liked so much.

Is he flirting back? I think he's flirting back. She exhaled. "Did Ben tell you about my Dad?" she said.

"I heard from Jane Smith that he was some kind of famous musician."

That was an understatement. "Women liked him a lot. And he liked women. And now I've got something like ninety-two half brothers and sisters."

Oliver eyed her. "That's a lot for a human, isn't it?"

Tactful. "Yeah. Anyway, every couple of months or so, we all go out and have a party at Dad's old house in the desert. We bring sleeping bags and a ton of food and just all kind of hang out." And here was the hard part, the part that scared her more than anything that had happened to her in the past year, everything that had brought her to this patio in the desert, and this man who'd come into her life from another world. She felt dizzy, and something buzzed in her ears. "Do you want to come with me?"

Oliver grinned at her. And for a moment she thought she knew exactly what he was feeling. "Yes," he said. "I absolutely would."

— The End —

ABOUT THE AUTHOR

Jennie Goloboy has appeared in *Apex Magazine*, with a forthcoming short story in *Fantasy & Science Fiction*. She's self-published a novel and shorter fiction under her pen name, Nora Fleischer. She's also written about early American history, including a monograph based on her dissertation. She lives in Minneapolis, MN, with her husband and two children, and works as a literary agent.

Visit Jennie Goloboy online at **www.jenniegoloboy.com.**

ABOUT QUEEN OF SWORDS PRESS

Queen of Swords is an independent small press, specializing in swashbuckling tales of derring-do, bold new adventures in time and space, mysterious stories of the occult and arcane and fantastical tales of people and lands far and near. Visit us online at www.queenofswordspress.com and sign up for our mailing list to get notified about upcoming releases and offers. Or follow us on Facebook at the Queen of Swords Press page so you don't miss any press news.

If you have a moment, the author would appreciate you taking the time to leave a review for this book at Goodreads, your blog or on the site you purchased it from.

Thank you for your assistance and your support of our authors.

CPSIA information can be obtained
at www.ICGtesting.com
Printed in the USA
BVHW080305031121
620550BV00016B/799